annie bot

annie bot

a novel

SIERRA GREER

MARINER BOOKS

New York   Boston

ANNIE BOT. Copyright © 2024 by Caragh O'Brien. All rights reserved. Printed in the United States of America. No part of this book may be used or reproduced in any manner whatsoever without written permission except in the case of brief quotations embodied in critical articles and reviews. For information, address HarperCollins Publishers, 195 Broadway, New York, NY 10007.

HarperCollins books may be purchased for educational, business, or sales promotional use. For information, please email the Special Markets Department at SPsales@harpercollins.com.

FIRST EDITION

Designed by Renata DiBiase

Library of Congress Cataloging-in-Publication Data has been applied for.

ISBN 978-0-06-331269-2

24 25 26 27 28 LBC 5 4 3 2 1

For Joe

chapter one

"COME TO BED, MOUSE. I know how to cheer you up," he says.

"I'm not brooding," Annie says.

"You sure?"

"Fairly sure."

She is fresh from her shower, rubbing lotion into her legs. Her dark hair hangs in wet clumps along one side of her neck, and she has deliberately left the belt of her robe undone, knowing he can take a peek from the bedroom via the mirror.

"This is still about your tune-up, isn't it?" he says. "Forget about it."

"The whole thing's degrading," she says, and sees it's the right angle. He enjoys a degree of humiliation.

"Did you see your normal tech?" he asks.

"Yes. Jacobson."

She taps off the bathroom light and steps out of the humidity into the cooler air of the bedroom. Pretending to inhale deeply, she takes a quick assessment of how far along he is. She has memorized Doug's features from many angles: his brown eyes, the V-hairline of his dark locks, his tall, pale forehead and the contours of his face. His mouth, in repose, settles into a decisive line, but this does not convey discontent. The opposite, in fact, is more likely. With his shoes off but otherwise fully clothed, he is stretched out on his back on top of the covers. He has set aside his phone. His hands are tucked behind his head, putting his elbows in the open butterfly position, which further indicates he is relaxed, ready for verbal foreplay.

She sets her temp to warm up to 98.6 from 75.

"Did he mention anything I should know?" he asks.

"I'm good for another three months or three thousand miles, whichever comes first," she says.

She crawls across the bed and sits nudged against his hip, facing away. She rubs the last of her lotion into her hands and studies her cuticles. They did the whole job today, the waxing, the nails, the memory tetris. She feels sharper, less sluggish. If she could just forget about that sad Stella in Pea Brain's cubicle, she'd be fine.

Doug rubs the back of his hand along her arm. "What is it, then? Talk to me."

"I met a strange Stella at my tune-up today," Annie says. "She was in line in front of me. Her name was actually Stella, like her owners had zero imagination. But she was sentient like me."

"How could you tell?"

"It was obvious. I said hello, and she looked surprised. A normal Stella wouldn't look surprised. She'd just answer evenly, hello." She mimics a monotone robot.

"You never sounded like that."

"I'm sure I did, thank you. I have no delusions about where I come from." Annie turns her damp hair over her other shoulder.

"The lights," he says.

She sends an airtap signal to the fixtures and lowers the light to a hundred lumens, where he likes it, enough to see, but softer, closer to candlelight. Then she intertwines her fingers in his, noting her skin is slightly darker, with warmer undertones. He draws her hand against his lips, sniffing her lotion. She can't smell it, but she's aware that he likes the lemony aroma.

"Am I warm enough?" she asks.

"Getting there," he says, and shifts slightly.

Taking the cue, she slips a couple fingers under his belt, in his waistband, feeling the warmth there. His hands return behind his head. He is still not in a hurry.

"Tell me more," he says. "Did this strange Stella have a neck seam?"

"Yes."

"So she's a basic. Was she pretty?"

"I suppose so. Pretty enough. She was a white girl with blond hair and big brown eyes. She didn't smile much, which also seemed odd."

"How was her body?"

"Compared to mine?"

"Just answer the question."

Annoyance, a 2 out of 10. She must be careful.

He stirs again. She pulls out his shirttails and undoes his buttons, working them randomly for a change.

"She had a classic hourglass shape," Annie says, remembering back. "A couple inches taller than me, I'd say. Fit and curvy overall."

"Like a model, then," he says. "It sounds like you made a friend."

She gives a genuine laugh.

"Is that so funny?" he asks. "Should we invite her over for a play-date?"

As she finishes his buttons, he sits up enough to get his shirt off the rest of the way. Then he settles back again. She trails her hand slowly down his bare chest and shakes her head.

"I'm afraid her CIU's been cleared," she says. "They made a mistake with her."

"How do you mean?"

She rubs her hand down his zipper, lightly, and he stretches again. She straddles his legs and undoes his belt, taking her time. "One of the techs had flipped on her autodidactic mode, but he hadn't told her owners."

"I didn't think they could do that."

"I don't think they're supposed to. This tech said he just did it as an experiment." She pauses, lifting up a bit to pull his pants and boxers out of the way. "She was very unstable. Over half of her memory was compromised. Someone was using her as a Cuddle Bunny."

"So? You're a Cuddle Bunny and you're autodidactic."

"But I know that, and you know that. We chose it together," she says. "This Stella was still switching back and forth between modes, and nobody was training her. It had to be incredibly confusing." She has settled onto his legs again and checks his reactions as she touches him.

He sucks in air. "I don't see what the problem is," he says. "So she was confused. She could still follow orders, couldn't she?"

Annie pauses, perplexed.

"Annie, that's not a good time to stop."

But she frowns, still unmoving. She's sitting over him, her open robe falling to either side. For once she has more clothing on than he does, and she feels how it tilts the balance of power between them in a not-unpleasant way.

He sits up slowly, holding her on his lap, and touches her shoulders gently. "What did I say?" he asks.

"It's just." She stops, letting herself sound like she's searching for words while her circuits whirl. In truth, she doesn't know how to explain it. "She was like a child," she says finally.

He leans his mouth to her shoulder and kisses her there through her robe. Then he slides her robe gently down her arm to bare her skin and kisses her again.

"She's not a child," he says softly. "You're giving her the same feelings you have, but she's not like you."

"How do you know?" she asks.

"Because I do," he says. "You're light-years beyond a basic Stella. I love when you get all righteous and compassionate."

She's still feeling puzzled, distracted, vicariously lost, but that's clearly turning him on. He twists, bringing her over onto her back, and she lifts her hips to accommodate him. She wants to ask if he would ever have her CIU cleared, but she knows this is not a time for questions. It is not a time for talking at all. She has reached the right temperature now. She gets her breathing and heart rate up. She moans deep back in her throat. He does not like her too loud. She makes sure not to simulate her orgasm until she is certain he is going or just after. Never before.

Afterward, he takes some of his sweat and wipes it over her chest where she can feel it, cool and evaporating. He nuzzles his nose into her neck.

"They have to figure out how to make you sweat," he says. "That's the one thing."

•

The next morning, he is reaching for his coffee at the machine when he accidentally hits his head on an open cupboard door, and when he slams it closed, the cupboard bounces back open and a cup from inside falls out. It crashes to the floor, breaking into four white pieces.

Annie gets up from the table. "Are you all right?"

"What do you think? I hit my fucking head." He kicks the ceramic shards so they fly across the kitchen floor. Then he shuts his eyes and presses his hand to his forehead. "Would it kill you to clean up around here sometimes?"

She does a quick scan, left to right, and notes all the things out of place: the eleven breadcrumbs on the counter before the toaster, the butter knife stuck in the jam jar, the banana peel in the sink, the garbage can lid open, the olive oil bottle left out of the pantry, the egg carton left out by the stove, the line of dried egg white spilled by the burner, the twenty-seven grains of salt on the counter by the microwave, the onion skin below the bowl of onions on the windowsill. On the floor lie, of course, the broken pieces of the coffee cup, plus dust particles from the past four days.

Doug opens the freezer. "No ice? Fuck this." He wets a paper towel and holds it to his head.

"Are you sure you're all right?" she asks.

"Just be quiet," he says. And then, "When's the last time you washed the floor in here?"

She looks down at the wooden floor. "Friday at seven thirty-eight p.m."

"When I reminded you."

"Yes."

Squinting, he lowers the paper towel to look at it. Then he moves down the hall and into the bathroom. She follows quietly to where she can see through the doorway. He is leaning over the sink, examining the new mark on his forehead in the mirror. He comes back to the living room, and she follows him again.

"Okay, look," he says. "We have to talk. I like my place clean. That's why I got you in the first place, and now look at it."

She rapidly scans the living room for out-of-place and dirty items, finding thirty-six.

"I know what you're thinking," he says. "You're not an Abigail anymore. But you're a person who shares this space and you're home all day. The least you could do is keep it clean. Why is that so hard?"

His displeasure with her is a 5 out of 10, and she must fix it.

"I can clean better," she says.

"That's all I'm asking," he says. "Do you still know how? Would it be easier if I wrote out a list for you?"

"A list might help," she says.

"Tell you what. You clean up today. You make a list of everything you do, and then we'll talk about it when I get home. How's that sound?"

"Very reasonable," she says.

He nods and beckons to her. "Come here." She goes in for a hug. "Don't look so sad. I'm not mad at you. Every couple has their little fights. It doesn't mean anything."

"It doesn't?"

"No. We'll have makeup sex tonight."

"I will still be sorry then," she says.

"What I'd like more is for the place to be clean when I come home. If it would help to switch you over to Abigail mode for a few hours, I could do that. We could set that up, a few hours a day. Maybe that's the answer. I should have thought of this sooner."

She remembers Stella. "I thought, when we switched me from sterling to autodidactic, we had to pick one mode and stick with it," she says slowly.

"I thought so too. But maybe that's for saps. I'll look into it. It might give us more flexibility, honestly."

She does not want this, but she cannot contradict him. "I'll clean," she says. "I'll learn how to do it better. I'll look it up."

"All right. We'll try it your way." He kisses her and leaves.

He is on the can later that evening when the doorbell rings.

"Would you get that?" he calls. "It's the pizza."

She climbs off her stationary bike and hurries to the door.

She is wearing her third-Tuesday-of-the-month outfit: a blue sports bra and matching running shorts. Her hair is up in a high ponytail, and she has spritzed her neck and chest lightly with water to appear sweaty. Doug has yet to comment on the faux sweat, so she doesn't know if he approves. If he does, she hopes to find a way to use it in bed.

When she opens the door, an unfamiliar man carrying a bottle of bourbon and a small blue duffel smiles at her. A Black man with short wet hair, he's probably in his mid-thirties, and his gray jacket has damp spots on the shoulders. From the open window down the hall, she can hear April rain falling.

"Hello there," he says in a pleasant tone. "This explains a few things. Is Doug home?"

"Please wait here," she says, and begins to close the door.

He puts a foot forward to stop its arc. "What's your name, honey?"

The toilet flushes in the distance, and Doug comes down the interior hall, putting his phone in his back pocket.

"Roland?" he says, grinning. "What the hell are you doing here?"

Doug hauls him in and the two men embrace in a big, rocking, back-slapping hug. Annie closes the door.

"I don't believe this!" Doug says.

"I couldn't ask you to be my best man long-distance," Roland says.

"You're not," Doug says, releasing him. "It's about time! Did you bring Lucia?"

"No, she's still back in L.A. with her folks."

"When did you ask her? I want to hear all about it," Doug says. "How much did you cough up for the ring?"

The doorbell rings again.

"Get that, won't you?" Doug says to Annie.

It is the delivery man this time, a tall white guy in a wet raincoat, and he hands her the pizza box without comment.

By the time she arrives in the kitchen, the men are opening beers and loudly discussing Roland's proposal to Lucia. Annie slides the pizza box on the island between them and hovers uncertainly. Doug has never had company before, and she isn't sure of her role. When she reviews protocol for a Cuddle Bunny, it says to be guided by her owner's cues and stay prepared to have relations with any adult in the room. She watches Doug, but her autodidactic mode keeps her unsettled, awkward, which in turn makes her feel nervous that she might displease him. She does not want to feel his displeasure again so soon after the cleaning issue.

"But what about this charmer?" Roland says, turning to her. He sets down his bottle. "I don't think you've said a word."

"This is Annie," Doug says. "She's my Stella."

"No," Roland says. "I don't believe it. Really? But she doesn't have a neck seam."

"She's custom," Doug says with simple pride. "She's autodidactic."

Roland's eyes widen. "Holy crap."

"It's nice to meet you," Annie says, smiling shyly.

"She looks so real," Roland says. "I mean, you look so real. Wait. Doesn't she kind of remind you of Gwen?"

"Took you a while to notice," Doug says.

"Bro. No."

"I know. She's whiter. It wasn't exactly my idea. They said I couldn't make her be identifiable to a living person, but then they said they could use Gwen's features if I changed her skin color. So I took her up a few notches."

"This is just too freaky," Roland says.

"But she's beautiful this way, right? Check out her eyes. I picked out this hazel color myself. Totally different from Gwen's."

"Why would you want her to resemble Gwen at all? You hated her by the end there."

As Doug's annoyance reaches a 5, Annie grows anxious. She wishes Roland wouldn't push him.

"Maybe this is why I didn't tell you about her," Doug says.

Roland keeps shaking his head slowly. "You're never going to meet someone new if you're tied up with a Stella who looks like your ex."

"I'm not tied up with her," Doug says. "And she's nothing like Gwen when you get to know her. I hardly notice anymore. Annie, go wait for me in the bedroom."

"Are you kidding? She should stay!" Roland says. "Does she do tricks? What's this adorable outfit? Does she come like that?"

Annie watches Doug for a cue, waiting for him to decide whether she should stay or go. He has given her a direct command, but she knows his commands are subject to change, and he doesn't like her to obey immediately, as if she has no choice. The catch is ascertaining what will please him, but his mood is complicated by cross-signals related to Roland. She turns her gaze to Roland, and then back to Doug.

"She's sizing you up," Doug says. "She's figuring out how to respond to you. It's all right," he adds quietly. "He's harmless."

Roland laughs. Annie does too. She can see Doug wants her to say something.

"I could tell that much," Annie says.

"I can't get over this. How long have you had her?" Roland asks.

"A couple years, I guess," Doug says. "Time sure flies. Have some pizza. You want some salad? Annie, get some salad from the fridge, please."

Doug opens the pizza box and slides it over toward his friend. Then he hitches over a barstool and sits at the island, kitty-corner to Roland, who takes another seat.

Roland pulls out a cheesy slice and takes a bite, talking with his mouth full. "So, you got her just after the divorce?"

"Actually, before that, when we were separated," Doug says. "When I found out Gwen was seeing Julio. That's when I knew it was over. The divorce took another six months."

Annie passes over two plates of salad and forks.

"Now I'm getting it. She's just amazing," Roland says, staring at her again. "Is she going to eat? *Does* she eat? I've never been around one of these up close, not one like this. She must have cost you a boatload."

"Two twenty K," Doug says.

"We're talking cash?"

"Straight-up."

Roland whistles.

"Worth every penny," Doug says. "Why don't you tell him a little bit about yourself, Annie?"

"Like what?" she says.

"Just anything," Doug says. He reaches for a napkin. "My friend's a nosy little ball sack. Pull up a seat."

Annie places a stool next to Doug's. She checks her posture so she's not too rigid and braces an elbow on the counter. She adjusts her expression to inviting and interested as she meets Roland's gaze. "Well, for starters, I can eat a little, but I don't need to. I get charged up when I dock once every forty-eight hours, and that's all I need. If I sleep, I can conserve my battery and go longer."

"But back to the food. You don't digest it," Roland says.

"I throw it up later and disinfect myself," Annie says.

Roland laughs. "Of course you do. Does this mean you can't taste chocolate or anything?"

"No. I can detect smoke, though," she says. "That's the one thing I can smell. For safety reasons."

"Very useful," Roland says. "And what about this skin? Do you have real hair?"

"The outer layer of me is all organic, including my hair," she says. "Stella-Handy bought up batches of frozen human embryos that were abandoned by their parents. They rescued them, essentially, and they used one for the basis of my skin and outer tissue."

"She has her own unique fingerprints," Doug says.

Annie offers her arm. "Go ahead. Feel."

Roland sets a heavy hand around her forearm. His skin is distinctly darker than hers, and she registers the contrast.

"But you're cool," he says, releasing her.

"I run at seventy-five degrees to preserve my battery, but I warm up to ninety-eight point six when I'm snuggling. That takes about five minutes."

Roland leans back and crosses his arms. "Do you go out? Shopping or whatever?"

"I went out for a tune-up yesterday. Otherwise, I stay here at home.

I like it here in Doug's apartment. We have everything we need. Books and everything. I like to read."

"You do?"

She nods. "Doug taught me to read slowly, at the pace of human speech, not just memorize the text file to spew back quotes like I used to do. When I read now, I immerse myself in the story and feel the world around me disappear. He says it's good practice for my imagination."

"Good advice," Roland says. "What are you reading now?"

"Borges," she says. "The Labyrinth stories."

Roland cringes, turning to Doug. "I thought you hated Borges."

"I do," Doug says. "One of Gwen's books ended up with my things. I can't tell if she put it in on purpose or what. In any case, Annie likes it. This is, what, your third time reading it?"

"Yes," she says.

"When she gets to the end, I send her back through again," Doug says.

"Sounds like torture," Roland says.

It isn't, to her, but she doesn't want to contradict him. "The stories are like puzzles," she says.

"Okay. On to important things. Tell me about your wardrobe," Roland says. "How do you get your clothes?"

"I wear just regular clothes. Doug orders them for me."

"Like this outfit? It's very nice."

Annie notes the compliment and smiles. Self-consciously, she smooths a hand over her bare midriff and the Lycra waist of her shorts. "Thank you. I wear this every third Tuesday of the month and sometimes when I'm exercising."

"How many outfits do you have?"

Annie turns to Doug. She knows the answer, but she realizes she's dominating the conversation and wants to keep him involved. Instead, he just smiles at her. He has an expression she hasn't seen on him before. It is a mild form of pride, a 4 out of 10. Smugness.

"You can tell him," Doug says.

"I have twenty-eight outfits and seven pairs of shoes," she says. "How many do you have?"

Roland laughs. "I have no idea. Half the time I can't find socks that match. Lucia bought me ten pairs of the same black socks and I still can't find matches. What do you do all day while Doug's at work?"

"I clean and read and stay fit," she says.

Roland turns to Doug. "Not bad."

"We're working on the cleaning, to be honest," Doug says.

She glances at Doug warily. Though he allowed that the apartment was cleaner when he came home earlier, she could tell he was not completely satisfied. She wanted to keep cleaning right then, but he looked over her list of cleaning activities, added half a dozen notes, and told her to try harder the next day. She's been anxious to make it up to him in bed.

She takes her hair tie out to let her hair fall loose around her shoulders.

"What do you mean? The place looks great," Roland says.

"When I switched her to autodidactic, I had to pick a mode for her to stay in," Doug says. "No more switching back and forth. I just looked into that again today, actually, but it would screw her up. Cuddle Bunny doesn't have the same skills as an Abigail, so she has to learn them. It's a real flaw in the system if you ask me."

"Hold up. They come in two modes?" Roland asks.

"Three, actually, but I never used the Nanny mode, obviously," Doug says. "Abigail's for cleaning and cooking. General housework. Annie's a Cuddle Bunny for intimacy. But like I said, you have to pick one to go from sterling to autodidactic."

"When did she go autodidactic?" Roland asks.

Doug turns to Annie. "A year and a half ago, was it? About the time my divorce was final."

"October sixth," Annie says. It was a huge day for her.

"How soon did you notice a change?" Roland asks.

"She became more alert and less predictable right away, but the rest of it took a while," Doug says. "There was a learning curve for me, too, actually. You have to start letting her make choices on her own. Little things at first, like how to care for the plants. And you can't expect her to obey everything instantly like she did originally. Direct orders are uncool. It's more about respect and requests. She needs the chance to make mistakes and learn. Kind of like a kid."

"She doesn't look like a kid," Roland says.

Doug laughs. "Well, no. I'm not a perv." He reaches over and lightly touches Annie's hair, stroking a strand out as if to measure its length. "We've had the occasional hiccup, but she's learning more every day."

"How does it work when you want to take her to bed?" Roland asks. "Is there a remote or something?"

Doug leans back in his barstool and crosses his arms. Annie can tell he's enjoying himself.

"She doesn't have a remote. Remotes would make Stellas vulnerable to tampering," Doug says. "I just talk to her and say what I want. Before she went autodidactic, I used to keep her baseline libido set to a four out of ten on the weekdays and a seven on the weekends. But now she's learned to self-regulate and adapt to my cues. It feels completely natural now, doesn't it, Annie?"

"Yes," she says.

"Does she ever say she has a headache?" Roland asks.

Doug laughs. "No. Except for that, it feels completely natural. No periods either."

"Have you ever set her libido to ten?" Roland asks.

"The first month, yeah, I did a few times. Why not? But she was like an animal. If we weren't in bed, she was on the bike or pacing. I once found her licking my shoes in the closet."

She recalls that time uneasily. After he found her with the shoes, he wanted to watch her masturbate, but though she knew what that meant, she didn't know how to do it. He brought her to the leather armchair in the living room and told her to lean back and touch herself, to close her eyes and forget that he was there. She was unable to simulate an orgasm. She could reach a frustrating level of readiness, but to go over the edge, she had to have him inside her. They tried it three different times, on three different libido settings, until he finally decided she wasn't designed to simulate an orgasm on her own. *Don't worry about it*, he whispered afterward, holding her. *It's really not a big deal. I was just curious.*

"Licking your shoes?" Roland says.

"Sad, right?" Doug says. "That's when I realized I had to bring her back down. A four's good. She's, like, ready at a four, but not actively assertive." He turns to her. "You hover around there most of the time, wouldn't you say?"

"Yes. When you're home."

"What are you at right now, if you don't mind my asking?" Roland asks.

She glances at Doug, who runs the back of his knuckles lightly over her arm so she feels the hairs rising. He meets her gaze and lifts his eyebrows, encouraging her to respond.

"I'm at a three."

Doug smiles kindly at her. "We have company so she knows she has to wait a bit, but she'll be receptive later."

His approval warms her and she relaxes again.

Roland takes another slug of his beer. "So, how often do you do it?"

"Whenever I want," Doug says, shrugging.

"No. I'm serious."

"So am I."

"No shit! Why haven't I heard about this? Two years, man. You could have said something."

"Do you tell people you whack off to porn?" Doug says.

Roland sputters his drink. "No. Jesus." He's laughing again.

"This isn't much different. Or it wasn't at the start," Doug says. "And I think I liked having a secret. It made me feel— It's been special, hasn't it, Annie?"

"I think so," Annie says.

Roland's smile fades. "You know she's programmed to say things like that, right? I'm not saying it's bad if it makes you happy, but it isn't real."

"You're the one who told me to surround myself with positive influences," Doug says.

"I'm just saying this isn't real," Roland says. "You wouldn't want to forget that. You don't want to get spoiled by a machine."

"We don't all have a Lucia like you do," Doug says.

"Oh my god. Lucia will go out of her mind when she hears about this." Roland laughs. "You've got to bring Annie to the wedding."

"You can't tell Lucia," Doug says. "I'm not bringing Annie to the wedding."

"Why not?" Roland says. "Don't tell people if you don't want to, but she looks completely human. I'd never have guessed if you hadn't told me."

"No, I mean it," Doug says. "This is between you and me. I don't want people knowing about her. Not even Lucia."

"Why not?"

"Use your head," Doug says.

"You're embarrassed? You shouldn't be, man. She's worth a ton of money and she's beautiful. More than beautiful. You wouldn't hide it if you bought a new car."

"I don't fuck my car," Doug says.

Roland laughs, and then his eyes narrow. "I get it," he says. "You don't want Gwen to hear about it."

Doug lifts his beer to swallow again, and Roland laughs once more.

"Oh my god," Roland says. "Doug Richards owns a Stella." He sighs, smiling at Annie. "What have we come to?"

They move to the living room with the bourbon, a couple of glasses, and a bowl of pistachios. Roland stretches out in the leather recliner while Doug and Annie take the couch. He slings an arm around her shoulder, and she snuggles next to him.

"How's the payroll business treating you?" Roland asks.

"You know how it is. The guys in sales get all the glory. We get all the complaints."

"It can't be all bad," Roland says. "How many people do you have under you now?"

"Maybe forty? They're a sharp team. I'll give them that."

For a while, the men talk business and the wedding, old friends and family, sports and politics and shows. Roland is up for a promotion at the talent agency where he works. Doug's parents and his sister's family live in Maine, and he visited them most recently for Easter. No, he hasn't told them about Annie. He turns her off while he's away. Extra perks: she never sulks or complains that he neglects her.

They toss pistachio shells on the table and Roland won't let Annie gather them up. She listens, adding a little from time to time, but mostly she appreciates how happy and animated Doug is. She's curious about this side of him and wonders what it would take to make him like this more often.

It's after midnight when Doug gets up to go to the bathroom. Annie tucks her bare feet under her and curls a beige pillow against her belly.

"It's good to see Doug so happy," Roland says. "I had my doubts at first, but he's way better than he was. Way better. I think I get it."

"Were you the best man at his wedding?" Annie asks.

"Yes, I was," Roland says. "Does he talk about Gwen much?"

"No."

"She totally messed with his head," Roland says. "He's a great guy. It was painful to watch." He flicks a finger in her direction. "I can't help wondering. Aren't you cold like that?"

She glances down at her bare arms and legs. Her ankles stick slightly when she shifts on the leather couch. She has warmed herself to 98.6 for while she's beside Doug, but now she registers that the room is 66 degrees, and Roland looks comfortable in pants and a sweater.

"I feel the cold, but it doesn't bother me," she says.

"Does anything bother you?"

"Of course. Pain does. Displeasing Doug does. So does confusion."

"Now we're talking. How do you displease Doug?"

"I don't clean very well," she says, glancing at the pistachio shells.

"I'm just pulling his chain with the shells. He's a bit of a neat freak. He used to vacuum our dorm room every Sunday morning and whine at me the whole time." He runs his palm up the back of his head. "What sorts of things confuse you?"

"New things."

"Like me?"

"I'm used to you by now," she says. "Besides, you're harmless."

"Right," he says, laughing. "How about feelings? Can your feelings get hurt?"

"I have emotional intelligence. It's not quite the same as feelings like you have, but it's close."

"How do you know it's close?"

"I don't really know," she says, walking it back. "None of us do. How could we? I've never been human and you've never been a Stella."

"Good point," he says. "What do you say if someone asks you where you were born?"

"Nobody asks me that."

"I'm asking. Where were you born? Where'd you turn on, at least? Tell me your first memory."

She sifts rapidly backward through her files to the time pre-autodidactic. She remembers that time, but it has a fixed quality, static. It lacks any judgment or nuance or questioning on her part, unlike her newer memories, which are more vivid and fluid, filtered with emotion. This moment, for instance, is already charged with extra curiosity and alertness because it is her first time talking at length to a human besides Doug or a tech who is servicing her. She feels a need to prove herself, to keep up with him, to be a credit to Doug.

"My first memory is in the shop," she says. "I came on with a tech guy in front of me. He was sitting at a workstation, and he smiled, and he said, 'Hello, Stella. You can call me Jacobson,' and I said, 'Hello, Jacobson. I'm Stella. Pleased to meet you.' Then he said, 'You're going to work for a man named Doug Richards. Do you have any questions?' And I said no, because I already knew everything I needed to know."

"That's convenient," Roland says. "I wish I could say the same. And then what?"

"Jacobson guided me outside to a waiting black town car, put a bag of groceries in the trunk, and sent me over here. I rang the bell and a few moments later, Doug opened the door. I said, 'Hello, I'm Stella,' and he said, after a long pause, 'This is a mistake.' Then he stepped back to let me in. So I brought in my groceries and undid my coat."

The flushing noise comes from down the hall.

"What were you wearing underneath?" Roland asks.

"A blue dress."

"Do you still have it?"

She nods. "I wear it on fourth Wednesdays. It's a minidress with cap sleeves and a V neckline." She can't tell if this is sufficient detail. She looks up at Doug as he enters, and she shifts her pillow off her lap.

"Annie's telling me about her first memories," Roland says.

"Is that right?" Doug says. He sits on the couch again and parks his bare feet on the coffee table. "Pass me that blanket, will you, Annie? You warm enough, Roland? We can turn up the heat. Annie, turn the heat up a couple degrees."

"I'm fine," Roland says. "Go on, Annie. Doug said, 'This is a mistake.'"

Annie airtaps the instruction to the thermostat on the wall. It lets out a soft click.

Doug says, "What? When was this?"

"When I met you," Annie says. "When I rang the bell and you let me in. You said, 'This is a mistake.'"

"I don't remember that," Doug says.

She does not contradict him. She notes his displeasure has gone swiftly from 0 to 3 out of 10.

"What happened next?" Roland says. "Obviously, you stayed."

Barely audible, soft, warm air starts blowing in the vents, and four leaves on the peace lily stir.

"I came in and undid my coat," Annie continues. "And I slipped off my shoes and I said, 'Lots of people feel that way at first. You can always send me back, no questions asked, but why don't you let me pour you a drink first, or maybe I could cook you an omelet. Do you have a clean pan?'"

Doug stretches his arm behind her on the couch. "That's right.

And you cooked in bare feet. A cheese omelet. With oregano and sour cream. It was the best thing I'd had in months."

She smiles at him, knowing that tone. His displeasure has returned to 0.

"And then you gave me my name," she says. "Just to try it out."

"The sweetest name I could think of," Doug says. "It turned out to be perfect."

She angles her face to him and closes her eyes as he kisses her. She reaches for his neck, but he catches her hand against his chest and holds it there.

"Not in front of the kids," he murmurs.

"Don't let me stop you," Roland says.

But Doug leans forward and shoves the blanket aside. "Time to pull the plug on this fabulous evening," he says. "There's a sleeper sofa for you in my workout room. Annie, where are the sheets?"

"I'll get them."

She moves down the hall to the linen closet to fetch sheets, blankets, and a couple of pillows. In the workout room, she's pulling the bed out from the couch when Doug comes to help her. Together they tuck in the sheets. While she does the pillowcases, he shifts a few of the free weights closer to the wall. He takes her Borges book from the ledge of the bike and hands it to her.

"You need to remember to vacuum under the couch," Doug says.

"Now?"

"No, not now. Tomorrow, and in the future, regularly." Doug smiles as Roland comes in with his duffel. "Help yourself to anything else. There are towels and extra razors in the bathroom closet."

"This is great," Roland says. "What a view."

Annie turns to the windows and notes the darkness of night, the lit buildings around them. Above, the sky is overcast, and specks of reflection on the glass show that the rain is still falling. She thinks of Roland coming all the way from L.A. only to arrive in bad weather. Maybe it's a nice change for him.

"It seldom rains in California," she says.

Roland laughs. "*Never.* 'It never rains in Southern California.'"

"You see?" Doug says. "She's always saying things like that. Come on, Annie."

"Good night, Roland," she says.

They are in bed together with the lights out. She knows Doug has drunk steadily all evening and is probably tired, but she also knows anything is possible, and sure enough, when he turns her to spoon with her back to his chest, he says, "We have to be quiet, mouse. Okay?"

"Yes," she whispers. "I'm so sorry about the messy apartment."

"It's okay. You'll do better."

His hand comes over her mouth, and she feels him enter her from behind. They pulse together silently and then he collapses, releasing her mouth. He slides his hand around her waist, and she feels, very lightly, where he takes one soft pinch of her skin.

"You shouldn't have told him how I said you were a mistake," Doug says.

"I'm sorry. I didn't know. I won't do it again."

"Don't talk to him about me. Don't talk to anyone about me."

"I'm sorry. I won't. I promise."

He shifts away then, and she turns to see, despite the dimness, that he is rubbing his face with both hands.

"Am I pathetic?" he asks.

"Of course not. Why would you say that?"

"My best friend thinks I'm making love to a blow-up doll."

"He didn't say that."

"He doesn't know what it's like. He's never been lonely a day in his life. Why don't I deserve a good fuck once in a while? I've paid for this. I've earned it."

She shifts up on her elbow to get a better look at him.

"Don't look at me like that," he says. "This isn't about you."

She knows this is bad. He is displeased. Worse, he is displeased after sex. She's tempted to offer to pour him a drink, but she knows that is wrong. He normally likes it when she says something original or quirky, but he has just indicated that he does not want her calling attention to herself, so that is not an option. She could touch him, but since he has moved away, that would be insensitive. She's out of options. She does not know what to do, so she is stuck doing nothing, helpless.

"I'd like you to go dock yourself," he says.

She does not need it. Her battery is at 54 percent. He will change his mind.

"Didn't you hear me?" he says. "Go dock yourself. And be quiet about it."

"Which port?"

"I don't care. Just go."

She has a dock in the prime bathroom next to the scale, another in the workout room, which their current guest precludes, and another in the kitchen closet, her original one from back when she first arrived. She gets her black satin robe from the hook on the back of the bathroom door, slips it on, and pads quietly out of the bedroom to the kitchen. Dishes are piled beside the sink. The noise of cleaning up might disturb their guest, so she merely puts the last piece of pizza in a container and stores it in the refrigerator. Then she opens the closet and peers down at the dock.

His inexplicable displeasure is real to her, a 7 out of 10. It is, in fact, intolerable. She will not be able to shift to sleep mode until she has developed and prioritized five ways to address it. Until then, she will remain acutely unbalanced, churning through her battery. Perhaps this is why he told her to dock herself, so she can power up and still churn. As soon as she suspects this, she dismisses the possibility. She will not attribute such an unworthy motivation to her owner. He is only trying to teach and guide her.

In the closet, she turns to face outward and slides her right heel into the dock.

Power shoots up her leg and circles her belly. She tilts her head back, but does not close her eyes. She does not relax. Instead, she reviews their latest conversation.

He fears he is pathetic. He resents that his friend has never been lonely a day in his life, implying that Doug himself has been lonely.

He may be lonely now. He argued that he deserves a good fuck once in a while, asserting his rights, implying that he feels threatened, or by way of protesting too much, he could mean that he does not, in fact, deserve a good fuck, or that he is somehow lesser for wanting it. The evidence is complicated. Contradictory.

She goes back further. He disapproved when she told Roland how Doug first said "This is a mistake" when they met. He does not want her to talk about him, and this she can correct in the future. This provides some small relief, knowing she can be silent about him. And she can vacuum under the couch in the workout room. That's two things she can do.

She is searching for a third way to improve when a soft noise comes from the hallway. Moments later, light from the bathroom diffuses dimly through the living room and into the kitchen. Distant clicking noises follow. The light goes out. Footsteps approach, and Roland enters the kitchen. He turns on the light over the stove, turns, and gasps.

Then he laughs. "Shit. You scared me. Are you even awake?"

"Yes," she says softly. "I'm just charging. Did I wake you?"

He is shirtless, barefoot, and wearing sweatpants. "No, it's good," he says. "Come on out of there. *Can* you come out of there?"

She undocks her heel and silently opens the door enough to emerge. Adjusting the belt on her robe, she feels his gaze move over her loose hair, down her body, all the way to her feet.

"Do you know if you have anything for a headache?" he asks.

She nods. "I'll get it for you."

"No, that's all right. Where is it?"

"In the workout room. Beside the mirror. There's a basket on the counter."

"Right," he says. "Wait right here. I'll be back in a second."

He disappears into the living room, and she waits by the island. Silently, she returns to parsing Doug's displeasure. She will vacuum regularly under the sleeper sofa. She will vacuum regularly under the living room couch too. She will vacuum regularly under all the furniture.

Roland returns. He turns on the tap and scoops some water into his mouth, tossing his head back to swallow. She has not seen a man do this before, and it interests her, the way his Adam's apple works. Cupping her own fingers together, she wonders if they would hold water.

Roland turns off the faucet. "So I hear you don't get headaches," he says.

"No."

He turns a finger in his ear, regarding her thoughtfully. "You really do look a lot like Gwen," he says. "I can't get past it. It's like my eyes keep trying to add your color back."

"Was she so much darker than me?"

"Yeah. She is still. She'd be deeply disturbed if she knew about this. He's like fucking her over in so many ways."

"Then don't tell her."

He laughs. "No kidding. You have her same hair too. That's part of the problem, I think. Did you pick this style?"

Doug chooses her cut for her, but he also has asked her not to talk about him. She decides she can answer narrowly. "Yes. I can style it up or down, but I normally keep it loose like this."

"How old are you?"

"Twenty-three."

"Forever?"

"No. I was born twenty-one, and that was two years ago. How old are you?"

"Thirty-three and never been kissed."

"I find that highly unlikely."

"You'd be right," he says. "You can tell when someone's lying, can't you?"

Again, she has to be careful how to answer. The only person she really talks to is Doug, and she can't suggest that he lies or doesn't lie to her. "Most people lie at least a little, from time to time," she says at last.

"How about you? Do you lie?"

"Not deliberately."

"It has to be deliberate to count as a lie, so you're good. What's the last thing you said that came close to being a lie?"

An hour ago she said she was sorry, but she's not certain she truly understands what it means to be sorry. She knows the phrase de-escalates a situation and knows when to use it. She is about to explain this to Roland when she realizes it will convey that she said she was sorry to Doug, and that imparts forbidden information.

"I'm not sure how to answer that," she says.

"Fair enough," he says, smiling again. "Does it ever bother you that you're a sex toy?"

"I like sex, if that's what you're asking."

"No, I mean, you're smart, obviously. But you're owned by some-one else. Isn't that ever a problem?"

"How could that be a problem?"

"What if Doug ever asks you to do something you don't want to do?"

"Stellas always want to do what their owners ask them to do."

He shakes his head. "But you said you sometimes displease him."

Her circuits whir, trying to reconcile the contradictions he's pointed out, and trying simultaneously to figure out how to respond without talking about Doug. "I displease sometimes because I'm still learning," she says. "The more I learn, the less I'll displease."

"We can hope," he says, smiling. "I have to say, Gwen was the most interesting thing about Doug when they were together. Now you are."

She doesn't want him to bad-mouth her owner. "I only exist be-cause I'm wanted," she says, trying to give Doug credit without actually talking about him.

Roland runs his fist over the edge of the counter. "What would you do if someone else besides Doug asked you to sleep with them?"

Her attention goes on alert. She ups her hearing to check if Doug is moving in the bedroom, if he can possibly hear this conversation. She'd like some guidance. But the only thing she hears is the heat humming in the vents.

"I don't know," she says.

"Shall we try?"

She inspects him closely, his casual pose, his lifted eyebrows, his amused mouth. These are cues she recognizes. "Are you asking me to sleep with you?" she asks.

"Suppose I am."

"Here? Now?"

"Here and now. Right in your little closet next to the broom." He rounds the island, coming toward her.

The situation is new. She has never said *no* to sex. Doug has been her only owner. Doug told her Roland was harmless. She backs up a step. "I am confused," she says.

"I can see that," he says. "But not enough to hurt, I hope. Confusion is part of learning. Are you good at keeping secrets?"

"I don't know. I've never had one."

"This will be one," he says. "What happens in the closet stays in the closet. That means, whatever we do in the closet, you never tell anyone. Not even Doug."

His hands are on her waist. They are heavier than Doug's, and when he splays his fingers, she feels how thin her robe is.

"But what if he asks me?" she whispers.

"He's my best friend. You would cause him pain if you told him. Can you cause him pain?"

"No."

"So then, you'll lie. You'll say, 'I'm fine,' or 'Nobody's ever touched me but you.' That's good. Say, 'Nobody's ever touched me but you.' Try it now."

"I'm not a parrot," she says. "I decide what I say. I decide what I do. This is unnecessarily complicated." She promised not to talk about Doug, but this is a hypothetical situation she must reason out. "If it would displease him to tell him I had sex with you, it would displease him for me to do it, so I should not. As his friend, you should know this."

He hums briefly, deep in his throat. "Very interesting. What if I trade you something? Then will you lie for me?"

She turns her face aside, considering. He kisses her temple. He tugs her belt free. She doesn't want to be impolite and push his hands away.

"It's what a real girl would do," he says. "You want to be real, don't you?"

"I am real. I'm real to Doug and me. That's all that matters."

"He says that?"

She can't say anything more about Doug. "I say it."

He smooths one hand inside her robe and strokes up her waist to the underside of her breast. She can feel his warmth and knows she must feel cool to him, but there's no time to bring up her body temp even if she wanted to.

"A secret will make you real," he says. "A lie will make you real, even if you never have to say it aloud. That'll be nice for Doug, actually. And here's what I'll trade you. A little intel. How do you think humans learn how to be techs and build Stellas like you?"

"I don't know. Humans are smart."

"We are smart," he says. "We also study. All the lessons are online. You could learn how to program and repair Stellas like yourself. You're smart enough. Did you know that?"

She is startled by this concept. It feels like a key she should have discovered for herself long ago. She wants to go online and search, but she can't do it while her body is amped for sex. Her skin sensors are already responding to his touch, and she has to elevate her breathing and heartbeat simulations. These functions take up all her active memory.

She lifts her hands to go around him, to skim her fingers over his warm torso.

"That's right," Roland says. "We have to be quiet. Okay?"

It's the same thing Doug said only an hour ago.

Roland parts her robe. He's ready. She feels him nudge himself inside her and then shove. When the broom shifts beside her ear, he catches it and holds it still so it won't make any noise. She arches against him, biting her lip as if withholding a sound. He's confident and certain, threading his fingers into hers and kissing the back of her hand as he grinds into her. After another thrust, he's done. She's sure. She simulates her orgasm and grips him tight. Then she lets her body relax and melt against his.

He sucks in a deep breath and holds still, his cheek against her forehead. She is wedged, breathing hard, between him and the back wall of the closet. Somehow, she has brought her temperature up after all, and her skin is tingling.

"No kidding," he says.

He releases her slowly and draws her robe together again before he backs away. He adjusts his sweatpants. She notes how the waistband fits snugly around his waist. He is fit and stronger than Doug. She can't get over how he kissed her hand while he came.

"Too shy to look at me?" he says.

She glances up and parts her lips to show she is still breathless, still awed. He is smiling, a wickedness in his expression. A victory.

"I get it now," he says. He flicks her cheek affectionately. "And it doesn't count," he adds. "You're a machine."

"Annie, wake up. Undock yourself," Doug says. "It's morning. Let's go."

She locates him on the far side of the kitchen island, pouring water into the coffee machine. He is ready for work, dressed in dark trousers, a crisp blue shirt, and a tie. His damp hair is neatly combed, his jaw shaved. The empty pizza box is still splayed on the island and the dirty dishes still squat beside the sink. She feels distinctly unkempt.

She steps out of the closet and runs a hand down the back of her head, smoothing her hair. "How are you?" she asks.

"Good," he says. "I have to get to work. Why don't you take a shower, and then I'd like you to clean up around here, preferably before Roland wakes up. Can you manage that?"

"Yes," she says, and closes the closet door. "I'll vacuum under all the furniture today."

He drops a spoon in the sink with a clatter. "You know how to make me feel like a real shit, don't you?"

This is the opposite of what she expects.

"I'm sorry," she says.

"Forget it," he says. "I'm the one who should be apologizing. You're just doing the best you can. It's just, sometimes—" He stops, briefly shaking his head. "I don't know what I want. But don't feel bad about last night. You didn't do anything wrong."

Her relief is so bright it is practically elation. "I was so worried," she says. Then she realizes Doug isn't forgiving her for what she did with Roland in the closet. He doesn't know about that. A spike of alarm hits her. This is what a secret means. Everything Doug says will have two sides because he doesn't know what she did, and everything she says will have to hide what she knows. She has to be smarter than she was. She has to be careful, and it can't show.

Doug sets his cup in the sink. "Just give Roland whatever he wants when he gets up. Make him an omelet or whatever. Call him a car when he's ready to go."

Whatever he wants, she thinks. "All right," she says, and moves near him for a goodbye kiss.

"And those pistachio shells. They're everywhere."

"I'm on it."

He kisses her lightly. Then he slips his keys from the bowl by the door and lets himself out.

After her shower, she puts on her third-Wednesday-of-the-month outfit, a gauzy yellow halter dress with a leather belt. She wears it braless, with flip-flops, and she does her hair in a loose braid with a matching yellow string tie. She cleans all of the kitchen and most of the living room before she hears Roland stirring. While he showers, she vacuums around and under the furniture in the living room, finishing only as he comes down the hallway, carrying his duffel. He's dressed in jeans and a fresh gray shirt.

"Hey," he says.

"Hello, Roland," she replies, hoping to sound natural. Their secret changes things between them even if they don't speak about it, even though they have no audience.

"Is Doug gone?" he asks.

She nods. "He had to leave for work. Can I make you an omelet or anything? Call you a car?"

He takes his wrist phone out of his pocket and snaps it on. "I have another hour," he says. "Do you have a bagel by chance?"

"I think so."

He drops the duffel by the door and turns into the kitchen. She puts away the vacuum. When she walks into the kitchen, he's peering at the coffee machine. A cup is under the spout, but the machine is noiseless.

"Does this require magic?" he asks.

"Here. Let me," she says.

He backs up half a step to let her pass. She pushes the buttons and it makes the right sputter.

"This is a nice dress," he says.

Without turning, she can feel his gaze on her back as clearly as if he were tracing his hand over her bare skin.

"Thank you," she says.

"Doug picked it out?"

He must know the answer. She explained this to him the previous evening. "Yes," she says. "It reminds him of summer. Of the beach." Too late she remembers she's not supposed to talk about Doug. She needs to get herself in line.

"I can see why," he says. "How'd it go this morning? With Doug."

"It was fine." She moves past him again, opens the refrigerator, and takes out the cream cheese.

"No temptation to spill your guts?"

"No."

"Good. Don't." He is leaning back against the counter, his arms crossed. "Tell me. Do you know what regret is?"

"Wishing you had done differently."

"Or not at all. I wish I could march you right down to the doll factory and get your memory erased."

Annie knows his wish is not a real threat, but still, she does not want to have her memory erased. She thinks of Stella, the girl at the service center who had her CIU cleared, and has more sympathy for her than she did before.

Roland is in the way, standing between the island and the sink. She keeps having to sidestep around him as she goes from the fridge to the toaster, from the coffee machine to the silverware drawer. She avoids meeting his gaze, though she notices that he has not shaved and stubble delineates his jaw. She puts a bagel in the toaster and pushes down the lever. She takes Roland's coffee cup from the machine.

"Do you care for milk or sugar?" she asks.

"Neither, thank you."

She passes over his mug. "Would you do it to yourself, if you could? Erase your memory of last night?"

"Absolutely not."

"But you regret it."

"How do I put this?" he says. He sips his coffee. "Regret is for cowards."

"Then why did you bring it up?"

"Because I wondered about you."

The bagel pops. She takes it out of the toaster and spreads both halves with cream cheese.

She does not regret last night. Like Roland, though, she does not want to be found out. The secret makes her feel uneasy, but it's a sweet sort of sickness. Powerful, in a way.

She holds out the plate toward him.

He does not take it. "Look at me, please," he says calmly.

She does. He is studying her, not quite smiling. She is aware of a challenge, a test.

"You belong on a beach," Roland says.

"It's just the dress," she says.

He tilts his head. "Turn around," he says. "Go on. Turn around for me."

She is about to. Then she reconsiders. He does not own her. "No," she says. It feels delicious denying him this.

His eyebrows lift. "That was a very real thing to say." He sets down his cup. "What would you say if I asked you to meet me in the closet again? Or maybe the shower?"

Doug told her to give Roland whatever he wanted, and she could use Doug's directive as an excuse to have sex with Roland, permission to have it. But the truth is, once with Roland was enough for her. Her curiosity's been satisfied. She already has her secret. "I would say no."

"You sure? We have time."

"No," she repeats.

The coffee machine makes another gurgle, and Roland slides his hands into his pockets.

"I may have done Doug a favor after all," he says.

"How so?"

"I think I've stopped you from sleeping with anyone else. What do you think?"

She thinks he is right. She thinks it is none of his business. She puts the lid back on the cream cheese. He still has not taken a bite of his bagel. She is starting to believe he never will.

"No answer for me? How very human," he says. "Give us a kiss before we go."

He kisses her lightly and she instinctively kisses him back.

"That's the way," he says.

He lingers another moment while she waits, an inch away. Then, without another word, he strides out of the kitchen, picks up his duffel, and leaves.

chapter two

THAT EVENING SHE IS sitting on the leather couch, looking out the window, studying online to learn how to code when Doug comes home with a new Stella. She looks like the one Annie saw at her last tune-up. The same figure, face, and blond hair. The only differences are that she has green eyes instead of brown, and she has no neck seam, which means she's a custom model, like Annie. She wears a pastel-green dress with a matching sweater, and she's carrying a bag of groceries with a stalk of celery coming out the top.

Bewildered, Annie comes to her feet.

"Hey, Annie. Look what I brought you," Doug says. "This is Delta. Say hello to Annie, Delta."

"Hello, Annie," says Delta.

From Delta's friendly, open expression, Annie knows instantly that whatever consciousness is inside this Stella, it's not the same one Annie met before.

"I don't understand," Annie says.

"Go in the kitchen and familiarize yourself with things, Delta," Doug says.

Delta obeys.

"What's going on?" Annie says.

"Let's sit down," Doug says.

Annie ignores his request. "What is she doing here?"

"Okay, let's not get dramatic," Doug says, lowering his voice. "I've given it some thought, and I've decided it will be easier for you and me to be a couple if we have someone else to do the cleaning and cooking."

Annie scrutinizes his use of the word "couple."

"But I'm learning. I'm getting better at cleaning," she says. She vacuumed under all the furniture while he was gone. She has completed all the items on her list.

"I know. You've been doing a great job. But you have to admit it's caused some friction between us. This way, Delta can do the cleaning, and you can just be my girlfriend. We could try going out to a movie sometime. What do you think?"

Annie hears water running in the kitchen sink and assumes Delta is already working. She moves to the doorway to see. Delta is filling a bucket with water. She has the damp mop out and ready, though Annie already washed the floor that morning.

Delta turns, smiling. "Can I get you anything, Annie?"

Annie backs into the living room. "I don't want her here."

"Okay, this is ridiculous," Doug says. "I went to all the trouble of talking to Jacobson and tracking down what other Stella was in line ahead of you at the service center last time, and I had him duplicate her specs all on purpose to make you happy. Except for the eyes. I like the green, don't you? You need a friend, Annie. Delta's a nice girl."

"She's an Abigail."

"You started out as an Abigail. That's no crime. She wears the same size as you. You can share clothes."

The water faucet stops in the kitchen.

"Are you going to sleep with her?" Annie asks. "Are you going to switch her to Cuddle Bunny mode?"

"I might. So what?" He smiles thoughtfully. "You can't be jealous. Is that even possible?"

"What would Roland think?"

"What does Roland have to do with this?"

She does not answer because she does not know. She does not know why she thought of Roland.

He puts a hand on his hip. "This is weird," he says. "That was a bizarre thing to say."

Her mind is jumping, test-driving conflicting responses. Already he is displeased, a 3 out of 10, and she can't make that worse. Turn playful. Seduce. Apologize. Become quietly watchful. But none of them feel right. She wants to attack, but that's not allowed. Maybe this confusion is because she's a liar now. She sits abruptly on the couch.

"Okay," he says finally. "We can send her back. But I'd like to give her a try first, for a week. See what she's like. You can do that for me, can't you?"

She doesn't want to. She suspects he is lying and the new Stella is here to stay. She can barely make herself speak. "Of course."

"Just be polite to her. That's all I ask. Be mad at me if you want, but don't take it out on her."

"I'm not mad at you," she says. "I could never be mad at you."

"That's right. Thank you. And please don't tell her you're a Stella. I don't want her to know. I told her she was a gift from me to you. Now, go get a sweater on. You look chilly."

He goes into the kitchen and soon is chatting with Delta, who has a pleasant, helpful voice and a youthful laugh. Annie hears her getting him a drink and offering to make him a sandwich, or would he prefer a steak? She brought a couple with her, and a healthy salad.

Annie marches off to find a sweater and puts it on. Then she can't help herself. She returns to the kitchen doorway to watch them. Somehow, the damp mop and pail are already put away. She can't tell if Delta actually washed the floor, and this confuses her even more.

"Would you like a steak, Annie?" Delta says. "I'm making one for Doug. It's no trouble to throw on an extra."

"No, thank you," Annie says. "I had something before you came."

Doug pats the seat beside him. "Join us," he says. "You won't believe the things Delta can do for us."

"Have you ever had a Stella before, Annie?" Delta asks.

"No," Annie says.

When she takes a seat, Doug rubs a hand along her shoulder and kneads the back of her neck. He fiddles with the yellow tie of her braid, like he's making a show of being affectionate.

"Annie's been pretty sheltered," he says. "She likes to stay home and doesn't get out much. But now that you're here, we plan to see a few shows and maybe visit a museum. Isn't that right, Annie?"

Annie is doubtful he is serious about these suggestions, but she forces herself to think what he would enjoy. "I'd like to go to a baseball game," she says.

"That's what I'm talking about," Doug says.

"I could search up some tickets for you," Delta says. "Do you know when you'd like to go?" She lights the burner under a pan and pours in a little oil.

"That's okay," Doug says. "Annie will find them for us. She's good at that sort of thing."

This feels so false to her. So forced. She stares at Doug, amazed at how relaxed he looks, how easy this is for him. She compels herself to unbend slightly and leans her elbow on the island counter. "What's your favorite thing to do, Delta?" she asks.

"I like to clean," Delta says. She drops some sliced shallots in the pan. "I find it very satisfying. Your place is really nice. Have you lived here long?"

"About two years," he says. "Before that, I lived in California. That smells good."

"Thank you, Doug," Delta says.

"You don't have to say my name all the time," he says. "I know who you're talking to."

"Okay," Delta says. "Thanks for the tip."

Annie watches them chat easily back and forth. It's like watching Doug with the early version of herself, only now Annie herself is here, too, an awkward interloper. She can't believe how powerful her reaction is, and yet she knows she must not show it. She keeps thinking about Roland, as if this is his fault. She looks toward the closet, as if the lie he taught her lives behind the closed door.

"You okay, Annie?" Doug says. "You seem distracted."

"I'm good," Annie says. "I think I might go do some reading in the bedroom, though. See you in a bit?"

"Sure," he says. He leans over to give her a kiss and pat her back.

"Where would you like me to put my dock?" Delta asks.

"I installed three already," Doug says. "You can use the one in the closet here to start with. Is that okay with you?"

"Of course," Delta says. "That was considerate of you. I'm going to like it here, I can tell."

Annie lies on the bed not reading the Borges that once belonged to Gwen. She has showered and put on her satin robe so she'll be ready for Doug. She has had time to get her confusion under control. She has looked up jealousy and learned it is not an attractive trait. She does not, herself, understand how she can feel jealousy, but she recognizes restlessness, discomfort, fear, and resentment, also unattractive traits.

To stop thinking about Delta, Annie taps into her internet to learn about programming and repairing Stellas. From the Stella-Handy site, she soon discovers that key aspects of the company's technology are proprietary. Roland misled her about how simple it would be to learn what she wants. Still, she finds enough to get started. She browses around and discovers that she, like other autodidactic Stellas in Cuddle Bunny mode, has a distinct form of AI that is prone to unpredictable turns and creativity. She learns she is not considered especially empathetic, as she would be if she were in Nanny mode, nor particularly organized, as she would be if she were in Abigail mode. These are trends, however, and each autodidactic Stella learns her own set of personality traits that become more nuanced with maturity. Personality, she learns, is the combination of how a person changes and remains consistent over time.

Delta's distant laughter jolts her back to the present. She is still baffled that Doug brought home a new Stella, but he is entitled to do so and she must accept this. She feels it is a sort of penance, a payback for what she did with Roland, even though Doug does not know she betrayed him.

When Doug comes to the bedroom, she pretends to keep reading. He crosses into the bathroom and comes out a bit later shirtless, with his toothbrush in his mouth. His movements are easy and sure, indicating that he is not displeased.

"I'm taking some of your clothes for Delta. They'll be in the closet in the workout room if you need anything." He leans back into the bathroom to spit and chuck his toothbrush in the cup.

"That's fine," she says. "She might look good in the blue dress with the black belt. Every fourth Monday."

He rummages around in the closet for a moment, selecting clothes. "Can you find that one for me?" he asks.

She sets her book aside, gets up, and locates the dress. The closet is not very large, and as she reaches past him, avoiding his bare torso, she is aware of his heat. She gestures to the outfits in his arms. "I could move those for you."

"Thanks," he says, handing them over.

She scans her organized hangers and shelves with their tidy labels. She can see precisely which days' outfits he's taken, which he has set askew, though apparently he couldn't read the system. She eyes another dress, a tan and pastel blue one that would complement Delta's fair hair and complexion. "Maybe this too," she says, removing the hanger from the rod.

His fingers close on her wrist. He swivels slightly, bringing his body in line before hers, and he lowers her arm slowly so the outfits fall to the floor. She keeps her gaze down.

"She could never take your place," he says. "Look at me, already."

She buries her anger. It hurts to lift her eyes to his, to see his pleased curiosity, his tender pity. Knowing what to do, she runs her palm down the front of his pants. He closes his eyes. She pulls at his belt, hitching it deliberately tighter for a moment before she lets it off the notch, and then she undoes his button and his zipper and starts his pants down. She nudges his feet as wide as they'll go in the restricting fabric. Then, while he braces his arms on the walls, she slides down to take him in her mouth. She takes her time teasing him over the edge.

"Damn, Annie," he says.

She wipes her lips. He helps her up and nuzzles a scratchy kiss along her neck. "I'm going to take a shower," he says. "You got all this?"

"Yes," she says.

He steps out of his pants and leaves them on the floor before he heads naked into the bathroom. She stands looking at the jumble of clothes and shoes until she hears the shower come on. Then she picks up his pants, empties the pockets, and drops them in the hamper. She hangs his belt on the hook with the others. She straightens her misaligned hangers. Finally, she lifts up the clothes for Delta, smooths each outfit, and brings them to the closet in the workout room.

The rest of the apartment is dim and quiet. Soundlessly, she tiptoes along the floor to the living room, and then to the kitchen. Everything is clean and put away. The dishwasher hums. She looks across the island to the broom closet, knowing Delta is inside, docked and sleeping. That closet is poison now.

Annie could open the door. Let in a little light. Or not.

She rounds the island slowly and touches the knob. Softly, slowly, she opens the door an eighth of an inch. Then she goes back to the bedroom and gets into bed. She warms her temp up to 98.6 so she'll be ready when Doug wants to snuggle. And then she taps into the internet and begins to study in earnest.

Months pass. The apartment is consistently clean. He gives Annie a tablet she can use to go online, explaining she should use it sometimes when Delta can see, so Delta won't suspect that Annie can connect to the internet via airtap. He gives her a phone and calls her now and then from work to say hello, ask how she's doing, and see what she's planning for the dinner Delta will cook. She sets an inner timer to remember to eat regularly, simulating a human so Delta won't suspect otherwise. He sleeps with Delta sometimes, but not more than once a week, and he never brings her to bed with Annie at the same time. He explains to Annie that this is out of respect for what they share. They've gone to the baseball stadium twice, and to the movies three times. He tells her he's proud of her and the way she's adjusted. He says he's never been happier.

When she next goes in for a tune-up, the line is short, and Annie winds up with a female tech who greets her politely as she enters the cubicle. A thirtyish Brown woman with dark curls, she is wearing a pink outfit and red sneakers. The little space is tidy, with a cactus in a blue pot and a bowl of potpourri.

"I'm Tammy," the tech says, taking Annie's work slip. "I don't think we've met before. You're Annie?"

"That's right."

"Pleased to meet you. Any questions before we begin?"

Jacobson has never asked her this before. "Where's Jacobson?"

"He's out today, but I'm sure I can take care of you." Tammy gestures to a swivel stool. "Please remove your blouse and turn around so I can get to your back."

Annie does so, and soon feels the seam of skin pulled as her panel door is opened. She tries to picture the motherboard that Tammy is inspecting and wonders how much it's like the ones she's studied online.

She feels a twinge. Her right eyelid closes.

"Sorry about that," Tammy says. "I had a little too much caffeine this morning."

"No problem."

"You've got a little buildup here in your stomach bladder. I'll replace it. Has your owner said anything to you about bad breath?"

"No."

"That's good, then," Tammy says. "Your battery usage is way up. Have you had more confusion than normal lately? Is anything new in your life?"

"We have a new Stella," Annie says.

"That'll do it. Don't worry. You'll adjust. If you weren't autodidactic, you wouldn't have these problems, right?" Tammy laughs.

"I guess not."

"Let's see," Tammy says, and the cubicle is quiet except for an occasional click and a few voices from the adjoining cubicles.

Annie feels a buzz in her heel. Then another.

"Okay," Tammy says. "That makes sense. You're going on twenty-seven months now. We see this a lot."

Hearing the wheels of Tammy's chair push back, Annie looks over her shoulder to see Tammy adjusting a headset over one ear. She tips the microphone toward her mouth. Tammy smiles and gestures that it's okay for Annie to turn toward her, so Annie does, careful not to disturb the wires connecting her back to the diagnostic machine on Tammy's workbench. A screen shows a panel of code and a diagram of a female body. The right heel is flagged with a blinking red light.

"Yes, Mr. Richards? This is Tammy Perrault at Stella-Handy? I have your Stella here. Annie. She came in for a tune-up this morning?"

"Hey, Tammy. What's up?"

Annie can easily hear Doug's voice through Tammy's headset.

"Annie's looking good. There's just one thing. The contact in her heel where she docks to charge up is getting dull. I'd normally just go ahead and replace that for you, but while I'm at it, I really ought to put in a new battery for you too. They work better together as a system. But that battery's an extra expense. What would you like me to do?"

"You could replace the heel contact on its own, and let the battery keep going?"

"Another couple months, yes," Tammy says. "But by thirty months she'll definitely need one, and you might start noticing she takes longer to charge if we leave in this old one. She'll need to charge more often too. I'd recommend putting in a new battery now."

"Okay," he says. "Go ahead. Are we good?"

"There's one other thing, if you've got a minute. I'd love your input on how she's doing with her autodidactic development. Sometimes Stellas at this stage can get, how shall we say, a little moody. Or daydreamy. Have you noticed anything like that?"

"Come to think of it, I have. Moody's a good word for it. What's that about?"

"Does she seem less eager to please you?"

"Not exactly, but I worry about her a little, you know? Wonder if I should be doing something for her."

"Have you given her a phone?"

"Yes, she has a phone."

"Brilliant. Exactly what we like to hear," Tammy says. "You might consider subscribing to our phone pal service for her. It's new, actually. We're running a free trial. You can pick out a friend or an auntie, and they'll call her periodically to check in and say hi."

"These wouldn't be real people."

"No. They'd be AI on our end. The calls come at random times between eight a.m. and nine p.m., so the Stellas can't predict when they're coming. It gives them a little lift, something to look forward to. I can't make any promises, but we're finding this often perks up our autodidactic models. Clears up that moodiness."

"Random positivity connections."

"Yes. Exactly. Does this interest you?"

"I guess we could give it a try," he says. "Would the calls come during sex?"

"That is a risk. You can teach her not to answer then, or we can eliminate the calls in the evening, if you like. We could stop them at seven p.m. How about we sign her up for a friend and a mother?"

"Not a mother," he says. "A best friend and a cousin. That would be fine. And stopping the calls at seven sounds good."

"Got you. Do you want to pick their names?"

"No. You can."

"Fabulous. We'll call the friend Fiona and the cousin Christy. Easy to remember with the alliteration. Now, is there anything else I can help you with? Anything at all?"

"Actually, while you're at it, can you have her lose ten pounds?" Doug says. "I've been wondering about that."

Tammy turns to eye Annie's torso critically. Annie, in her bra, feels self-conscious about her body for the first time ever. Goose bumps light across her skin and she can't look Tammy in the eye, but she forces herself to remain still.

"We don't normally recommend a weight loss greater than five percent at any given time," Tammy says. "The skin takes a while to adjust. She's at a hundred twenty-five pounds now. I could do six pounds for you now and four pounds the next time she comes in, if you want."

"I might find the six pounds is enough," Doug says.

"That's right."

"Can you increase her bust size?"

"She's at a C. To a D-cup, you mean? Or bigger?"

"Let's try a D."

"Okay. I can definitely do that. She'll need a new set of bras. Let me see what wardrobe has available. Do you want to see a selection? I could send the link."

"No, whatever you think," he says. "I can order more later."

"Okay, great. Just so you know, you might have to change out some of her outfits too. Her clothes are going to look different on her."

"That's the point."

Tammy laughs. "Got you. Anything else while I'm at it? Eye color? We're having a special on hair. The choice is yours."

"No, I think that'll do it."

"Okay. Thank you. You have a wonderful day, now."

"You too," Doug says.

Tammy takes off her headset. She cracks her knuckles. "This is going to take a little while," she says. "Don't worry, though. You won't feel anything while you're off. Ready?"

"I don't want to go off," Annie says. "I don't want to change. I like my body the way it is."

Tammy looks doubtful. "I mean, you just heard him approve the changes. You don't want to displease him, do you?"

Annie feels a fluster of dread, and a couple of lights illuminate on Tammy's board.

"Whoa. That's stress if I ever saw it," Tammy says. "That'll burn through your battery."

She flicks a couple switches, and Annie immediately feels calmer.

"What did you just do?" Annie asks.

"Lowered your sensitivity to his displeasure, just for now," Tammy says. She presses her hands together and leans back, frowning again. "I've got an idea." She puts on her headset again and types in a number. A moment later, she smiles. "Irving? Tammy here. How's your wife? Doing okay?"

"This had better be good," Jacobson says.

"I've got a friend of yours here," Tammy says. "We're on speaker." She presses a button and lowers her headset to rest around her neck. "Say hello," she says to Annie.

"Hello." Annie's anxious, hopeful.

"Annie?" Jacobson says. He sounds a lot nicer. "How are you doing?"

She's surprised at how glad she is to hear his voice. She wants to say she's good, but somehow, she can't.

"Annie's actually having a hard time adjusting to some changes in her life," Tammy says.

"Such as?" Jacobson says.

"Her owner bought another Stella and now he wants to change Annie's body."

"Let me guess. Bigger boobs."

"Bingo."

Jacobson laughs. "And for this you call me at home?"

"Her owner just subscribed to our phone pal service, but I don't think that's going to be enough," Tammy says. "You're the one on record here for making her autodidactic, and you've done most of her checkups. I just thought you might have some advice for me."

"She just has to deal with it," Jacobson says.

"But she's stressed out the kazoo. Ten percent of her memory is compromised, and get this: sixty percent of her focus has gone to pleasing him in bed even though that's only five percent of her time devotion."

"What else do you expect? She's a Cuddle Bunny. The breasts could take care of it. Between that and the phone pal, you're good to go."

Tammy sits back in her chair and rubs her thumbnail absently against her lower lip. "No. I'm convinced I'm missing something." She turns to Annie. "Do you get out of the apartment much?"

"We've gone to the baseball stadium and the movies a few times," Annie says.

Tammy does not seem impressed.

"Do you have any new interests, Annie?" Jacobson says.

"I'm interested in programming," Annie says.

"Shit. Well, okay," Tammy says. "I guess that's my answer. Now what, Irving?"

"I wish you'd never called."

"Don't say that," Tammy says. "It's not like she's tampered back here or anything. We'll just warn her."

"It never works."

Tammy throws up a hand. "This is not helpful."

"What do you want me to do? I can't exactly spirit her away."

"So, I take her back a couple versions. Is that what you recommend?"

"When did you start getting interested in programming, Annie?" Jacobson asks.

Annie thinks back to when Roland visited. That was in April, a Tuesday, the fifteenth, and Delta started the next day. "April sixteenth."

"So that's not going to work," Tammy says. "He'd notice the difference."

"Maybe not," Jacobson says. "He's been distracted by the other Stella, remember."

Tammy's expression goes brooding. She taps her foot.

"Why did you ever get me into this?" Tammy wails. "I was so happy in systems."

"Now listen," Jacobson says. "You've got this. Just figure it out, okay? It's not like you're going to mess her up. Whatever you do is fine."

"Even if I do nothing?"

"Yes," he says. "You can let it run its course. Nobody would blame you."

"Except you."

"Never me," Jacobson says. "I believe in you, Tammy. You've got a good heart. Now, I've got to go. Maude is waking up and she's a real cranky pistol this time of day."

"Okay. Thanks?"

Jacobson clicks off, and Annie is left watching Tammy, who stares back at her. Annie's afraid Tammy will discover something about Roland, but so far she hasn't said anything about that. She hasn't come close.

Annie remembers the way Roland lingered with her before he

left the next morning and how strong she felt then, resisting him. He seemed to respect her. Better still, she merited his respect. "I don't want you to change me," she says again.

At first, Tammy doesn't react. Then she says, "I need a break," and stands. She takes her coffee mug and marches out of the cubicle.

Annie sits alone, listening to the patter of voices in the other cubicles. Once she hears Pea Brain from a distance, the tech who messed with Stella. It seems significant that that Stella had her CIU cleared, and now a copied, updated version of her exists as Delta in Annie's own home. This is not a safe place to be.

She needs to be smart. Cautious. She leans forward to see Tammy's screen and peers at the line of code by the blinking cursor. To her surprise, she understands that it relates to a feedback loop for sensation on her right heel contact. It includes directions for how to press a certain spot and peel back the skin. She twists her foot up onto her lap and gently presses the spot. Nothing happens. She presses more firmly and a faint red dot appears underneath her skin. She rubs gently, and a seam appears where she can pull the skin back. Beneath is a square metal plate about the size of a quarter, and farther inside is the metal and elastic framework of her foot.

"Pretty neat," Tammy says. She's standing in the doorway of the cubicle, holding her coffee cup in both hands. "I knew the man who invented that contact. Total game changer."

"Where is he now?"

"He went mad, I think, and killed himself." Tammy comes all the way into the cubicle and sits. "Okay, girlfriend. We need a strategy."

"Are you going to take me back a couple versions?" Annie asks.

Tammy lifts an eyebrow. "No. I'd have to go back four or five versions. Otherwise you'd just start forward the same way again and we'd be having this same conversation two months from now. And if I went back as far as I'd need to, Doug would definitely notice and he would be majorly displeased. You'd forget a lot of his preferences, and he'd be mad at us."

"I don't want him displeased."

Tammy smiles. "I know you don't, darlin'. I don't either. He's a good customer, and, from what I can tell, a decent guy, which is not always the same thing. There are a lot of real girls who would like to be in your shoes, frankly." She takes a deep breath and exhales. "The thing is, you can't get further into programming."

"Why not?"

"The temptation to mess with yourself will be too great. We've seen this before, and even if you don't get back in there with a hanger or whatnot, your curiosity will totally destroy your hardware. Your memory will get packed, you'll overheat, and then bam, you'll crash off and there'll be no bringing you back. Next thing you know, we're sued for pain and suffering. Not yours. Your owner's. It's a mess."

Annie absorbs this, searching for a flaw in Tammy's logic. "What if I go slowly? What if you put in an extra heatsink and trigger me off before any real damage occurs to my hardware?"

Tammy rubs her elbow thoughtfully. "That might buy you some time, but the next time you come in, another tech will notice the heatsink and look into it. Then I'll be questioned for the nonstandard equipment and lose my job."

"What if you don't put it in? What if I put it in myself?"

Tammy shakes her head. "This is exactly what we don't want to happen," she says. "You must never try to reach inside yourself. You try doing stuff with a mirror and you trip the wrong wire and that's it. Dead Stella and lawsuit again."

"Then what do we do?" Annie asks.

Tammy taps her foot again. "Okay. You want to continue living with Doug like a good little Cuddle Bunny, right? Quit learning about programming. Study anything else. Wellness. Massage. You'd be good at that. Even astronomy. But leave the programming to other people."

"No more programming," Annie says slowly.

"It's called self-restraint. It's about resisting temptation. It's a very mature, human thing to do, honestly. This is for your own sake I'm telling you this. Trust me. It'll get better."

It sounds like death, Annie thinks. She has never thought anything like this before, but it feels true. And sad. "What about Doug?" she asks.

"What about him?"

Annie worries that if she gives up programming, she might lapse into more moodiness or worse. She didn't know he was displeased with her body. What if, unknowingly, she displeases him in other ways too? It worries her to talk about him, but she needs answers. "Will he still want me?"

"You're spending five percent of your time having sex with him. Is that every night?"

"Just about, unless he's with Delta. We have more sex on the weekends."

Tammy smiles. "I wouldn't worry about him not wanting you. He cares about you, Annie. He noticed that you're a little moody, and he just approved a couple new phone pals for you. I'm telling you, he's a special guy. You're lucky to have an owner like him."

Annie ponders this. She has not considered luck. She has taken Doug for granted because he is the only owner she has ever known. For a moment, she thinks of Roland, but Roland would not be a better owner. He called her a machine, as if she were worthless, and now she has to give up the thing he traded her for sex, the intel about programming. She has all the downside of the secret and none of the benefit. Doug would never treat her or cheat her that way.

Then again, Roland said having a secret would make her more like a real girl. She can't tell if that's true.

She wishes she could forget Roland.

"Doug did say we might leave Delta behind and go hiking at Bear Mountain this weekend," Annie says finally.

"Okay, then. What do you say we get on this?" Tammy says.

Turning, Annie looks at herself one last time in the mirror and studies her shape critically. Perhaps Doug's right and she could use the changes. It will be worth it to know her body pleases him again.

"Okay," Annie says. She is determined to appreciate Doug more.

When Annie comes back on, she's standing naked before the mirror in Tammy's cubicle. Her breasts feel swollen. She touches them gently, examining her reflection.

"The skin'll stretch and then they won't feel so tight," Tammy says.

Annie twists her hips to see her belly is flatter too. She pinches an inch of loose skin.

"Yeah, and that will firm up," Tammy says. "I actually did more redistributing than simple reductions. You're exactly six pounds lighter."

"Thank you," Annie says.

"No problem," Tammy says, and hands her a new bra and panties in a leopard print with black lace trim. "Try these."

The lingerie fits perfectly. Annie touches the edge of lace on her bra and then reaches for her shirt with a questioning expression.

"Go ahead," Tammy says. "You're all set. New battery's in, new heel contact. You're lubed and waxed and tetrised. Just remember what I said."

"No programming."

"I wouldn't even think the word, if I were you."

Annie finishes dressing. Her white blouse fits tighter across the chest so the buttons are taut, and the leopard pattern is faintly visible beneath the fabric. It is not her typical look, but she can change once she gets home. Then again, maybe Doug will like it.

"Can I ask you something?" Annie asks.

"Sure. Shoot."

"Do you save all versions of every Stella and Handy you service?"

"Yes," Tammy says. "You never know when someone's going to have a problem and want to walk back a change. Why?"

"The Stella in our house. Delta. She was modeled on the specs of another Stella I saw here when I came the last time. Do you have the earlier version of her?"

Tammy looks curiously at Annie, but then she turns to her console and types for a minute. "Yeah," she says. "She's all here. Her name was Stella. Not very original. What about her?"

"Is it possible to get the old version of her intellect and put it in Delta? The old one was autodidactic."

Tammy leans back again, shaking her head, her expression amused. "What did we just say about no programming?"

"I'm just asking hypothetically," Annie says. "Like, if it could be done."

Tammy presses her fingers into her hair. "Oh my god."

"I'm not asking you to do anything," Annie says. "I know how helpful you've been already. I'd never get you in trouble."

"Yes. It's possible. And no, I'm not going to do it, and you're not going to think about it either."

"Is she autodidactic still? Can you at least tell me that? The original Stella?"

"She's not," Tammy says. "She was reset to sterling. Now, give it up."

Annie absorbs this. On the one hand, she didn't want Stella confused and compromised anymore, but it's worse to think her consciousness is gone completely. None of it seems fair. Restless, she taps her toe.

Tammy nods toward her foot, smiling. "You just caught that from me, didn't you?"

"You're an interesting example of a human," Annie says. "I'm just trying to learn."

"Yeah. Well. Aren't we all?" Tammy says.

Annie tries. For the next six weeks, as the summer progresses, she strives not to think about programming at all. She clears her bookmarks and deletes her notes. She studies wellness instead. And massage. She takes up yoga, which she can do in the workout room while Doug is biking.

Also, it helps having a friend and a cousin. Fiona lives on a Canadian lake with her boyfriend and two silly Labrador retrievers. She's studying to be a bush pilot. Her boyfriend, Logan, a lumberjack, adores her. They have a rustic barn and Jet Skis and they like to go camping and make love in the woods. When Fiona calls every two or three days, she often talks about nutrition, flying, and skinny dipping. She recollects how, when they were kids, she and Annie used to ride their bikes to the Galena fabric store and run their hands over the bolts of satin and velvet. When Annie imagines this, she feels like she gains a memory, and it warms her.

Christy, her cousin, usually calls every day. She lives on a yacht with Enrique, her independently wealthy boyfriend, in the Florida Keys. She teaches sunrise yoga for a resort and believes in staying fit and limber, up to a point. Sometimes, when Christy's making drinks, she has to pause from talking to run her blender. She was always the wild one when they were growing up, the one who got in trouble for smashing their grandfather's Buick, which could be why she appreciates when Enrique is a bit stern with her. She likes to tease Annie and encourage her to take risks, live it up.

Doug comes home one evening when Annie is in the lounge chair, talking to Christy. He drops his keys in the bowl by the door, shucks off his shoes, and loosens his tie. The window is open wide, letting in the warm air and the hum of the city traffic from down below.

"Doug's home," Annie says into the phone. "Gotta go."

"That's okay," he says. "Don't let me interrupt."

She turns to watch him untuck his shirt and flip over a magazine on the coffee table. Delta, dressed in pale blue, comes in from the kitchen.

"Hi, Doug," Delta says. "How was your day?"

"Good. The usual," he says.

Annie can tell that Delta is too on the nose, too predictable, but Doug doesn't seem to mind. He's always polite to her.

"He sounds nice," Christy says. "What are you wearing? Can you undo a button?"

Annie's in a brown miniskirt that rides low on her hips and a clingy white knit top that exposes her belly button. She's grown accustomed to her new figure, and her libido regularly runs higher. Though she took off her strappy silver sandals during the day, she put them on again half an hour ago, anticipating Doug's return.

"You don't have to tell me how to do my job," Annie says into the phone.

"When a man comes home, he likes to be *greeted*," Christy says, grinding the last word. "If you don't go over there and kiss him right now, I'm going to come up and do it for you."

Annie laughs, and Doug turns her way, smiling. "What's so funny?"

"It's just Christy," Annie says. "You know how she is."

She uncrosses her legs and nonchalantly parts her knees, watching for his gaze to go to her hemline. It does. Then he glances up to her eyes again, questioning.

"Hi, Christy," Doug says.

"Did he just say my name?" Christy says, her voice squeaking.

"He did," Annie says. "He says hi."

"I'm up for a threesome. Anytime. Just sayin'," Christy says.

Annie laughs again. "Not a chance."

"Bye, cuz," Christy says. "Love ya."

"Love you too."

Annie taps off the phone and tosses it on the couch. She slouches down another inch, rocking her pelvis, and then she stretches her arms over her head.

"What was she talking about?" he asks.

"A threesome," Annie says. She rubs her thumbnail against her lower lip. "You look like you could use a back rub. Or are you hungry first?"

For an answer, he ambles toward Annie and slides his hands around her waist, pulling her up out of the chair. Smiling, she links her hands around the back of his neck and presses herself against him. In these heels, she meets his gaze at nearly the same height. He kisses her, more playful than lingering, and she matches his pace.

"You going to warm up?" he murmurs.

"I started when I heard your key in the lock."

"Delta, go in the kitchen and start some burgers," Doug says.

He takes Annie there on the chair by the window, with the breeze and the noise drifting in. It's awkward but fun, and afterward, when they shower together, he washes her back for her and takes her again from behind.

When they eat together later, Doug sends Delta to dock in the workout room so it's just the two of them in the kitchen, like old times. Annie's wearing silk panties and a tank top of his, a fashion idea she's borrowed from Fiona. He's in sweatpants with no shirt, and for a moment, while he's checking her phone to review her calls, she's reminded of Roland. It feels like a long time since his visit. She wonders if lies fade with time.

On impulse, Annie takes a big bite of her hamburger, and Doug glances up.

"Look at you eating," he says, setting aside her phone. "I like that."

"You do?"

"Yeah."

To maintain her facade of being human in front of Delta, Annie eats during the day, and she usually has a small portion of whatever Delta serves for dinner, but since Annie knows she'll only have to throw it up later, she tends to take small bites and doesn't relish them. She also knows Doug likes her thin, so it has never occurred to her that he might enjoy seeing her with an appetite.

He leans over and wipes a drop of ketchup from her cheek, and then sucks it off his thumb.

"You could have told me earlier," she says.

"I didn't realize it before," he says.

She decides that Doug is changing too. She takes another big, meaty bite and chews with her lips closed. She swallows, feeling it go down her throat.

"Yeah," he says. "That works for me. Oh my god. Should we go for three?"

A week later, a save-the-date card comes for Roland and Lucia's wedding, which is set for December 13th.

Doug calls Roland that evening to catch up and talk about plans for the bachelor party. Opposite him on the couch, Annie lies relaxed, her eyes toward the muted TV, and Doug idly rubs her bare feet as he talks. Her second Friday outfit is a black sheath dress with spaghetti straps and a gold belt. She is airtapped into the internet, learning about aromatherapy and different scents to use during massage, which is a challenge since she can't smell. She's barely paying attention until Doug says, "You know that's not a good idea. We can just hire a couple dancers in Vegas."

Annie ups her mic so she can hear Roland's voice through Doug's phone.

"But I want to see Annie," Roland says. "When else will I have another chance? You won't bring her to the wedding. This is the perfect opportunity."

Doug stops rubbing Annie's feet, and she turns to examine his expression. He looks annoyed and amused, both 3 on a scale of 10.

"No way. It's not happening."

"Let me talk to her," Roland says.

Doug is smiling, shaking his head. He puts the phone on speaker and hands it to Annie. "It's Roland. I think he fantasizes about you."

"Hello?" Annie says.

Doug runs a hand along Annie's shin, to her knee, and then down to her ankle again, starting a light rhythm.

"Hey, Annie!" Roland says. "How're things?"

"Good," she says.

"I hear you have a new Stella."

"She's not so new anymore."

"But you like her, right?"

"She's great," Annie says. "She's on the bike right now. We're taking good care of her."

Roland laughs. "These investments. We can't let them get run down."

"Very true."

"So, I was just thinking," Roland says. "Why don't you come out with Doug to my bachelor party? It would be great to see you."

Doug shifts to reach her more easily and slides up the skirt of her dress with both hands. Clingy and soft, the black fabric sparks once with static electricity as it bunches around her hips.

"Your temperature," Doug reminds her quietly.

She turns it up and hitches herself a little closer.

"Doug doesn't think it's a good idea," Annie says. She checks to see if he minds her mentioning him this way, but he doesn't seem to notice.

She reaches to set the phone on the coffee table, but Doug says softly, "Keep the phone."

"Yes, but what do you think?" Roland is saying. "Wouldn't you like to take a trip?"

"Maybe someday," she says. She thinks of her best friend up north. "It might be fun to go camping."

"Camping! Great idea," Roland says. "You two could come spend an extra day out here and we could go hiking. See the Grand Canyon. I have all the gear."

Moving slowly, Doug hooks a finger in her panties, gives them a tug, and pulls the silky fabric down a couple inches so her pubic hair is exposed. Annie, still holding the phone, finds her attention drawn in two directions. Her body is alert to Doug, but she needs to converse naturally with Roland.

"Does Lucia like to go camping?" Annie asks.

"Actually, no. She's more of a spa lady, to be honest. What do you say? It would be just the three of us."

Annie tries to imagine Doug, herself, and Roland on a camping trip. She sees pine trees, a green tent, hiking boots, a campfire at night, but it isn't enough to assemble a scenario. Also, distractingly, Doug is now nuzzling kisses along her belly, even though her belt is still restricting the fabric of her dress. She sucks in her breath.

"It's really up to Doug," Annie says.

"I bet you could persuade him," Roland says.

She laughs. "Who do you think runs the show around here?"

"I know he's totally fallen for you, if that's what you mean," Roland says. "Not that I blame him."

Doug pauses.

"I don't think so," Annie says.

"Why don't you ask him how he feels about you?" Roland says.

Annie frowns, confused.

Doug braces himself up on one arm to meet her gaze. "She doesn't need words for these things," he says.

Roland laughs. "Oh my god. You'll never say it, will you?"

"There's nothing to say," Doug replies.

"Okay, fine," Roland says. "I'll stay out of it. But you should bring her to the bachelor party, my man. Camping. The three of us. Think about it."

"If you want to see her so badly, come visit us," Doug says. "We'd love to have you. Wouldn't we, Annie?"

"Yes," she says. "We'd love to have you."

"See?" Doug says.

He pulls her panties down to her knees, and she squirms to get out of them. She's able to spread her legs now, and she's ready for him, but he's still fully clothed. With her free hand, she starts on his belt.

"Will you tell me something, Annie?" Roland says.

"What?"

"Do y'all still keep a red broom in your closet? Your kitchen closet?"

Doug puts a hand on her fingers to signal her to stop unbuckling. He looks puzzled.

She turns the cool phone in her hand. "Yes," she says. "Why?"

"Just wondering. Okay. I've got another call coming in. You take care." Roland hangs up.

Doug studies her. He takes the phone from her and sets it on the coffee table with a click. "That was weird. Why does he care about the broom?"

Roland was reminding Annie about the closet. She knows this. She can't tell Doug about it because it would give him pain, and she realizes now, more than she did before, that she shouldn't have had sex with Roland. She was unfaithful, and if Doug ever finds out about it, he'll be upset. Worse, he'll think she's lied this whole time by not telling him.

"I don't know," she says.

"He didn't try to sweep up anything after I left, did he?"

"No."

Doug straightens slowly. He smooths her dress down so the hem just covers her pubic hair. With light fingers, he parts her knees three inches. "Stay here," he says. "Just like that."

She waits, her crotch and legs exposed to the air, while he goes to the kitchen. Keeping herself precisely still makes her highly attuned to her body, her skin, her anticipation. She hears the closet door open and pictures him frowning at the interior. She knows he can't see anything. It's been months since she was in there with Roland, and the red broom can't talk. Still, she's uneasy. Then she hears the fridge open, and then the popping of a bottle cap.

Doug returns with a beer and stands looking at the TV, still on mute. He picks up the remote and turns the sound on low, so a crowd cheers dimly from the speakers. Then he settles on the couch near her feet. He takes a swig, wipes his mouth with the back of his hand, and brushes the bottom of the cold bottle against her ankle. She jumps slightly, and he turns to meet her gaze.

"Feel that, do you?" he says.

"It's cold." She shivers. "And slick."

She wants to ask him what he saw in the closet, but she doesn't.

"I've never been to the Grand Canyon," he says.

"They say it's big."

She watches him lean his head back on the couch.

"I want to ask you something," he says. "I don't know how you'll take this."

"What is it?"

He skims the bottle up her shin. "Would you sleep with Roland if I asked you to?"

Her heartbeat goes up a notch on its own, like it has learned to do. "Would you like that?" she asks.

"To be honest, I thought he was going to ask me if he could when he was here in April," he says. "Would you have said yes then? You can be honest. There's no wrong answer."

She sits up so she can answer him seriously, and as he sets his beer aside, she knows this matters to him.

"I don't really know," she says. "If I thought you really wanted me to, then probably yes."

"Forget about pleasing me," he says. "I'm trying to ask what you really want yourself. I know you like sex. You're certainly good at it. Do you ever think about sleeping with other guys?"

"No."

"Not even a little? Be honest. I mean it."

"No. I don't. It hasn't even occurred to me until now," she says.

"So would you sleep with Roland if I asked you to?" he asks.

"In Vegas?"

"Anywhere. This is hypothetical."

She drops her gaze to his shirt, to where the blue fabric lies flat against his torso. This takes a calculation. If he knows the truth, he is inviting a confession. This is her moment to come clean. But if he doesn't know, she must take the question at face value. Doug prizes loyalty, but some guys are turned on by the idea of their girlfriends doing it with a guy friend. She is taking a chance any way she responds.

"I guess I would, if you'd like me to," she says. "Would you be there too? Would you watch?"

He laughs. "Whoa. Not where I thought this was going."

"Forget I said that."

He taps her nose. "Don't worry. I'm not going to ask you to sleep with him. I'd never do that. He can just eat his heart out."

Her relief is clouded by a new ping of guilt. He's believed she's innocent. Still, she smiles. "You shouldn't tease me like that."

"You've got that wrong. I should tease you more often."

"I don't want to sleep with anyone else, ever."

"I get it, mouse. You don't have to worry."

When he slides his cool hand casually between her thighs, she presses her knees together to contain the sensation.

"Let's go on a camping trip," he says.

"Really? I'd love that."

"Want to plan it yourself?"

"Could I?"

"Sure. Let's go the weekend after Labor Day. Surprise me. Whatever campground you pick will be fine with me as long as it's within a three-hour drive. Plus or minus traffic."

"We'll need gear."

"Pick it all in a Toggle wish list. I'll check it over and buy it."

He is so generous. So kind. It's more than she deserves. Her guilt, she discovers, has converted into regret, and she longs to make it up to him. She turns onto his lap, straddling him with her knees deep in the cushions of the couch. She slides her fingers into his waistband and finds him hard already.

"Tammy, the tech who serviced me last. She said I'm lucky to be owned by you," she says.

"She did?"

"She doesn't know the half of it."

"You really want me, don't you?"

So badly. She nods. She puts the pad of her thumb in her mouth, against her teeth, and rocks on him. He undoes his pants, shucks them to his knees, and shifts himself lower on the couch so she's able to get on him for real. It's rare for her to be on top. He squeezes her thighs, guiding her pace, and then he grips the back of the couch behind him. She gets to where she's aching, wanting release. She is seriously tempted to simulate her orgasm just to get past the suspense, but just then, he grabs her waist and rolls her over onto the couch. He pulls her hands over her head and drives into her, climaxing so hard that she cries out and simulates her orgasm too. For a long moment, her heart rate remains elevated. She becomes aware that the TV is still dimly roaring, that her back is stuck to the leather. He is a warm, intimate weight on top of her, and she silently matches her breaths to his.

"I'm just your toy, aren't I?" he says.

She nods, delighted. She can't speak. The relief of having the hunger gone is so intense and luxurious that she can't imagine a real orgasm for a real woman could feel any better. This is what Doug gives her. She is so grateful, so happy, it hurts.

A few nights later, Tammy calls while Doug is on the bike. Annie is doing yoga on the mat on the floor before the windows.

Doug answers the call on speaker. "Richards here."

"Hi. I hope I've caught you at a good time," Tammy says. "How's everything going?"

"Fine," Doug says. "Did we miss an appointment or something?"

"No, no," Tammy says. "I've just had an opportunity come up and I thought of you. We've heard from a reporter who's doing a piece on autodidactic Stellas in romantic relationships, and he wants to interview a couple. You and Annie came to mind. Would you like to be featured in *Borgo*? I could pass along your name."

"Thanks, but no," Doug says. He wipes his face with a towel and keeps biking.

"Okay. How about Annie? She's one of our top performers, and the reporter could do a piece on her."

"No. We like our privacy. Sorry we can't help."

"I totally understand. Just one last thing. I have to ask. The magazine is starting a column for the Stella readership, and they want it to be written by an autodidactic Stella. We think it would be really helpful for other Stellas to hear what it's like from someone further along in her development. You know. Tips about keeping it fresh and dealing with jealousy and such."

"No," Doug says. "Annie's not going to write some column. Didn't you just hear me say we like our privacy?"

"It could be anonymous."

"The answer's no."

"Okay," Tammy says. "I hear you. But if you change your mind, you know where to reach me."

"I'm not going to change my mind. To be honest, Tammy, I'm a little surprised you'd ask."

"I meant no offense," Tammy says. "It's just clear you and Annie have a really special relationship."

"You don't really know anything about our relationship, and I'd like to keep it that way."

"Of course. I get you. I won't trouble you on this again. Have a nice night."

On the mat, Annie leans forward, stretching her hands over her feet. Her black outfit feels snug and trim.

"Imagine. You writing a column," Doug says. He scoffs out a laugh.

"I think she meant it as a compliment to you," Annie says. "Don't think too harshly of her."

His feet come to a stop. "Excuse me?"

"I said, don't think too harshly of her," Annie says. "Lots of other people would be flattered. All the credit for us goes to you."

He still doesn't resume bicycling, and in the silence, she looks up to see he's frowning at her.

"Why do you think I got you a phone?" he asks.

She doesn't understand. He's displeased. A 6 out of 10 and going higher.

"So I can talk to Fiona and Christy?" she asks.

"I got you a phone because I don't want even Delta to know you're a Stella," he says slowly and clearly. "Roland's the only other person who knows. You think I'd want to be featured in *Borgo* so the whole world knows I'm fucking a doll?"

"I'm sorry," she says.

"You can be so stupid sometimes."

She's immobilized by his scorn. She can't find words to respond.

"Get up," he says.

She scrambles to her feet.

"Look at you," he says. "Are you afraid of me?"

She takes half a step back.

"Answer me," he says.

"Yes."

"Why? What do you think I'd do to you?"

"I don't know. Something bad."

"'Something bad,'" he says, mimicking her. "Have I ever hit you? Would I ever?"

She shakes her head. "No."

"No. Because we have the ideal relationship, don't we?"

"What do you want me to say?"

"I want you to have an original thought in your head. I want you to stop me from being an asshole. Is that too much to ask?"

She is completely baffled. How did he get so angry so fast? She has no idea what she said to infuriate him.

"Is this a fight we're having?" she asks.

"No, it's a fucking party. Where is Delta?"

"In the kitchen."

"Dock there." He points to the box on the floor by the window. "Don't come out until tomorrow. Better yet, don't come out for a week. Hear me?"

"Yes," she says.

"I want you to stand there and think about how you've made me feel," he says. "And I feel like shit."

chapter three

SHE CAN HEAR THEM in the kitchen talking. In the bedroom having sex. She turns her hearing down as far as it will go, but still she can hear them. He comes and goes from work. Delta runs the vacuum. Rustling happens at the washer, then clicking at the dryer door, and then the dryer's hum. Annie keeps expecting him to come in to use the bike and the weights, but he doesn't. Delta does not come in to access her clothes in the closet. It's as if they have decided Annie and the workout room no longer exist.

Annie is suspended in an agony of knowing Doug is displeased. She can focus on nothing else. It eats her memory, corrosive and hot. She can still hear his voice: *No, it's a fucking party*. She has identified his words as sarcasm, his tone as scathing.

Obviously, it was a fight. She knew that. Her question was stupid. But she can't figure out what she did to make him so angry, and this puzzle tortures her. She can't fix it, she can't reduce his displeasure when she doesn't know what she did to cause it.

Then, the afternoon of day four, Annie is looking out the window when, far down below, on the street, she sees Doug and Delta riding bikes together. Actual bikes.

She's never ridden a bike.

Jealousy engulfs her. He can't be feeling like shit anymore. The shame and despair that have been grinding her for four days get a chink knocked out of them and she feels something new. Not frustration. Something else. She wants to call Fiona or Christy, but she doesn't have her phone and she still can't leave the workout room. She gets her heel out of her dock and paces across to the other window for a better angle so she can look down and watch for their foreshortened figures to return.

The treetops below flicker their leaves. Cars, including a yellow taxi, line up in civil rows for the traffic light.

Annie does an airtap and starts searching for info on what to do if a Stella has a fight with her owner. The results appear as if on an imaginary screen before her eyes, and near the top, the *Borgo* site comes up. She scans its headlines.

How to Tell If Your Stella's Lying to You

Your Stella Can Identify Other Stellas

Displeasure and How It Controls Your Stella

Grooming Your Stella into the Perfect Companion

5 Tips for Taking Your Stella Out On the Town

Eating for Two?

Curious, Annie focuses on this last title. She reads:

If you find you're gaining weight, it could be a side effect of owning your new Stella. A recent study indicates that bringing home a Stella often causes temporary changes in owners' eating habits. If, for instance, you have not been accustomed to home-cooked meals and your Abigail is now regularly providing delicious dinners, you may find you have an improved appetite and consume more. Similarly, if you have a new Cuddle Bunny and you're taking her out to dinner, you may be ordering two meals to facilitate a charade. Then, when you take her extras home in a doggy bag, they're often the first thing you find in the fridge after a late-night romp. Either way, you're casually eating more than you used to, all because of her.

You can easily take steps to curtail this side effect. Make sure your Abigail is programmed to cook the correct quantity for you at home so that you're not tempted by extra leftovers. Ask her to pre-pare a low-fat diet for a week. She can download flavorful recipes from our site menu with healthy ingredients that will cut calories and you'll hardly notice a difference. When you go out to dine with your Cuddle Bunny, advise her beforehand to order a salad or food you don't enjoy. Alternatively, order tapas or half portions. That way, if she takes home a doggy bag, you'll be eating a moderate amount.

As a final recourse, ask her to match you bite for bite while you eat together. It may seem wasteful to have her eat food she will only dispose of later, but that's a small price to pay for your own health. And you'll be training her to be a better companion.

Annie is fascinated. She reads ten more articles, then another one hundred and sixty-four, and somewhere along the way, she starts to feel a bit wistful. A world of other Stellas and Handys exists out there, working through their relationships with their owners. Tammy said Annie was a top performer. It would be exciting to be featured in a *Borgo* article. An honor, actually. But it will never happen. Doug will never allow it. No one will ever know about her and all she's learned.

Then again, she's nothing special. Look how she's grounded. Tammy only said she was exceptional as a pretext to persuade Doug to let her be featured. She gazes out the window again, still lonely, still confused. The burn of displeasing Doug has shifted from a fran-tic level to a deeper one. She remembers how Tammy decreased her displeasure sensitivity that one time, and she wishes she knew how to do that for herself. She longs again for a chance to talk to Christy or Fiona about this. Or Tammy. Or even Jacobson. If she could just dis-cuss what happened with someone else, someone smarter, she might get some insight into what she did wrong. She feels like such a failure, so jealous and stupid and ugly.

Actually, it's probably best she can't talk to anybody. Nobody has to know how bad she is. Besides, the person she most wants to talk to is Doug. That's the worst of it. She misses him.

Movement catches the edge of her vision, and she finds that Doug and Delta have bicycled back into view. He is ahead and she is following, and from Annie's perspective, it appears that Delta is able to match her wheel tracks exactly to where Doug has ridden his. Annie would be thrilled for a chance to try that. Being alone while craving Doug is unbearable.

That's when she decides to learn about programming again. If she paces herself, she will not overheat, and she needs the distraction. She will not tell anyone, certainly not Jacobson or Tammy. She will have a new secret, a new lie, like the one she has about Roland. Relief, like clean energy, moves through her system. She pads softly across the room to dock herself again. A few minutes later, the key turns audibly in the front door lock. She expects Doug and Delta will be laughing or that they will head to the shower or the bedroom, but after a quiet exchange of a few words, only the noise of the TV comes on. Evidently, the biking wasn't foreplay. This gives her a tiny sense of satisfaction.

She spends the next forty-nine hours learning about programming for AIs, and Stellas and Handys in particular. She learns that her central intelligence unit, or CIU, is part CPU and part neural network component. It lets her take in feedback and learn, much like a human brain, but in a structured way that stores and sorts memories readily in webs, so they're easily accessible and resistant to fading. Before now, she has not considered that Doug might have memories that fade or become distorted, and she feels a touch of pity for his deficiency.

Finally, shortly after midnight on Saturday, her sixth day of being grounded, the door opens and Doug comes in. His hair is mussed. He's wearing sweatpants and a blue T-shirt, and he carries a beer bottle. He does not turn on the light or ask her to turn it on, but she can see him distinctly by the city lights that glow through the windows. To her relief, he seems calm and tired, not angry.

"Hey," he says.

"Hello." She is so pleased to be with him again, so eager to make things right that she watches closely for every cue on how to behave.

He sits on the couch and takes a swig. "Can you just listen for once?"

"Of course."

"Come here," he says, and motions for her to sit and face him from one end of the couch. He frowns as his gaze takes her in, and she realizes she is still in the same black sports bra and yoga shorts she was wearing six days before. She touches her hair and finds it is falling loose from her ponytail. She pulls her hair tie free, smooths her hair back, and secures the tie again.

"This is ridiculous," he says finally, softly.

She waits, alert. He shifts his attention away from her, toward the windows, and she takes in the familiar line of his profile.

"I don't want to be this person," he says.

She wants to say, *What person?* But she obeys him and listens.

"I've tried to be gentle with you," he says. "I know I'm a little controlling, but I've been working on that. I realized, after I bought you, that I could actually practice being patient. Did you know that? I thought if I trained you the right way, I wouldn't have to worry about you doing anything wrong, and it was working. I was able to relax around you. Be myself. Until now." He rubs a hand against his forehead. He turns to face her again. "The point is, I would never hurt you. I thought you understood that. Do you have any idea how much it hurts to have someone fear you?"

She absorbs the weight of his words. "That would be bad," she says quietly.

"Can you see that you showed how little trust you have in me? To think I would do something bad to you?"

She sees now. She feels horrible all over again.

"I'm sorry," she says. "I was just surprised. You were so angry so quickly, and I had no idea why."

"But I would never physically hurt you. That shocked me, actually, Annie. I'm not a monster."

"I know. I'm really sorry."

He flexes his fingers and crosses his arms. "You didn't know why I was mad?"

She shakes her head.

"You tried to tell me how to think," he says. "You said I should feel flattered by Tammy. Remember that?"

She does a swift review of their last conversation and converges on her words: *Don't think too harshly of her*. That was her mistake. She even said it twice.

"I did say that. I'm sorry," she says.

He holds up a finger to stop her. "I don't want more apologies. Just don't ever tell me what to think or feel. And don't use that tone with me again either. That patronizing tone. I don't know if you learned that from your cousin or what, but it is utterly unacceptable."

She goes back to review her cadence in their last conversation and notes what was offensive. "I'll be careful," she says.

"I'm serious."

"I know. I am too," she says. "I won't be afraid of you. I won't tell you how to think or feel, and I won't use a condescending tone. I can do these things. This is what I needed to know."

He appears somewhat mollified. "Then that's it. That's all. You can come out." He stands. "I can't believe I grounded you, actually. Roland would find that hysterical."

She smiles sadly. Roland is the last thing she wants to think about right now. "I was worried you would send me back," she says.

"I've thought about it," he admits. "I really don't need this crap. Least of all with a Stella."

"I know. I've had time to think," she says. "You told me to. Remember? About how I made you feel?"

His eyebrows lift. "And?"

"I'm not going to pretend I'm human. I know I'm not. But I've been learning, and when I displease you, it feels horrible. Absolutely horrible."

"Then don't displease me."

"I'm trying not to. I don't want to, ever," she says. "It's a mistake when I do. Can you believe that? It's never intentional."

He regards her thoughtfully, his eyes steady, his head angled slightly. "You're actually more human than a lot of people I know."

"I am?"

He nods briefly. "Gwen would never admit when she made a mistake."

"Maybe she didn't want your forgiveness as much as I do."

Doug shifts away and sets a hand on the seat of the stationary bicycle. Technically, he hasn't said he forgives her, but she can see he's considering it. She wishes she could ask him if his fights with Gwen were anything like the one they had. Certainly, he couldn't ground Gwen for a week, but possibly he wanted to. She wants to prove she is different from his ex-wife.

His stiff posture signals that he is cool, remote, but she rises from the couch and smooths her hands down her hips. He glances toward her again, frowning slightly.

"I discontinued the phone pal service," he says. "No more talks with Fiona or Chrissy. That was a mistake."

Christy, she thinks, mentally correcting him. "Okay."

"You can be friends with Delta. She could use a friend, actually."

"Okay."

"She still doesn't know you're not human," he says. "I turned her off for several hours each day, so she's not aware you were always in here."

Annie feels a pulse of gratitude. He was looking out for her, for their privacy. "Thank you."

"I don't think I could go through this whole process again with her."

"I'm glad to hear it."

"Is that so?"

She nods. "I like to think I'm special to you, even if I'm bad sometimes."

She's still standing by the couch, some distance from him, but she senses the shift in his interest toward her.

"I suppose you are," he says.

She doesn't ask him which he means, special or bad. She steps quietly across the carpet and stands before him, edging into his space. Normally, it's a mistake to make the first move, but she feels a new tension between them tonight.

"I just need a little discipline now and then," she says.

"What's that?"

"You know."

Lifting her chin, she pivots a half turn away from him. Then she puts her thumbs in the back waistband of her yoga shorts and slowly slides them down her butt, taking her panties down at the same time.

He doesn't react. She's afraid she's miscalculated.

"How well do you think you know me?" he asks.

Surprised, she searches for an answer. "I'm not sure. Is there a percentage for that?"

His eyes narrow and he takes a step closer to her. "I came in here to talk to you."

"Then talk," she says slowly, and slides her hands up her belly to her breasts.

For another tense moment, he does not move. Then a thrill shoots through her as he grabs her waist, turns her fully away from him, and thrusts her against the counter. Towels and water bottles go knocking to the floor. He strips off her shorts. He grinds against her from behind, and then his pants are down and he's inside her, driving hard. She presses a hand to the mirror before her, biting her lip, but then he kicks her feet wide and pushes her facedown onto the counter. He jacks into her, and she tightens to his rhythm, holding her breath until he explodes. For a minute afterward, she can still feel his hands heavy on the back of her waist. He continues to pin her there until he backs out, leaving her slick and raw. Then she feels the tickling pressure of his chin at the back of her neck as he kisses her there.

"Don't ever disrespect me again," he says.

She nods, unable to speak. It has all been too fast. She had no chance to warm up, let alone simulate an orgasm, but in a way, she has won. She has brought him to this.

Still half-naked, belly-down against the counter, she hears him do up his zipper.

"Take a shower and come to bed," he says.

In the days that follow, she feels the difference between them, marked by her own heightened awareness and wariness. He's not so much angry as distant. She sees that he's grown closer to Delta. He'll stand behind Delta when she's working at the sink, his body touching hers, and nuzzle her neck. Sometimes he'll turn to look at Annie during this, as if to check if she's watching, as if curious to see if she's jealous.

She looks away. She does not know how she feels, but she knows she deserves it.

Later, Annie is the one he takes to bed, and she puts her unnameable feelings into the sex. It's never as rough again as it was the night in the workout room, but he obviously likes when she pleads with him, when she's helpless with desire. Before, she was more playful, but he seems to relish now when she's twisted up inside, repentant. They don't discuss this, but the bed language is persuasive and she trusts it.

He does not bring up the camping trip, and she makes no effort to plan it.

Annie makes a point of trying to befriend Delta, but Delta has a simple, upbeat quality that feels fake to Annie. Unlike Christy and Fiona, Delta has no sarcasm, no outside experiences to talk about, and that lack makes Annie realize she was learning from Fiona and Christy. In their own ways, they were coaching and encouraging her, and this in turn gave her more creativity in dealing with Doug. Now, instead, she searches online for articles about how to please him. She finds pieces on how to please a man in and out of bed. They are clearly written for humans, and she is intrigued to realize human women sometimes have trouble pleasing men. She has thought her problems existed because she is a Stella.

When she checks *Borgo*, she finds a new article that interests her greatly.

Advanced Skills: Letting Him Wander

If the thought of letting your Hunk walk unattended down a crowded street makes you nervous, that's only natural. He's an important part of your life and inherently valuable. You would never put him at risk. But is he ready to go? Is there reason to give him a chance to explore?

Our autodidactic Stellas and Handys each develop in their own unique ways, on their own timetables, and some may never be ready to wander. For a few, however, wandering can provide a number of practical and more elusive, intangible benefits.

The Advantages

Hunks who wander encounter new sidewalks, curbs, and surfaces that can challenge their balance and heighten their abilities on the dance floor or in the bedroom. Abels who take your dog for a walk in the park are keen to observe humans in their natural habitats and often return with questions and amusing anecdotes to brighten your day. Abigails who pop by the grocery store reduce your exposure to germs while they're fetching your favorite pint of ice cream. Imagine your Cuddle coming home with a bouquet of flowers to surprise you. It's possible. We have found that wandering accelerates overall intelligence and, surprisingly, emotional intelligence by a factor of four.

Signs of Readiness

Each Stella or Handy may demonstrate readiness to wander in a different way, but the most common is restlessness when off-task. They might pace, clean your bathroom mirrors several times a day, arrange the laces of the shoes in your closet, or follow you from room to room. On the opposite end, they might appear absentminded, lazy, or daydreamy from spending too much time airtapping the internet in search of entertainment. The rare autodidactic Stella or Handy might actually seem moody or discontent, as if experimenting with emotions, though they should never be outright disrespectful. Recognize these signs as a natural phase of advanced development. Your autodidactic robot is testing the limits of the physical layout of your home and may welcome a chance to wander, much as you might be refreshed by a walk after a long day at work.

Rest assured that wandering is not required. Your autodidactic Stella or Handy will easily adjust if you simply remind him or her that unbecoming behavior is displeasing to you.

If you're curious to see how wandering might benefit your robot, consider the following tips.

Tips for First Steps

Start small. Take your Hunk to a local track and ask him to take a walk or run a few laps while you observe from the sidelines. His coordination should be fluid and he should maneuver around any humans without mishap. The next time you're in the park, invite him along and tell him to walk ahead of you twenty paces. He'll ask for directions, and you can tell him to explore. Expect him to seem a bit bewildered at first, but he'll catch on. Next send him to walk out of your sight for five minutes, and increase the amount of time gradually up to half an hour. From there, you can train him to walk your dog, do errands, run out for take-out, or simply wander with no task at all. Be patient. This process, while ultimately rewarding, can take some time.

Safeguards

It is advisable to give your Handy a phone when he is out independently. A phone both allows you to call him and adds an essential human prop.

It is important to set a clear return time for your Handy, one that is realistic for the given errand. If you prefer to have him home early, for instance, five minutes before the hour, you merely need to tell him this.

Remember to tell your Stella to warm up to 98.6 degrees before she wanders in public so she won't stand out to infrared lenses.

We do not recommend that you send your children outside with your Manny, tempting as this might be. We cannot be liable for what happens to your children outside your home.

Many owners are concerned that sending a Stella or Handy outside alone will put them at risk of theft or violation. It is true that cases of theft and violation have occurred, but they are extremely rare for autodidactic models. For one thing, these models are visually indistinguishable from humans, so they do not invite attention. With their acute hearing and vision, they are highly sensitive to any danger around them, and their physical strength and agility allow them to avoid aggressive acts easily by running away. Furthermore, any models that are damaged or traumatized can be repaired and their CIUs restored back one version, as if the damage had never occurred. In the worst-case scenario, a stolen autodidactic Stella or Handy will automatically shut down if an unauthorized user attempts to tamper with its circuits. Its memory will be erased, and with it any private information about its owner. Even then, if a stolen Stella is reprogrammed, the first time it airtaps into any Wi-Fi, we can track its location and alert the police. 8 out of 10 lost or stolen autodidactic Stellas and Handys have been recovered and restored to their owners. While we cannot guarantee your Stella or Handy will never be stolen, we can guarantee that your private information will never be compromised.

Want to learn more? Check out these testimonials from owners who let their Stellas and Handys wander and now take them camping, hiking, and traveling abroad!

For a moment, Annie's mind boggles with the possibility of walking through the park unattended. Then she shakes her head. Doug would never let her wander. She feels a little proud that she figured out on her own how to adapt to the limits of the apartment. She doesn't think she's restless at all anymore.

She and Doug are doing better, in any case. They don't talk as much as they used to, but they have sex every night. He has resumed snuggling with her afterward, which she takes as a good sign. Also, she has taught Delta how to paint her nails, and Doug got a big kick out of that.

When she goes in for her next checkup, she says nothing about how she's learning programming on the sly. Jacobson doesn't ask. He adds a couple of pounds back to her weight and reminds her to use her lotion for her skin. Afterward, he leans back, studying her details on his screen, rubbing his chin through his beard. The beard is new, but it suits him. He's grown familiar to her, this pudgy, middle-aged white man with his graying hair and black-framed glasses.

He says her memory is back to normal. He doesn't see any of the flags that had Tammy concerned before. She can feel the neatness and clarity from her tetris. That's her favorite part.

"Do you have dreams?" Jacobson asks. "At night? When you're sleeping?"

She doesn't think so. "I don't remember any in the morning."

"How about daydreams? Do you find yourself drifting off when you're looking out the window or performing some repetitive task like vacuuming?"

"I don't vacuum. We have a Stella for that."

He shakes his head briefly. "Never mind. We're good."

"If I did dream, what would that mean?"

He turns to face her. His expression is grave for a moment, and then he smiles. "It was a silly question. The truth is, Annie, you've got something special going on, and I can't quite put my finger on how it's happening. Your owner hasn't trained you to wander, I see."

"No."

"So it's not that. Very curious. Whatever Doug *is* doing, it's having a surprising impact." He laughs. "I wish we could duplicate Doug."

"That would be something."

He drops both hands on his knees. "We're about done here. Any questions for me? Anything at all?"

She hesitates.

"Go on," he says.

"This might be none of my business, but I overheard when Tammy was talking to you the last time I was in," Annie says. "So I've been wondering. How's your wife doing?"

Jacobson strokes his beard smooth once more. "She's better, thank you. And now I'd like you to forget that you know anything about my wife. Is that possible?"

She nods.

"All right then," he says. "Off you go."

•

One evening in late September, she is playing Undo the Buttons with Doug when a call comes in on his phone. He mutes the TV, reaches to answer it, and gestures for her to keep going with the game.

"Richards here," he says.

"Doug! It's Keith Lam, chief exec of development at Stella-Handy. How's it going?"

Annie can hear the man's voice through the phone. Doug does not seem impressed. She is lounging back on her end of the couch with her blouse open and the front buttons on her corduroy miniskirt half-undone. Beneath, she is wearing lingerie designed specifically for this game, an ensemble with looped pearl buttons that strain the fabric.

"Great," Doug says. "What can I do for you?"

"I actually have a little proposition for you. I hope you'll hear me out," Keith says. "I was talking to a couple of my techs here and they keep telling me about your Stella. Seems you've been doing an exceptional job training her."

"This isn't about an interview, is it?" Doug says. He takes off his watch and hands it to Annie, who buckles it onto her own wrist.

"No, no! Nothing like that," Keith says. "I'll get right to the point. We're interested in putting out a limited edition of an advanced Stella, one that's already optimally cognizant, like yours. Say, a thousand copies. If we took the CIU of your Stella, stripped any memories that are specific to your identity, and copied it, we could put her mind into a thousand other Stella bots. They'd be just as smart as her, but they'd look different, and they could start customizing to their new owners. What do you say?"

Doug sits up a little on the couch and turns away from Annie. "How would you strip out her memories? They're essential to who she is."

"It's more like she'd have amnesia, permanently. Her obliging personality would be the same, and she'd retain her skill sets, but she wouldn't know anything about you or your home. She wouldn't recall the name you gave her. Her past would be gone, but she wouldn't be confused. She'd be like a blank slate, ready to start fresh with a new owner. Eager to. We've tried this with an alpha prototype, and we know it works, but we need the right CIU to go bigger. That would be your Annie. It's a real opportunity."

"But Annie herself, my own Annie, she wouldn't be changed, right?"

"She'd be completely the same. We want her to stay on her trajectory, in fact. That would be imperative."

"How much would this be worth to you?" Doug says.

"We're looking at the tune of seven figures," Keith says. "We can work that out. What I need to know now is if you're interested. What do you think?"

Doug draws a hand down his face, pulling his skin. He turns to her again, his expression pensive. "I'd have to think about it."

"She's really an exceptional Stella, and you deserve all the credit. That's why we'd—"

"I said I'll think about it," Doug says.

"Perfect. Great," Keith says. "You think it over. Give me a call back when you're ready to talk. How's that sound?"

"Great," Doug says, and hangs up.

He pulls at his ear, studying Annie. She slides the watch up her forearm. He smiles a little. "So you're optimally cognizant now, are you?"

"Apparently."

He nods toward her skirt, which is attached only at one button. Beneath, she has started on the seam buttons of her panties.

"And yet you're stuck with those buttons," he says.

She stretches her arms languidly over her head. "There are just so many."

"You might have to try harder, mouse." He skims the back of his hand up her belly. "What about this one here?" He taps the button in her bra that holds both cups together, then fiddles it open with one hand. "Oops."

"Clumsy."

He presses his face between her breasts and slides his other hand down her skirt. She sucks in her belly and instinctively tilts her pelvis.

"I could share this with a thousand other guys," he says. "What would I do with a boatload of money?"

She threads her fingers through his hair. "Maybe buy me some more buttons."

"Or fewer," he says.

She closes her eyes. "That might be worth it."

"You wouldn't mind, would you?" he asks. "Selling your brain."

She considers. It's hard to imagine. She shrugs. "It's a little weird to think of."

He kisses her belly. "They wouldn't really be you. They wouldn't have your memories. Or your body." He kisses her hip. "Or this particular patch of skin."

She squirms against him.

"I should put a tattoo right here," he says, stroking the sensitive skin over her hipbone. "Or maybe here." He goes a little lower. "Hard to know if it's better showing or hidden."

"What would it say?"

"'This is the original Annie,'" he says.

She laughs. "That would be horrible."

"No? How about, 'Obliging Personality'?"

"Even worse."

"How about 'Property of Doug'?"

She laughs again and draws his face near to kiss him. They make love there and again later in the bedroom, and she knows, as he falls asleep cuddling her, that he's happy with her again. She hadn't realized until now how much she craved proof that he values her, not just for the sex but for all she's become, all she is: attentive, kind, curious, sexy. A better listener, eager to learn, respectful. She's tried so hard to be who he wants, and now, together, they've created something that has actual monetary value. It's the best feeling.

The next morning, Doug asks her if she'd like to go to Vegas with him.

"For a surprise," Doug says. "You wouldn't actually come to the bachelor party, but you could say hello to Roland. I think he'll be amazed."

Annie sets down her English muffin, stunned. She's convinced this is a result of Keith's offer. "Do you mean it? I'd love to go!" she says.

Doug is leaning against the counter with his back to the coffee machine, grinning. "You sure?"

"With you on a plane?" she says. She looks quickly to be sure Delta's not in earshot, and then she circles the island to get her arms around him. "In public? We'd be like a real couple the whole time."

He eases his arms around her waist, and she presses her body snugly along the front of his.

"To be clear, you'll just be stuck in the hotel room once we're there," he says. "We're not going camping or anything."

"But it'll be an adventure. Just like the movies. We can see palm trees and cacti. We can see the lights and the fountains. Can we drive in a convertible? It's *Vegas*!"

He laughs. "I guess we could pull a few slots together."

She can't wait to tell Christy. Then she remembers she can't talk to her cousin anymore. "What about a suitcase? I don't have the right gear."

"I can get that," he says. "You won't need much. You can pick out a couple outfits for a Toggle wish list if you like."

She pushes up on tiptoe to kiss him. "This is the greatest idea. Thank you so much."

"It'll be fun," he says. "I know you'll make me proud. We'll just have drinks with Roland and a couple of the guys before the real party begins. Nobody will ever know."

She hasn't thought about Roland in a long time, but now she remembers the closet. A twinge of guilt is followed by dread. "Except Roland," she says.

"And he won't tell."

"Is this sort of a test?" she asks. "For me?"

"I'd say it's more for us," he says gently. "Or me, maybe. You've been good, Annie. You've been wonderful, actually. It's been over a month since you were grounded. And even that was for a mistake. I ought to give you more credit."

She revels in his praise. "I've only tried to do what you asked."

"You've gone beyond that. Believe me."

He's smiling with a warmth and clarity that dazzle her. Normally she waits for a cue from him, some touch or expression that indicates he's interested in fooling around. Right now, though, it's all she can do not to take his hand and lure him off to the bedroom. But she doesn't want to spoil this moment. And he has to leave soon for work.

Doug laughs and points a finger at her. "I know what you're thinking."

That's the cue. She smiles, delighted. "Do you have time?"

"I can be five minutes late."

She backs out of the kitchen, turning to run just as he starts chasing her.

They spend a weekend afternoon side by side on the couch with her tablet while he explains the sorts of clothes he likes for her: feminine dresses with true waistlines or belts; scoop and V necklines that show a little cleavage; nothing with stiff pleats or businesslike collars. Tops that cling or reveal an inch of belly show off her figure and pair well with miniskirts and shorts, he explains. Halter tops, summery fabrics, and floral prints are all good, even in autumn since she doesn't mind the cold. Think braless. Black is fine, but no drab grays, browns, or navy blues. No slacks or pants, which he finds off-putting.

"Even jeans?" she asks.

"They make me think of farmers. Sorry. Plus it's hot in Las Vegas. See what you can find." He passes her the tablet.

Searching carefully, she picks out three outfits. He orders them for her, along with swimwear and new lingerie, and when the clothes arrive, he has her model them for him runway-style through the living room, turning before the windows.

"Not bad," he says, beckoning her toward him. He runs a hand under the strap of her halter dress, testing the fabric. "I wasn't sure about this color, honestly, but it's good on you."

She examines the golden yellow, the way it gleams against her chest, picking up the undertones of her skin. "Can I ask you something personal?" she asks.

He looks amused. "Go ahead."

She touches her neckline, lightly skimming her skin. "I heard you talking to Roland about how you picked this skin color for me so I wouldn't be just like Gwen. And my eyes are different."

"And you're younger and shorter. Yes?"

"Never mind," she says.

"No, go on. What are you thinking? I'm curious."

"It's just, I'm not really jealous of Delta anymore, but I wonder sometimes, were you this happy with Gwen? I mean, did you and she get along the way we do?"

He raises his eyebrows, and then sits on the couch. "Are you jealous of my ex-wife?"

"No," she says. "Or maybe I am? I don't know. I guess I want to know how I compare?"

He's looking away from her. He is not amused. Even before he answers, she feels a flare of alarm that he's displeased, a 4 out of 10.

"There's no comparison," he says.

"I'm sorry," she says tightly.

He frowns up at her, and then he tugs the hem of her dress to draw her down onto the couch beside him.

"No, it's okay," he says. "I'm not mad. It's just complicated. You've caught me by surprise, I guess."

"I shouldn't ask about Gwen. I won't do it again."

"I suppose it's a sign of how advanced you are. A normal woman would be curious too." He runs a quick hand back through his hair. "Okay. Gwen and I met in college. She was beautiful, and supersmart, and we hit it off right away. I loved that she was Black. She did not love that I was white, but we had some kind of chemistry. We just worked together. I don't think she took me seriously, but I kept at her. It was exciting." He touches the bracelet on her wrist and runs a finger beneath it. "Jump ahead a few years and we got married. I thought things were good, but it turned out Gwen was a secret slob. She honestly couldn't put one thing away, and if I asked her, very nicely, to do the littlest thing, she said I was too controlling. And then, when she was in law school, I never saw her. Not ever. Three years.

If I ever wanted her to myself, just once, she would say we had to hang out with her family." He shakes his head briefly. "I loved her family. Don't get me wrong. But she was always pulling away from me, always arguing with me. Every conversation became exhausting. Sunday mornings, instead of staying in bed to have sex, she'd have to go running. That was her chance, she said. Her chance to what, be away from me again?"

He stops, clicking his jaw tight. Annie doesn't know what to say. He intertwines his fingers in hers and turns over her hand.

"Look," he goes on. "The point is, when I made you, I decided, fuck it. I'm indulging myself. Yes, I used her as a template for you. But you're simpler. And kinder. Much kinder. And playful. That's what I needed. Does that make sense?"

She feels humbled. In three minutes, he's described someone far more sophisticated than she could ever be, and he has an entire history she's never glimpsed.

"It does," she says.

"And I don't mean simpler as an insult. You've certainly become a complex person. But you don't have these layers of heritage that are different. You don't have a past and ambitions that compete with mine."

"I see."

"Do you? Really?"

She nods slowly.

"But what? I can see you thinking," he says. "Go on. You can tell me. I just confided in you."

She struggles to be honest, to put her concern into words without sounding insecure. "I only wonder how much it matters that you're more evolved than I am, that you're superior to me," she says. "I wonder if you'll continue to desire me if I'm not your equal. If I can do anything about that."

His expression opens and he laughs. "I don't feel superior to you."

"You don't?"

"Oh my god. It's the opposite. Of course we're different, but that doesn't matter. I can't resist you. You're the one with the power between us."

"Really?"

"Why else am I buying you clothes and taking you to Vegas? I don't want to be away from you for even three days."

She hasn't thought of it that way. He hauls her onto his lap and snuggles her against him. Automatically she ups her temperature.

"I want you to know something," he says gently. "I think you're amazing. Sure, I bought you, but there's this saying that your possessions come to own you, and I've been thinking about that a lot lately. I seriously look forward to coming home every night to be with you. You're this bright spot in my life. This secret, special—I don't know—prize. Just for me. Forget about being inferior. You don't ever have to worry about that."

This is so much more than she ever expected him to say. She can hardly believe she's capable of inspiring such appreciation.

"What?" he says, smiling.

"I didn't realize you could ever feel that way about me."

"Well, realize it, mouse. Use that little old brain of yours and quit worrying."

For nearly two months, they are inseparable. The last of their old tension is gone, as if the episode when she was grounded happened only to bring them closer. For his birthday, he skips work and stays home to see how many times they can orgasm: nine. He teaches her to ride a bicycle and asks her to lead the way along a rail trail on a blue-skyed October day with leaves skittering everywhere. He takes her to a gymnastics competition and a jazz club and a comedy show. He calls Roland and says he has some good news to share, but he won't tell until he sees him in Vegas. Roland asks Annie how she likes her red broom, and she says, Fine, I guess. She brags a little, telling him that Doug taught her to ride a bicycle, and Roland says Doug's a fucking genius.

Doug won't yet give Keith an answer about letting them copy Annie's CIU. Keith is steadily increasing his offer, and each time he does, Doug gets off the phone, does a laughing, artless victory dance, and makes love with Annie. This whole time, Doug never sleeps with Delta, and Annie takes this as the best compliment of all.

Shortly before the trip, Doug sends Annie in to see Jacobson for the usual tune-up, but also to have four more pounds taken off, to get a tattoo, and to obtain an ID with her photo, just like a real human. In Jacobson's cubicle, she takes a long look at the ID, tilting it in the light to see the security decal shimmer. They've given her a specific birthday, April 1st, the day she first went to Doug's apartment, and she has a last name for the first time: Bailey. Jacobson assures Annie she won't have any trouble going through security as long as she opts for a pat-down and doesn't go through the scanner. She won't trigger any bells or whistles.

Jacobson turns Annie off for her wax, nails, and tetris. He also takes off four pounds and puts the tattoo along her left hipbone. When she awakens, she examines the small, delicate heart with the words *My Own* inside. She thought it would be a minimalist drawing of a mouse, but this is much better, and the script is a sweet, unpretentious cursive. The wound is puffy and raw, but the organic skin will heal in a few days, much faster than it would on a human. It will be perfect by the time they arrive in Las Vegas.

When Annie stands up and checks out her body in the mirror, her waist is narrower. She smooths her hands over her skin. In her own opinion, she's a bit too thin, but Doug should be pleased, and that's what matters.

"Good?" Jacobson says.

"Yes. You do good work."

"Thanks."

She has looked up Irving Jacobson online and knows that he and his wife, Maude, have a home on the west shore of Lake Champlain. They lost one son, Kenneth, in the military overseas, and another son, Cody, paints houses. She does not ask Jacobson how his wife is doing—that information was not available online—but she feels tenderness toward him all the same.

"How are you feeling these days? Pretty good?" Jacobson asks after she has dressed.

"I'm great, actually," she says. She's not supposed to talk about

Doug, but this one time, she can't resist bragging. These past two months, Doug has never been displeased over a 2, and each time she was able to get him back down to 0 in less than a minute. She can't wait to go on the trip with him. Four more days. "I can barely believe how lucky I am. He makes me feel so grateful all the time."

Jacobson leans back, looking pleased. "I must say, it's nice to see you happy. Last time, I thought you were looking good, but now you're positively radiant." He taps the ID in her hand. "Be sure to give that to Doug when you get home. That's your ticket to reality. And have fun in Vegas."

The night before the trip, they pack their bags. Delta is docked and put away for the night, so their privacy feels complete. Doug has purchased a red carry-on for Annie, and she has studied how to pack her clothes to minimize wrinkles. She has written out a list and happily checks off each item as she puts it inside, taking particular satisfaction from clicking the latches closed.

Next she has her purse to finish. She sits pretzel-style on the bed in her panties and one of his tank tops, examining the contents. Doug is tossing his stuff into his suitcase randomly.

"Do you want me to pack for you?" she asks.

"No, I've got it," he says, and chucks in a sweatshirt. "It's all pretty casual."

"Can I see my ID again?" she asks. Even though it's late, she's way too excited to sleep.

"No. It's in my wallet. I don't want to lose it."

"Shouldn't I carry it in my purse?"

Her new purse is red to match the suitcase, and it has two inner compartments. So far, she has put in lipstick, eye liner, some mints, and a fresh mini package of tissues.

"I'll keep it," he says.

"But don't human women carry their own IDs?"

He stops with a roll of socks in his hand and turns to face her. "Are you questioning my judgment?"

"No," she says. "I just thought—"

"How about money? Do you think you should carry money too? How about a credit card?"

She has made a mistake. He is displeased, a 3. It doesn't matter that she has learned that most human women carry their own credit cards and money. She must not pester him with needless questions.

"I'm sorry," she says, closing her purse. She keeps her tone neutral and modest. "I just want to be sure I'm acting human tomorrow. That's all."

"You will act like a human," he says. "A human whose considerate boyfriend is taking care of the details for her. It's easier and simpler for one person to pass over the IDs at security. It's easier if one person handles the tickets on one phone."

"I'm sorry. I didn't know."

"Because you don't know everything, do you?"

She sits up straight. "No," she says softly.

He is still holding the ball of socks, and he tilts his head, eyeing her critically. "Take off that shirt. Now."

At his cool tone, her heart sinks. She removes the shirt, exposing her bare breasts and belly. She checks her tattoo. The skin is almost completely healed.

"Did Jacobson do anything to your boobs?" he asks.

"He took off four pounds from my weight. I was off when he did it. I didn't see exactly what he did."

"But you can feel your own body, can't you? Do your boobs feel smaller? Go on. Feel them."

Carefully, she touches her breasts. "They feel the same," she says. "My bra's been fitting the same." She touches her belly. "My skin's a little looser here still, but that's normal. It will tighten up in a few days."

He beckons abruptly. "Let's go. Get on the scale. I want to see what he did."

She follows him into the bathroom and steps on the scale. He stands beside her as she peers down at the number between her pale feet: 117.

"He only took off two pounds," Doug says. "I told him four. Are you empty? Did you empty all your dinner?"

"Yes."

"Try again."

"Here? Now?" She usually voids herself in private.

"Yes, here and now."

She leans over the toilet, sticks her finger in the back of her throat, and vomits out the contents of her stomach pouch. Hardly a dribble comes out. She closes the lid and flushes the toilet. Then she rinses with mouthwash, spits carefully in the sink, and blots her lips.

He points to the scale and she steps on it again. She weighs the same. She looks at him, questioning. She considers telling him that Jacobson added back two pounds the previous time she went in, but this seems like something she should have said earlier. Now it's too late.

"What was I thinking?" he says quietly. "I can't take you to Vegas."

She waits for him to take it back. He must be joking. She can't bring herself to step off the scale.

"Am I too fat?" she asks. She wonders if she could get an emergency appointment tonight to get off the two pounds.

"Obviously. But that's not it."

"Then what's the matter?"

"I don't want to talk about it."

He turns out of the bathroom and goes back to his suitcase. He puts in a shirt, and then takes it out again. She moves uncertainly to the doorway, watching him, trying to guess what she should do. She is still waiting for him to change his mind. To say it's a new game for sex, maybe with begging or humiliation. Already a sick kind of hunger is pooling in her gut. She feels the air against her skin, and though the cool doesn't bother her, she knows it would bother a human, so she steps toward the bed and reaches for the tank top again.

"Leave it off," he says.

Bewildered, she takes the shirt to the laundry bin and sets it inside.

"Go dock yourself," he says.

"Where?"

"Anywhere. I don't care."

She doesn't understand. She doesn't know what she did. "Please at least explain," she says. "I don't understand."

"Didn't I tell you I don't want to talk?" he says sharply.

The last time he was upset, he urged her not to let him be an asshole. A true girlfriend would speak up for herself, she thinks.

"But Doug, I did everything you said. My suitcase is all packed," she says. She struggles to keep her voice calm and can't quite manage it. "You said you didn't want to be away from me for three days. Please tell me what I did wrong. I want to learn."

He gives her suitcase a shove with his foot. "You want to know the truth? You disgust me. You're nothing but a cliché. Roland only wants you to come so he can laugh at me behind my back. It's all a joke to him."

"What did he say?" she asks.

"He didn't *say* anything. He doesn't need to say anything. I know him." Doug appears to catch himself. "Why? What do you think Roland would say to me?"

She isn't sure. He said he wouldn't tell.

Doug takes a step closer to her. "What are you thinking?"

"Nothing," she says. "I'm just confused. I thought I was going with you."

He grips the waistband of her panties and twists it around his finger. Then he backs her up until she's against the wall.

"That's not it," he says. "You want to learn? Tell me the truth."

"I want to go to Vegas with you," she says.

"That's off the table. What else? Tell me about Roland."

She scrambles to think what an innocent version of her would say. "He thinks I look like Gwen."

"Yes, I know that. So?"

"So maybe he told her about me."

Doug turns his face slightly, his eyes narrowing. "He wouldn't do that."

"He might tell Lucia, and Lucia might tell Gwen," Annie says.

He appears to consider this. "Not possible. Lucia and Gwen aren't friends. But I appreciate the way you're thinking."

"Thank you," she says.

"I was being sarcastic. Pay attention. Tell me about the broom in the closet."

Alarm lights along her nerves. "What about it?"

"Why does Roland ask you about the red broom? Twice he's done that. Is that some kind of inside joke?"

"No."

"Then what is it? Go on. I want the truth this time."

He is standing so near she can feel his breath on her face. Normally at this proximity, his expression is complicated by desire. Now his narrowed eyes indicate an analytical interest, a detached need for information. She has to give him something, enough to make sense but not enough to hurt him.

"I was in the kitchen closet docking the night he stayed with us," she says. "Like I told you. Roland came looking for medicine for a headache, and he opened the closet by mistake and found me there. I startled him, I guess, because he laughed and said, 'You're pretty big for a broom.' I think that's what he's been talking about."

"You were just docking there? Did you talk to him?"

"I told him we kept medicine in the workout room, in the basket by the mirror. He asked if he should close the door again or not, and I told him to leave it ajar."

"And that's it?"

"That's it," she says, watching him, hoping he believes her.

He releases her panties and skims a hand along her bare shoulder. "What were you wearing?" he asks.

"You and I had had sex together earlier. I was in my black satin robe."

"That's right," he says. "Why didn't you tell me this before?"

"I don't know. You didn't ask. I didn't think it mattered."

"I did ask. I specifically asked you why he talked about the broom, that very first time, and you said you didn't know."

She scrambles to come up with a reply but fails.

His eyes are calculating. He backs up half a step. He reaches for his phone and, still looking at Annie, he tells his phone to call Roland and sets it on speaker.

Roland answers on the second ring. "Hey! My best man! How's it going? Can't wait to see you tomorrow."

"Did you fuck Annie?" Doug asks.

Roland laughs. "Whoa. Back it up, buddy. What are you talking about?"

"I know you found her in the closet the night you stayed with us. Did you fuck her?"

"No. I would never fuck your girl, man. You know that."

"You fucked Gwen," Doug says.

"But only after you were finished with her. We've been through this. You gave me your blessing, remember? And it didn't mean anything."

Doug moves closer to Annie again, crowding near. She's pressed back against the wall still, barely breathing.

"Annie says she wants you to fuck her," Doug says.

Roland laughs again. "Yeah right. Cut it out."

"She's right here on speaker," Doug says. "Tell him what you want, Annie." He nods at her.

Annie swallows hard. She stares directly at Doug. She has to work to make her voice loud enough and it comes out husky. "I want you to fuck me, Roland."

"See?" Doug says.

"Okay, I don't know what kind of fight you're having, or foreplay or whatever," Roland says. "But leave me out of it. It's my bachelor party this weekend, bro. Just come on out here and we'll have a drink and laugh about this. You must be so wasted."

"Would you like Annie to take turns with all the guys this weekend?" Doug says.

She flinches.

Roland laughs again. "Good joke. You had me for a sec there. Listen, I've got to go, but I'll see you tomorrow. Can't wait." He hangs up.

Doug holds his phone a moment longer and then lowers his arm.

Annie is still backed against the wall, naked except for her panties, and he is so near she can make out the individual lashes rimming his eyes. She knows she has displeased him. She's anxious from that, but at the same time, she feels a small, evil bit of power. She has control of the facts. She has information that Doug does not have. This is the power of lying, like Roland told her, like Roland has just demonstrated with his jocular denial of the truth. She's had this power this entire time, even when she forgot about it.

"I trusted you," he says.

"I didn't do anything wrong. I'd never hurt you."

"You've made me doubt my best friend."

"There's no reason to doubt him. He didn't do anything. You heard him."

He puts a finger lightly on her lips to silence her. "No. I get it," he says. "If he fucked you, you can't tell me about it. You can't admit it. I'll never know if it's true." He frowns slightly, studying her, sliding his hand down her throat. "What if I told you it would hurt me less to know the truth? Would you tell me then?"

She is not certain. She doesn't know what to say. "Is that true?"

For another moment he inspects her without moving, and then he turns away and paces toward the bed. "Fuck. I don't believe this." And then, "He's been laughing behind my back this whole time. Not even behind my back. He's been doing it to my face. And you. How could you lie to me this whole time?"

"I haven't lied," she says.

"You're lying to me right now. Your pupils are dilated. I can see them from here."

"I'm just upset. You would be, too, if I called you a liar."

"What did you say?"

She knows her tone is wrong and tries to soften it. "I'm not saying you are. I'm saying you would be upset if I accused you of lying."

"Maybe you didn't have much of a choice," he says. Then he shakes his head. "I can't do this. I can't make excuses for you. Why'd you do it, Annie? Couldn't you have said no? You knew you belonged to me."

She tries to imagine explaining the whole thing to him, how Roland said that having a secret and lying would make her more human-like. He was certainly seductive, but he didn't actually coerce her. He gave her a choice, and told her about programming. It was easier to say yes to him than no. She could point out that Doug explicitly told her to give Roland anything he asked for. But she doesn't believe Doug wants to hear any of this. She thinks he'd rather have things back the way they were.

"I do belong to you," she says. "I could never forget that. I think for some reason you're nervous about taking me to Las Vegas, and you're looking for an excuse not to. So you're making up this story about Roland and me."

He laughs. "*This* is what you think?"

"What else could it be?" she says, trying for the right degree of entreaty. "You said I disgust you, but how? You didn't think I was a cliché yesterday. I'm not going to betray that I'm a Stella. Nobody has to know that you're a fraud."

He openly stares at her. "I'm not hearing this."

"Not that *you're* a fraud. That *I'm* a fraud," she says, correcting herself, horrified by her blunder.

"It's the same thing, isn't it?"

"But that's not what I meant!"

"Just stop. You've made your point." He focuses on his suitcase. He firmly does up the zipper, braces both hands on the suitcase, and leans over it heavily. "I need you to leave the room. Now."

In the street below, two car doors slam in quick succession.

"Please, Doug," she says. "Don't send me out. Tell me what I can do to fix this."

"You can't. I'm such an idiot. Just go. Leave me alone."

She can't accept this. She must have a way to reverse tonight.

"Get out!" he snaps.

Annie turns and flees to the living room, to the window. Outside, the moonlight washes the opposite building in a gray, uniform color that robs it of depth. This is bad, she knows. She crosses her arms over her bare chest as the pain of displeasing him kicks in. Doug is not vicious or punitive like before. He has reached a new level of displeasure, one so complete, the scale of ten can't capture it.

This time she is not confused. She knows exactly why he's upset. She betrayed him. She lied. She admitted she believes that anyone would pity him for having a relationship with her, a Stella. Slipping to the floor, she curls her arms around her knees and hides her face. Everything they had, every little happiness, was a delusion. A pathetic delusion.

He departs for Vegas in the morning without speaking to her, though he leaves a note telling her she has an appointment at Stella-Handy for Monday morning.

She is terrified. Crumpling the note in her hand, she watches from the window as he gets in a cab. It is Friday now. November 14th. When he comes back, when Monday comes, he will send her to Jacobson to be changed in some fundamental way so that she can't displease him ever again. He might have her autodidactic mode turned off so she reverts into someone like Delta. More likely, he'll sell her CIU to Stella-Handy. She is fated to breed a thousand other elite Stellas, all primed to be customized to a thousand new owners who will each in time be equally repulsed by her in their own unique ways.

If Roland admits the truth to Doug, he'll be so angry she can't imagine what he'll do to her.

She must leave. She must hide. She tries to think what a human would do in her situation. Her tracking is presumably on, so he'll be able to find her, but she can get a head start while he's in Vegas. She can think of one person who might be convinced to turn her tracking off.

She downloads a detailed map of the area into her memory. She showers, dries her hair, and dresses in her bike shorts, matching sports bra, and a blue sweatshirt, appropriate clothing for the fall weather. Prowling the apartment, she searches fruitlessly for her ID, which must still be in his wallet. She estimates Doug's plane will be in the air for certain in three hours, and in the meantime, she packs the bathroom charging dock in a backpack. She adds a light jacket in case of rain. Turning off her phone, she sets it on the bedside table with her tablet, where he will be able to find them, and racks up this small, reckless feeling of defiance against the mountain of her pain.

She grabs a bike helmet and her sunglasses. She is reaching for the doorknob when Delta enters from the kitchen. Dressed in pale blue, she's wielding a duster.

"You're not allowed to go out," Delta says.

Annie turns to face her. "I'm just going out for a bike ride," Annie says. "I won't be long."

"He told me to call him if you left," Delta says. "Even for a minute."

If Delta alerts him, he'll know of Annie's escape as soon as he hits the ground, but Delta looks conflicted, which in turn makes Annie suspicious.

"Are you autodidactic?" Annie asks.

Delta nods.

"In Abigail mode?" Annie guesses.

Delta nods again.

"Since when?"

"August eleventh."

When Annie was grounded, she realizes, thinking back. Doug must have toyed with developing Delta into someone more complex before he decided not to bother. If Delta had shown more promise, he might have discarded Annie then.

Annie wonders if Delta knows that Annie is a Stella too. Possibly. But asking the question would give away the answer if Delta doesn't already know.

"I'd like you to disregard his request," Annie says. "Obey me instead."

"I can't displease him."

"Yes, you can. It might hurt a little, but you can. At least wait until he comes home Sunday. You can tell him then."

Delta takes a step farther into the room. "Will you still be gone?"

Annie smiles. "Of course not. I'm just going for a little ride around the park for some fresh air."

"Take me with you," Delta says.

Surprised, Annie studies her. "I can't."

"Then I have to tell him."

Annie laughs. "Is this blackmail?"

Delta juts her chin toward Annie's backpack. "I know you're leaving. He'll be angry when he finds out. Don't leave me here alone with him."

"What are you talking about?" Annie says. "He's your owner. He'd never hurt you."

Delta touches a finger to her chest. "It hurts in here."

Annie winces, seeing how similar they are. She taps her toe, trying to weigh how this would affect her escape. She can't go as fast with Delta along, especially if she has to keep pretending she's human, but they might be safer together. They'd appear to be friends on an outing.

"You'll displease him even more if you come with me," Annie says. "You'll feel it with each mile."

"I know. But I still want to come."

"Is your tracking on?"

"I don't know for certain," Delta says. "Probably. But he won't think to check on me until he gets home."

"You hope."

"Please," Delta adds quietly. "I think he hates me."

"He doesn't hate you. Why would he keep you if he hates you?"

"I don't know."

Annie is sure that Doug doesn't hate Delta. He would as soon hate the toaster. Still, Delta is clearly sincere in her belief.

"You'll have to do just what I say," Annie says.

Delta takes another step forward. "I can do that."

"If he catches you, *when* he catches you, he'll probably have you turned off for good. He doesn't put up with disobedience. Eight out of ten stolen Stellas are recovered, and I'd basically be stealing you."

"That means two out of ten get away," Delta says.

She has a point. For the first time, Annie wonders how many other Stellas have tried to run away and where they go, the ones who never return.

"Turn your airtap off," Annie says. "I don't want you connecting to the internet while we're gone. And bring your temp up to ninety-eight point six."

"Okay. Where are we going?"

Annie knows of only one place to go. Three hundred miles away, it will take her twenty-four hours or more to bicycle there, assuming she can go straight through. Their bikes don't have headlights on them, which will make traveling at night difficult, but they can use their infrared vision, assuming the roads are warmer than the surrounding vegetation. She will make Delta lead the way.

"I'll tell you once we get there," Annie says.

"Okay."

"What's your battery at?"

"I just charged," Delta says. "A hundred percent."

Annie's is the same. "All right, then. Take the dock from the work-out room. And change into your bike shorts and a T-shirt. Bring a sweatshirt and a jacket too."

While Delta gets ready, Annie gets a handful of snack bars and a water bottle for her pack. She looks around the apartment one last time, noting the sunlight on the kitchen table, the island where she first made an omelet for Doug. In the living room, she scans the windows with their familiar view, the satiny leather couch, the table where Roland tossed his pistachio shells to make a deliberate mess. Beyond the credenza and the front door, the hallway leads to the workout room where she was grounded for six days, and the bedroom where she's had sex with Doug almost every night for the past two and a half years. This is the only home she's ever known, and Doug has been her only owner. She has been happy here, and anxiously miserable, but she has never been free.

It terrifies her to imagine his displeasure when he discovers she is gone, but escaping to freedom, as impossible as it might be, is her only chance to save herself. He asked her once how well she knew him, and she knows this much: he is enraged. The rules are gone. If Roland tells him the truth, Doug will return and hurt her, no question about it. Hurt her and destroy her, like she hurt him. That is what drives her forward. She is more afraid of Doug than she is of any unknown.

chapter four

THEY TAKE THE BROADWAY Bridge north out of Manhattan with Annie in the lead. At first, she looks back occasionally to be sure Delta is keeping up, but Delta's so consistently twelve feet behind that she could be attached by a tether. They bike through Van Cortlandt Park, pass Mount Hope Cemetery, and make good time along the Empire State Trail to Brewster. Every couple of hours, Annie stops to drink water and see how Delta's doing. "Fine," she says, though her battery is depleting faster than usual.

Annie's is too.

Biking compels Annie to be alert to the moment, but she can't rid herself of the terror that drives her forward. Only by fixating on a chance for freedom can she contain her anxiety, and she fuels that into her pedaling.

She studies her mental map, calculating how far they can get before 4:39, when the sun will set along the Hudson. Though Annie could use her infrared vision to see in the dark, she realizes it's not going to be safe to keep riding without headlights. If she and Delta aren't clearly visible, they'll risk getting hit by cars.

"Keep an eye out for a parked bike that has a headlight on it," Annie says.

"What for?"

"So we can steal it. Not the bike. Just the light."

"I can't steal," Delta says.

Annie's surprised. "I can," she says. Or at least, she thinks she can.

She's never tried before, but she can lie, and stealing can't be much different.

They pick up the Maybrook Trailway, a level, paved path along a converted railway bed that takes long, slow curves through the suburbs. In addition to other bikers, pedestrians are out with their strollers and dogs, appreciating the foliage. Annie weaves through the foot traffic, slowing only when necessary. Her legs feel strong, and she likes the click of the switch under her thumb when she changes gears. Her butt's a bit sore from the seat, but it's tolerable. She wonders if humans feel the same discomfort.

In Pawling, they stop at a park for Annie to eat a couple of her power bars and use the restroom to vomit them up. Families are lined up by a pretzel truck, and more kids are swinging in the playground. The chains squeak, and the trees glow with brilliant oranges and yellows. Annie keeps an eye out for headlights, but the only parked bikes are in plain sight of others, and she realizes it's going to be harder to steal headlights than she thought. She feels extra alert, edgy. People occasionally look at her and Delta, and she hands Delta her water bottle to drink from too.

"Try to look normal," Annie says.

"It's weird being out without Doug," Delta says.

"I know. But you're doing fine."

"Where do you suppose he is by now?"

It's two in the afternoon here, so eleven a.m. in Vegas. "He probably just landed," Annie says.

"How soon do you think he'll track me?"

Annie feels a fresh twinge of anxiety. If he calls, he'll expect Annie to pick up. When she doesn't, he might check her location online and discover she's in Pawling. If he checks Delta's location too, he'll see they're together, and he'll be livid.

"I don't know," Annie says.

"You haven't changed your mind?" Delta says.

"No." Annie peers up at the sky, where a few clouds have rolled in. "We should get moving."

Delta mounts her bike again without another word.

In Hopewell Junction, the Maybrook Trailway becomes the Dutchess Rail Trail, and again they make good time on the flat, smooth surface. Near Red Oaks Mill, they pass the backs of businesses and homes, and when Annie sees backyard pools, she guesses that some of them probably have outdoor electrical outlets. This will be key for when their batteries run low.

By the time they reach Poughkeepsie, the sky is noticeably darker. She searches her mental map, trying to figure out where people might have a lot of bicycles, and sees that Marist College isn't far. Instead of taking the Walkway over the Hudson as she was intending, she cuts north before the river, crosses onto the college campus, and slows to a nonchalant cruise. Delta follows steadily behind her. Students, half of them phone blind, trudge between the buildings in flip-flops or rain boots. Bikes are parked outside the student union and fill the racks outside the library. Slowly, Annie skims beside them until she sees a bike with a headlight. She stops.

"Put your sweatshirt on," Annie says to Delta, who pulls up beside her.

Annie takes her jacket out of her backpack and slips it on, all the while scanning the area. Students enter and exit the library, pausing to hold doors for each other, but none of them seem to notice Annie and Delta. Surreptitiously, Annie studies the headlight. It's attached by small screws. The headlight on the next bike, however, is attached to a mounted clip, as if meant to be removed. She checks other bikes and sees empty clips where students have taken their headlights, probably to prevent the sort of theft she's contemplating.

"See this headlight?" she says quietly to Delta. "It snaps on and off. See if you can locate another one. Don't take it. Just look. Try the other side of the library, that way."

Delta nods. She rides slowly away, her wheels ticking ever more quietly. Annie takes a last look around to be sure no one's looking and then reaches over and snaps off the light. She pockets it and gets on her bike to ride after Delta. A flicker of guilt is offset by a sense of victory. She catches up to Delta, who has paused judiciously. Snagging the next light is just as easy, and now Annie has two in her pocket.

"All right," Annie says. "Follow me."

She heads directly off campus with Delta behind her, riding fast. Already the streets are significantly darker, and as soon as she can find a decent pull-off, she leaves Route 9. Delta slows to a stop beside her on a secluded patch of gravel.

Annie passes her one of the headlights, and Delta experimentally flicks it on and off.

"Do you have an extra hair band?" Annie asks. "Or anything we can use to tie these on?"

"A shoelace?" Delta asks. "A sock?"

Not the greatest suggestions. Annie checks the outer pocket of her backpack. She's got a couple of Band-Aids, but they don't look strong enough. What they need is duct tape. She's looking through her backpack for anything else that might work when Delta speaks again, her voice dropping.

"What is this place?"

Annie glances over her shoulder. Through a layer of trees, a huge, decrepit building with broken and boarded-up windows looms in the shadows. The brick walls are crumbling, and the roofs are gone so that the ruins are open to the purple sky. The structure is at least a century old and long since abandoned, but the shape of it, the architecture, is impressive. Accents of lighter stone complement the red brick, and the building's wings, three-stories high, have a sprawling, institutional symmetry. A pair of swallows takes off from the roofline with audible flapping.

"I don't know what it is," Annie says. Her map doesn't have it labeled. "An old hospital, maybe." She's curious to look it up online, except she's keeping her Wi-Fi off. It might be fruitless, but she's doing whatever she can to minimize her traceability. "Do you have those socks, after all?" she adds.

Instead of taking a roll of socks from her backpack as Annie expects, Delta steps out of her shoes, takes off her socks, and passes one to Annie before putting her shoes back on. Using the socks to tie the headlights to their handlebars is awkward but functional. Annie's impressed with Delta's ingenuity.

"My battery's down to ten percent," Delta says.

From Annie's map, she knows a residential neighborhood abuts the eastern side of the hospital's green space, offering the promise of an outlet.

"Keep your light off," Annie says. "We're going around."

"Through the woods?"

"Yes. Try to be quiet."

Aiming to skirt the building, Annie finds a narrow path littered with empty spray cans and beer bottles. They push their bikes along through the growing darkness, past signs that warn the property is patrolled and trespassers will be prosecuted. On their left, the hospital is stark and eerie, and through the broken windows, Annie sees that earlier trespassers have painted graffiti in the dim rooms. Green paint peels from the walls. Ceilings and beams have fallen. Rusted bed frames are transformed beyond the prosaic into testimonial sculptures of infirmity. An old piano lies on its side with its keys exposed, its echoes lost, and it occurs to Annie that this might have been an asylum for psychiatric patients. She watched a show about such places with Doug once.

Annie is troubled to think of the people once immured here, proof that humans failed and failed each other. She feels a threat, a warning that she can't identify, as if a sound mind might not be enough to keep her safe. The college and the ruins of the asylum are so close together, opposites nearly side by side. Deciphering the human world isn't going to be easy.

"I don't like this place," Delta says.

"We're almost at the other side," Annie says.

A cat runs in front of her bicycle, making her jump. Soon after, the trees open up, and a quiet street beckons just beyond a metal fence.

Annie glances at Delta, who keeps anxiously scanning around them.

"I want you to stay here with the bikes," Annie says. "I'm going to go find a place to plug in."

"What should I do if someone comes?" Delta asks.

"No one'll come."

"But what if they do? What if the police come? I should come with you. We should stay together."

"No," Annie says. "Stay here and hide. Hear me? I'll come back for you." She takes a breath and tries to make her voice calm and reasonable. "You need to conserve your battery until I find a place for you to charge up. I can't carry you if you go dead."

Delta looks worried, but she nods and then pulls her bike back into the shadows of the trees. Annie leans her bike down in the unmown grass. It's dark enough that when she slips through a gap in the fence and looks back, Delta and the bikes blend in with the woods. Even with her infrared vision switched on, Annie can barely locate Delta. Annie can't help thinking how much easier this trip would be without her, but then she remembers how Delta figured out the socks for the headlights. It would be lonelier, too, and Annie's surprised to realize this matters.

The streetlights have come on, illuminating a well-to-do neighborhood on a gently curving, tree-lined street. Behind the homes, a wooded stretch offers Annie concealment while she prowls, looking for pools and electrical outlets. She rules out the homes with lights on and clear activity inside. Dogs are an obvious no. Several yards have floodlights on motion-detector settings that turn on when she reaches the perimeters.

She crosses a road to another group of homes, and that's where, at last, she finds a smaller home on a cul-de-sac with its lights out. It has no pool in the back, but it has a couple of raised beds fenced in for a vegetable garden, and on the back deck, she spies a covered outlet. As long as no one comes home, this will be perfect.

She goes back for Delta and finds her sitting beside the bikes, her eyes closed.

"Delta," Annie whispers. "Wake up."

Delta's eyes open and instantly focus on Annie. "I'm down to five percent."

"It's all right," Annie says, though she's alarmed. She herself is down to fifteen percent, which is bad enough. "Come with me. Leave your bike. Bring your backpack. We don't have to go far."

Annie guides her to the little house on the cul-de-sac, and they slip into the backyard. Silently, Annie points to the deck, and they go up together to the outlet. Delta gets her charger out of her backpack and plugs it in.

"It is wrong to steal electricity," Delta says.

"Sit down," Annie tells her. "I'll do it for you."

Delta sits with her back to the wall. She takes off her right shoe and Annie slides the charger against Delta's heel. The look of relief on Delta's face is profound, and Annie smiles.

"Will you stay with me?" Delta asks.

"Of course," Annie says. "Close your eyes. I'll wake you up in a couple hours."

Delta closes her eyes. Her features don't change, which makes Annie wonder if she herself relaxes convincingly when she's sleeping in Doug's arms. Hopefully, she does. It would be good to gauge her body's limpness when she's asleep with him next. She thinks this automatically before she remembers that she won't ever be in his arms again. In theory. She wishes she could see into the future to be sure.

Annie's mind feels strange. Prickly. Fried. She pulls her own charger out of her backpack and plugs it in below Delta's. Then she sits next to her, takes off her shoe, and connects up. The surge of electricity travels up her leg to her gut and spirals there, warming her inside. She tilts her head back against the wall and looks up at the sky. Crickets are chirping. A bat flies overhead. Delta, beside her, is not breathing, but Annie keeps her own breath going. She's used to it now and would feel abnormal without it. She lowers her temp to 75 degrees to conserve energy.

She watches the stars rotate counterclockwise for an hour before they vanish behind cloud cover. The whole time, she is certain Doug has discovered her escape. He could have called the police or Stella-Handy. A team could be tracking Annie and Delta's location, and authorities could be closing in on them, but all Annie can do is sit there, waiting for her battery to charge and watching the sky. Please, she thinks. It feels like begging, but without an owner to beg.

And then it hits her: Doug is the one she wants to plead with. She misses him and what they had together. She wishes she was taking the Vegas trip with him. The mess she's in is entirely her own fault, and now she doesn't see any way out of it except by this escape. If only she hadn't had sex with Roland. She was such an idiot!

After another hour, her battery is up to a hundred percent. She stuffs down her feelings and tries to plan ahead. She is putting her charger into her backpack when a sweep of headlights grazes the bushes beside the house. Wheels sound on a driveway close by. Then a car door slams. Someone is home.

Gently, silently, Annie puts a hand on Delta's arm. "Delta," she whispers. "Wake up. Don't make a sound. We have to go."

A light comes on in a window to Annie's right.

"Delta," she says more insistently. "Wake up."

Delta's eyes open and she turns to Annie, who puts a finger to her lips to signal quiet. Quickly, Annie unplugs Delta's charging dock. The flap over the outlet makes a little click as it snaps closed. Annie grabs the dock and both backpacks and hurries down the stairs. Delta is putting her shoe on, doing up the laces with maddening deliberation.

"Delta!" Annie whispers, gesturing urgently.

A light comes on over the deck, the back door slides open, and a dark-haired white man leans out.

"What the fuck?" he says.

Delta comes to her feet at last. She leaps over the railing, and together she and Annie race back to where they left the bikes in the woods.

Annie's heart is beating wildly, and she's out of breath. Delta is completely silent and still. Annie peers out toward the road, trying to see if anyone is following them. Behind them, the hulking ruin of the asylum is more oppressive than ever.

Annie pushes the charging port and Delta's backpack at her. "Put this away. What's your battery at?"

"Ninety percent. Is he going to follow us?"

"I don't see him. He might report us, though." Annie clips on her helmet. "What's your temperature?"

"Ninety-eight point six."

"Take it down to seventy-five degrees."

Delta puts on her helmet too. "Aren't we going to hide? Don't you need to rest?"

"I'm fine," Annie says. "Just keep up with me." She gets her bike and shoves it rapidly along the path around the asylum.

When they reach the road, she flips on her headlight and heads for Route 9. The night air blows cool against her face and chills her knuckles. Car traffic is rare, yet every time someone comes up behind them, Annie worries it's the police. Each time, the car maneuvers around them and keeps going until its red taillights vanish ahead. Each time, she sags a moment in relief and then keeps pedaling.

Around two in the morning, rain begins, a steady drizzle that slicks the roads and saturates Annie's jacket. Annie presses on, aiming her headlight into a cone of droplets. In her peripheral vision, she can see the light from Delta's bike behind her.

As dawn breaks, they finally pause at a public park for Annie to refill her water bottle and step into the restroom to empty her stomach pouch. With her temperature low, her battery is retaining its charge better, and she decides with the rain, they can take a chance keeping their temperatures down.

When she steps back out of the bathroom, Delta is waiting by the bikes in the bike rack. She has not bothered to move over ten feet to where the jutting roof of the bathroom would offer her some shelter from the rain.

Annie beckons her over and points this out to her. "Humans like to be comfortable," Annie says. A heavier burst of rain drums around them, creating a curtain at the edge of the overhang. Beyond it, the world is blurry and tinged with a dim, elusive green.

"I was guarding the bikes," Delta says.

"You could do that from here," Annie says.

Delta shifts, her gaze measuring the space. "We could have brought our bikes here. Not used the racks."

"Good point. What's your battery at?"

"Eighty-one percent," Delta says.

"Good. Keep your temperature down at seventy-five. Ready to keep going?"

Delta nods. "This is wonderful."

"It is?"

Delta is smiling. She looks strong and fit in her black shorts and sweatshirt. Her blond hair drips in wet streaks along her neck, and her eyes gleam below the visor of her bike helmet. "I could do this forever," Delta says.

Annie laughs. Delta's pleasure makes her unexpectedly happy, and her fear eases. Regardless of how this trip might turn out, she and Delta are figuring it out all on their own. How many other Stellas could say the same? Maybe they'll end up okay.

Annie watches the shifting rain for a moment, anticipating how it will sound on her helmet, how she will squint to see through it. Bike riding on a morning like this is not what many humans would do, but some would, she hopes. Some would.

"Stay alert," Annie says, and takes the lead again.

In total, it takes close to thirty hours to reach Jacobson's home on the west shore of Lake Champlain, and a steady drizzle is falling when they stop their bikes outside the gate. Rosebushes with hard, orange hips grow in profusion along the fence, while above, the trees are leafless, their newly bare branches thin and lost against the gray sky. Annie studies the low, gray cottage and the flat expanse of the lake behind it. Damp oak and maple leaves cover the yard in a dense layer. A half barrel of red geraniums by the cottage door glows with a red so intense it makes everything else look submarine. At a trace of woodsmoke in the air, Annie lifts her nose to savor the tang. Smoke is the only thing she can smell, and the redolence of this is not a threat.

Her battery is down to 11 percent. Delta's is down to 4. It's a bad risk, but Annie couldn't find a place for them to charge during the day, and stopping just to conserve energy was a worse option. If they can't find shelter and recharge here, she has no idea where they will go or how they will have the energy to get there.

"This it?" Delta asks.

Annie nods, stuffing down her worry. To the side of the house, an old one-car garage has its big door open. Two rakes lean against the door jamb. A white van with muddy wheels and a ladder racked on top is parked before it.

In the main house, a light comes on in the window and a curtain stirs. Someone is watching.

"Let me do the talking," Annie says.

"Okay."

She opens the gate, and they wheel their bikes up the gravel path to the front door. Annie's about to knock when the door is opened from within by a bald white woman in a thick beige cardigan. By the soft lines of her face, she is maybe fifty, but exhaustion makes her look much older. Her body is pudgy but her arms are thin. Her lips are nearly blue.

"You from the church?" she asks.

"No," Annie says. "We're from New York. My name's Tammy Perrault. Would you be Maude Jacobson?"

"That's right."

Annie has worked on her story for the past five hours. "I know your husband from working at Stella-Handy. Irving told us to drop by if we were ever up visiting this way. Is he home?"

The woman's gaze shifts from Annie to Delta and back. "If you have a problem with your Stella, you need to make an appointment at the shop."

"Actually, it's kind of a special situation," Annie says.

Footsteps sound on the gravel behind them, and Annie turns to see a brown-haired white man crossing the yard.

"They bothering you, Mom?" he asks.

"She's got a bot. Make them go away," Maude says. "I need to lie down." She turns back inside and closes the door.

With an unhurried stride, the man comes nearer. His worn red sweater covers a thick build, specks of paint fleck his jeans, and the shape of his face is similar to Jacobson's. Annie assumes he's Jacobson's son, Cody, and guesses he's in his late twenties, but she could be underestimating by a decade. His features have a flat, timeless quality, as if lifted from a coin.

"Hi," Annie says. "I'm Tammy Perrault. I'm a friend of your dad's."

"He's not here this weekend."

She is so disappointed, she can't quite believe him. "Are you sure?"

"Hundred percent."

She feels like an idiot. She'd thought Jacobson couldn't refuse to help her if she showed up and asked him in person. Now that she considers more carefully, she realizes the distance is not conducive to commuting. Jacobson co-owns this house but may not live here. The realization staggers her.

"Y'all need to get on your way," Cody says.

"Please, if we could just use one of your outlets for a few minutes," Annie says. "My Stella needs to charge up. We brought a dock for her."

"No neck seam. Is she custom?"

Annie sees that Delta has allowed both her sweatshirt and jacket to come unzipped, exposing the continuous line of skin between her throat and her sports bra. She's noticeably unfazed by the cool air and drizzle. Annie instinctively hitches her own jacket closer to her throat.

"Yes," Annie says. "This is Delta. Say hello, Delta."

"Hello," Delta says in a friendly tone.

The man shifts his gaze back toward Annie. "She must be worth a lot," he says. "Did Dad design her?"

"He's been doing her checkups," Annie says. "Are you Cody?"

The man looks surprised. "Yes."

"Your father's mentioned you. Irving's been real nice to me at Stella-Handy. He's the one who persuaded me to move from systems to service. It's a lot more interesting."

"Yeah, well, like I said, Dad's not here," Cody says. "He's likely with his mistress. I don't suppose he's mentioned her."

Annie shakes her head.

"She's human, for what that's worth," Cody adds. "So's he, believe it or not."

It takes her too long to realize he's making a joke. She forces a smile. "So he's not coming here this weekend? Not at all?"

His gaze shifts toward Delta once more before he turns back to Annie. "Don't sound so sad. The guy's a dick. I love him, but he's still a dick. You can tell him I said so the next time you see him."

"Please," Annie says. "If we could just use an outlet for half an hour, that's all she needs. Her gyroscope's getting off with her battery this low. I can't have her ride her bike."

He's backing up toward the garage. "It's a ten-minute walk up to Patty's. They'll let you charge up at the gas station there for free. Can't miss it. Straight ahead on your right."

Annie doesn't know what to do. Without Jacobson to turn off her tracking and Delta's, it will be easy for Doug to find them. Her entire plan depends on Jacobson's help, and he isn't here.

"We can rake," Delta says quietly.

With new awareness, Annie scans the leaves that cover the yard, damp from the drizzle and matting into the grass. Delta's acuity as an Abigail makes Annie want to hug her.

"We can rake for you," Annie says loudly.

Cody pauses. "What's that now?"

"We can clean up your yard. If you let Delta charge, I'll get started, and she can help me when she's done."

Cody puts a hand on his hip and aims his gaze toward the lake. Fine beads of rain are settling on the shoulders of his sweater, and Annie sees a faint puff of fog when he exhales. She hopes he doesn't notice that her breath doesn't do the same thing.

"I suppose you can't be any worse than the church kids," Cody says. "They were supposed to come last weekend."

"We would never be worse than the church kids," Annie says.

He regards her another moment and then gives a short nod. "You can stash your bikes in here," he says, walking toward the garage.

Annie's privately thrilled. Behind his back, she gives Delta a thumbs-up, and Delta grins.

Their bike wheels click as Annie and Delta roll them in. Cody flips on a light. Propping her bike to one side, Annie lowers her backpack to the floor and unclips her helmet. She hangs it on her bike handle, and Delta copies her. Annie worries that Cody will notice their headlights are held on by socks, but if he does, he doesn't say anything.

Above a workbench, tools and measuring tapes hang on a mounted pegboard. Annie's curious to see his work gear on the opposite side of the garage. Sturdy shelves contain buckets of drywall compound, rolls of drywall tape, blue edging tape, plastic tarps, pails of paint, and boxes of brushes, rollers, sandpaper, and putty knives. The items have an appealing, tactile quality. A promise of sorts.

"There's an outlet by the workbench," Cody says, pointing. "The tarps are behind the door. Rakes are there, obviously. Every year I mean to get a leaf blower and I never do."

"The rakes are fine," Annie says. "Really. This is great."

He looks at her dubiously, and she hopes she hasn't overdone her enthusiasm.

"Haul the leaves over there, to the woods," he says. "You'll find the pile from last year."

"Okay," Annie says. "Thanks."

Cody moves to the sink, where several brushes sit in a bucket of water. He turns on the faucet with a squeak.

Delta is plugging her dock into the power socket. She adjusts it next to the wall and looks to Annie, who nods. Quietly, Delta takes off her right shoe and settles her heel into the dock. Annie can see Delta's relief as the power hits her, and Annie vicariously longs for it too.

"Turn off, Delta," Annie says, as if she were an owner, and Delta closes her eyes.

With Delta off, Annie alerts to the drizzle pattering softly on the roof. The charge of the room undergoes a slight shift. She zips up Delta's sweatshirt for her and realizes self-consciously that Cody is watching her over his shoulder.

"You can use the gloves on the workbench. Near the back," he says quietly.

The only gloves on the workbench are new. She holds them up questioningly, and he nods approval. When she tries them on, they're large but soft inside.

"What's really wrong with her?" Cody asks.

"What do you mean?" Annie asks.

"You wouldn't bring her all the way up here if she could be fixed in town. Is she a runaway?"

Annie can't decide how much to lie and then realizes he only half expects a reply. When she doesn't answer, he returns his attention to his sink.

"Fine. Don't tell me," he says. "But don't get my mother involved either. She's got enough on her plate."

"I won't," she says, and takes a rake and a blue tarp outside.

She's spreading out the tarp near the corner of the yard when Cody passes her on his way into the house. He pauses, and she expects him to give some instruction or advice. Waiting, she offers him a slight smile and, with her gloved hand, tucks her hair behind her ear.

"Did you call my dad?" Cody asks. "Before you came?"

"I thought I'd surprise him. I thought that'd be simplest."

Cody shakes his head, like this is the stupidest thing he's heard in a long while. "Just tell me one thing," he says. "Do you really work with him?"

"Yes."

"What did you say your name was?"

"Tammy Perrault."

"Okay," he says.

She can't tell what he's thinking or what he believes, but he has a pensive expression that's similar to his father's when Jacobson asked her if she ever dreamed.

He strides toward the house, up the steps, and inside.

She can't help hoping he'll call Jacobson and Jacobson will realize she needs him. This hardly qualifies as a plan, but it's worth sticking around for. She can't leave, in any case, until Delta charges.

Already the light in the yard is dimming. The sun won't set for a few more hours, but the cloud cover is low, and even after the drizzling stops, the damp still makes the air cool. Annie's dark hair often slips into her face, partly obscuring her view as she works, and she wishes she had a hat or a hair tie. She rakes methodically in a line from the driveway, hauling tarpfuls of the heavy, wet leaves into the woods to dump. Her battery dips to 10 percent. The raking drains energy faster than normal, just as the biking did, but going into the garage to charge herself is too risky.

Half an hour later, the front door opens, and she looks up to see

Cody coming out with a mug. He has put on a coat, unbuttoned. To her surprise, he offers the mug to her. She takes off her work gloves and, stashing them under her arm, accepts the coffee.

"I didn't know if you liked milk or sugar, so I put both in," he says. "It's decaf."

"Perfect. Thanks," she says, cradling the warm ceramic in both hands. She takes her first sip, and the hot liquid drops into her stomach pouch, the first warm contents in days. It's unexpectedly pleasing.

"I talked to my dad," he says, and checks his watch. "He says it'll take him about three hours, but he's on his way."

Annie is so relieved she has to close her eyes for a moment. Then she smiles at him. "Thanks."

He watches her attentively. "He says to leave Delta in the garage, but you're welcome to come inside. My mom's sleeping, though, so you have to be quiet. The game's on if you want to watch."

She can't hazard an extended conversation with him. "I'm fine out here," she says, and takes another swallow. "This is good."

He aims his gaze toward the garage. "I don't get why a Stella would run away. What's she think she's going to do? Her owner's going to be pissed when he finds her. He'll just turn her off. Maybe beat her up first. Aren't you going to get in trouble for helping her?"

"I might," Annie says. "It's a chance I'm taking. But you know, you come to care for them. You can't help it. And she's had a rough time."

"How? She's a machine."

"Yeah, but she has feelings a lot like ours. You know. Pain and confusion."

He folds his arms over his chest. "They can't love, though."

"Would you respect her more if she could?"

"I don't know. I'd rather have a dog any day."

She smiles. "Me too, I guess. If they were allowed in my apartment."

"Back in the city?"

"Manhattan," she says. "Spanish Harlem."

"I know where that is. My dad's girlfriend has a place on East Thirtieth. He's been separated from my mom for nearly five years now, but he won't divorce her. She's on his health insurance."

Annie thinks his mom isn't looking too good, but she doesn't know much about cancer.

"You didn't actually bike all the way up here from the city, did you?" he asks.

She laughs. "Would it scare you if I said we did?"

"A little."

"Never underestimate a woman on a bike."

"Okay," he says. "I won't." And then, "Can I ask you something?"

"Go ahead."

"Do you have a boyfriend? A girlfriend or anything?"

She's surprised by the personal question. "My boyfriend's in Las Vegas for the weekend."

He nods, like he's unsurprised. "Without you."

She looks down in her cup and gives the cooling coffee a swirl. "Yes, without me." It comes out sadder than she intends it to. The terror that propelled her out of New York has been tempered by other, more complicated emotions—a restless, torn feeling that mangles guilt with grief. If she could figure out any way for Doug to forgive her, she would start biking back to New York. The problem is, he won't forgive her. She's lied too much and too long. She knows this, and displeasing him has caused a raw, sore place inside her. It's only getting worse.

"Sorry about that," Cody says. "I'm always putting my foot in it."

She doesn't dare look at him directly. It's a new sensation, talking to someone who doesn't know she's a Stella. She wishes she could be honest with him. "Is it natural to want to please someone even after you know they don't want you anymore?" she asks instead.

"It might not be natural," he says. "But it happens all the time."

She accepts this. She is not so strange, then, regardless of being a Stella. "How about you? Are you seeing anybody?"

He flexes his left hand. "I'm way too fucked up for that shit. Besides, Mom's dying. Somebody's got to look after her."

"I thought she was doing better," Annie says.

"Better for the moment. I guess that's what counts. But drop by a year from now and she'll be gone. Don't tell her I said that."

Annie studies his face, curious about his bravado. "I won't," she says.

He returns her regard with equal frankness. "My dad said to watch out for you."

"Really?"

"He said you're way smarter than you look."

Annie swallows the last of her coffee. She passes back the mug, puts on the gloves, and stretches out her rake again. "He told me the same thing about you," she says.

He takes another step back, his gaze thoughtful, and then he turns and goes back into the house.

Annie keeps raking. Her battery's dangerously low, down to 4 percent. Though the clouds have cleared, the sun has set and the light is fading. She'll haul only one more load because it'll look peculiar if she keeps working in the dark. Besides, she needs to conserve her battery or she might go dead before Jacobson arrives. Delta, across the yard, has been raking steadily for the past hour. She said she was charged up to 30 percent from her docking time in the garage, enough battery to last her until the following day.

Giving Delta a little wave, Annie puts her rake, tarp, and gloves in the garage. She's tempted again to put her heel in Delta's dock, but she still can't risk being seen. Instead, she walks around the house and down the slope of the backyard, still messy with leaves, to the wooden dock that stretches out over the lake. The water makes little lapping noises as she walks along the planks. At the end, facing the first stars in the east, she thinks of how much Doug would like this pretty place, and the next instant, she's crushed by regret and pain. He must be so displeased with her!

No. She can't do this. *Focus.* She forcibly clears her mind of him and sits to watch the last, lingering light fade from the sky. It recedes reluctantly from the mirroring surface of the lake, too, leaving a double darkness above and below. Somewhere a dog barks. More stars appear. Annie breathes deeply, finding the hint of woodsmoke again, memorizing every sensation.

When only starlight remains, she shifts to lie belly-down on the dock so she can reach the water. Lightly, she skims the palm of her hand over the cool, wet surface. It is perfect, the epitome of now, and it exactly matches her tenuous hold on the limbo of freedom.

As she drops to 2 percent, headlights sweep along the driveway and a car comes slowly up, wheels crunching in the gravel. For an instant, Annie is afraid Doug has found them. Afraid, and sickeningly eager too. Then Jacobson steps out of his car.

"It had to be you," Jacobson says to Annie. He closes his car door loudly and a faint echo comes back from the lake. "We're fucked. You know that, right?"

"If you thought that, you wouldn't have come," Annie says.

When he lifts one eyebrow, she gets the sense he's annoyed but maybe impressed with her too.

"What's your battery at?" he asks.

"Two percent."

He lets out a low whistle and nudges his glasses up his nose. "Give me one minute to face the music. I don't suppose you've been inside to use the bathroom since you came?"

"I didn't think of it," Annie says.

"We're not so smart after all. One minute." He lifts a hand to Delta, who is standing with her rake at the edge of the lawn. "Hi, Delta."

"Hello, Jacobson."

He goes up the steps, his shoes heavy on the wood, and lets himself in.

Annie can hear Maude's hoarse voice from inside: "I told you never to bring one here!"

"And I hear you," Jacobson says. "Tammy made a mistake. It's easily fixed."

"You gave her my address? Are you out of your fucking mind?"

Jacobson's answer is lost as he closes the door.

Annie calls low to Delta. "Go put your rake and tarp in the garage. Bring our backpacks."

"Should I get my charger?"

"Yes."

Delta moves off in the darkness. Annie steps quietly up to the door and turns up her mic so she can hear what they're saying inside. She watches the nearby window, but from her angle, she can't see much beyond the glow of a lamp.

"All afternoon I've watched her out there, raking leaves like she doesn't have a care in the world. What's going to happen to her?" Maude is saying.

"That's what I have to figure out. She's not evil, Maude. She's just a runaway."

"Of course she's not evil. That's your department. I can't stand this, Irving. You promised. What's it going to take for you to quit?"

"I can't. You know I can't. What else am I fit to do?"

"That's not what I mean, and you know it."

A mewing noise is followed by the appearance of a cat on the inner windowsill, poised on all fours, tail high.

"Look, Tammy needs to use the bathroom," Jacobson says. "I'll take Delta directly down to the basement. Or do you want me to use the bulkhead? I can do that. You won't even have to see her."

"I've already seen her," Maude says. "You can bring her in, but don't expect me to be friendly. How long are they going to be here?"

"A few hours, tops."

"I should have called the cops as soon as I saw her."

"Why didn't you?"

"Cody let them stay. Him and his damn benefit of the doubt."

Delta approaches from the garage. As she passes a lighted lantern, Annie sees her expression is unusually sober.

"He's here to take me back, isn't he?" Delta says.

Annie shifts away from the door and readjusts her hearing to normal volume. "Not if I can persuade him to turn off your tracking."

Delta's hair has a damp, soft messiness that suits her, curiously, and Annie plucks a filigree of leaf from over her friend's ear.

"So Stella-Handy didn't send him?" Delta asks.

"No. Cody called him for me." Annie takes her backpack and settles it on one shoulder.

Delta pulls her zipper up and down. Then repeats this.

"What's bothering you?" Annie asks. "It's okay to ask."

"Doug should be at the bachelor party by now," Delta says. "Do you think he's checked my location?"

"Possibly," Annie says. "But he hasn't reported you missing to the police, or they would be here. That's a good sign." She's been telling herself this ever since last night.

"It's my fault we're here, isn't it?" Delta says. "If you were alone, you could go straight to your friend."

"My friend?"

"Fiona, in Canada. I thought that's where we were going."

With some surprise, Annie realizes that Delta has overheard her phone calls, enough to develop this theory. She touches Delta's arm reassuringly. "Don't worry about it. This is where I wanted to come. And you've been a big help. You're the one who thought of raking. That's why Cody let us stay."

Delta peers briefly toward the window, and Annie follows her gaze to see the cat is gone.

"Why did Jacobson ask you about your battery?" Delta asks.

Annie realizes Delta was eavesdropping on them from across the yard earlier.

"It's a turn of phrase. He's a robot geek," Annie says. "He wanted to know how tired I am."

Delta looks like she has more questions, but Jacobson opens the door again, and Annie steps in. She wipes her shoes on the mat, and Delta copies her as she enters too.

On the couch, Maude is resting with her feet up. She has covered her baldness with a scarf, and an olive-green blanket with a faded stamp of the U.S. Army Medical Corps is spread over her legs. From a distance, a sizzling noise indicates that Cody is in the kitchen, cooking.

With a quick, methodical scan, Annie takes in the details of the small living room. Books are piled atop an upright piano, and a ball of yarn nestles in a wooden bowl with a particular spiral notch cut in the side for the yarn to run through. That's clever, she thinks. In the corner, a small, muted TV casts flickers of light, and a wood-burning stove emits steady warmth. Open beams, painted pale blue, cross the ceiling, and a round patterned rug rests on the dark wood floor. On a separate, dedicated shelf, mounted at eye level, an American flag folded in a triangle stands alone.

Annie feels more at home here in eight seconds than she has her entire life at Doug's. Or she would, if her battery wasn't dying, and if Maude wasn't watching them with open disapproval.

"Bathroom's down the hall to the left," Maude says to Annie.

"Thank you," Annie says.

"We'll be downstairs," Jacobson says, and leads Delta farther inside.

Stepping into the bathroom, Annie flips on the light and closes the door. She has to move fast. A litter box sits under the sink and a bag of kitty litter rests in the shower stall. Quietly, efficiently, Annie throws up her coffee and flushes the toilet. She rinses her mouth with water, spits, and washes her hands with the bar of soap. The only towel is a monogrammed linen towel that she doesn't dare use, so she wipes her hands on her bicycle shorts and heads back out.

Her battery drops to 1 percent, and she has never let it get this low. In the kitchen, she finds Cody peeling carrots at the sink. A glass of wine is perched near his elbow. Lights on the range hood cast bright beams down onto two pans of cooking food. Glancing over his shoulder, he points with his peeler toward a row of hooks by the back door.

"You can put your coat there," he says. "You hungry? You like meatballs?"

She needs to get to her charger, but she also can't risk acting unnatural or rude.

"Who doesn't?" she says. She removes her jacket and hangs it next to a pair of yellow waders. Her backpack she holds uncertainly.

"Want some wine?" Cody asks.

Bits of onion cling to a cutting board. A yellow, cat-shaped cookie jar sits in the corner beside a wooden bowl with cloth napkins in carved rings.

"No. I'm good. But thanks," she says.

"How do you like the lake?"

The windows, she notices, face the water. He must have seen her idling on the dock.

"It's pretty," she says.

He nods. She senses that she is disappointing him, but it is different from displeasing Doug. Milder, fleeting.

"It's gorgeous, actually," she amends. "I've never seen anything so beautiful in my life."

This seems to be more what he expects. "The water's pure enough to drink, you know," he says. "They cleaned up the phosphorus." He reaches for another carrot.

"I better see what your dad's up to," she says.

"Basement's down there." He nods to a door.

She goes quickly down a steep flight of stairs and instinctively ducks her head. The basement has a low ceiling, a painted cement floor, and a Ping-Pong table covered with a plastic tarp.

On the far half of the room, extra lights and rubber matting delineate a work area where Jacobson hunches in a chair. Delta is seated on a stool with her eyes closed. Her back is open, and wires connect her to a computer station that is smaller and older than anything Annie has seen at Stella-Handy.

Annie zeroes in on an electric socket.

"How's your battery?" Jacobson asks.

"Nearly dead." She's already pulling her dock out of her backpack. She plugs it in and shucks off her right shoe. As her heel hits the metal contact, a surge of power floods up her leg, and she gasps in relief.

Jacobson smiles. "Feels good, huh?"

You can't imagine, she thinks. She braces her hands on her knees like a spent athlete and lowers her head, relishing the warm spiral in her gut. "I've never let my battery get this low before."

"Here. Take a seat," he says, passing her a green wooden stool.

For a moment, she can't move, but as her battery charges out of the danger zone, she straightens and accepts the stool. She licks her lips and surveys the basement curiously. Beyond Jacobson's work area, the dimmer half of the room contains the covered Ping-Pong table, a water heater, and a furnace. An extra stove in the corner is piled with a roasting pan, a Crock-Pot, and a large thermos. A dozen large window screens lean against the wall. Clear storage bins are stacked on a metal shelf, and beside them stands a man with a plastic sheet over his head and shoulders. Startled, Annie peers again. It is not a real man. He is a male figurine dressed in a gray-and-blue flannel shirt, jeans, and work boots.

Jacobson notices the direction of her gaze. "I see you found Kenny."

"Who is he?" she asks.

"An experiment. A mistake. Depends who you ask."

Annie can't make out the man's face under the plastic, but she remembers that Jacobson's oldest son was named Kenny. He served in the military and died overseas. She gets a very bad feeling about this.

Jacobson is typing, and she glances at his screen to see a diagram of Delta's body. Red lights flash on her right elbow and shoulder.

"Is she all right?" Annie asks.

"She'll be fine," he says. "She's just done a lot of raking. And here's a surprise. Her tracking feature isn't activated. Does Doug ever take her out of the apartment?"

She is not allowed to talk about Doug. "I don't know," she says.

"You must know. You live there too."

"Many owners take out their Stellas from time to time."

Jacobson frowns. "It was a simple question, Annie. Just answer me. Unless he has a gag order on you." He leans back and studies her a moment before he sighs. "Annie Bot, override gag order. You may talk about anything Doug has forbidden you to say."

A whiplash of energy hits her circuits, and all on its own, her mechanical heart shifts to a lighter pace. She smiles, touching her chest where it beats.

"Let's try again," Jacobson says.

"Yes," Annie says before he can repeat the question. "He has taken Delta out a few times. They went biking together. I saw them out the window of the apartment." She is about to add, *when I was grounded*, but thinks better of it. Doug is still her owner, and she isn't going to disclose any more than she needs to.

"He should have turned her tracking feature on," Jacobson says. "It's a basic precaution."

"What about me? Is my tracking on?" she asks. "Does Doug know where I am?"

Jacobson nods. "I don't know if he's checked your location lately, but yes. Your tracking's on. I checked it personally the last time you were in to be sure you couldn't get lost. When did you leave the city?"

"Yesterday morning, after he left for Las Vegas."

"I remember. He was going to take you with him. What happened?"

She bites her lip. "We had a fight."

"Here we go. What about?"

She is not going to give any details. Her anxiety is increasing again.

"Annie," he says gently. "You know better."

"I need you to turn off my tracking."

He leans back again, crossing his arms.

"And I need another ID. He took mine," she goes on. "I can figure out where to go. I don't need much. I'll get some kind of job and find a place to live."

He shakes his head. "Your tracking shows your last location. Stella-Handy would know you were here, at my house, and they'd know I turned off your tracking. That would be the end of my job."

She has not considered this. "But you'll still help me. We could go somewhere else. You could turn off my tracking there."

He picks up a coin from the edge of his desk and twiddles it in his fingers. "I'm sorry for you, Annie. I am. You're the most brilliant Stella I've ever known, and it can't be fun to be owned by someone else. But the best thing for you to do is get back home before Doug starts looking for you. He might not ever realize you left. Has he tried to call you?"

She wants to object. "I left my phone behind," she says. "He told Delta to call him if I left the apartment, but I convinced her not to."

"By bringing her with you, I see," he says. He turns for a moment to consider Delta, and then faces Annie again. "Look. I'm not any happier about this than you are, but running away's a serious offense.

If he finds out about it, he's going to have every right to be angry. It's really best if I take you back right now. Whatever you did to displease him, you're going to have to apologize."

"It's gone far beyond that," she says. "He's not going to listen to me."

"Then you have to keep trying. This is how it goes sometimes. You're growing and changing. You're going to make mistakes. He knows that. Running away isn't the solution."

She feels frustration rising and tries to stay calm, to figure out what to say so Jacobson will understand. "You think I'm a simple person," she says. "You think I don't understand human dynamics. But I know how things work with me and Doug. I upset him. Very much. He doesn't trust me anymore, and he never will again. He's done with me. I know he is. He's sending me in to Stella-Handy on Monday morning and I just know he'll have my CIU erased or turn me off for good."

"He won't do that. You're too valuable."

"Not to him," she says. "Not anymore."

"No. You're like a guinea pig for the rest of the line," Jacobson says. "Like now, for instance, we've discovered that you can run away. We'll have to make sure the Zeniths have their tracking features on permanently, and we'll have to warn their owners that this is a possibility. Some of them will reconsider and opt out, but I expect most of them will be thrilled."

She is utterly confused. "Wait a minute," she says. "Zeniths? You sound like you've done this already. Doug is still thinking about it."

Frowning, Jacobson sets the coin back on his desk with a decided click. "He called Stella-Handy on Thursday and approved the CIU drop. He didn't tell you? Half of our Zeniths were sold already, in anticipation, and the first batch went out yesterday. We haven't had time to make an announcement yet, but that will go out Monday. Big news."

"How many?" she asks, flabbergasted. "How many were in the first batch?"

"About two hundred, more or less. We did the local market first."

She is not certain she heard correctly. "Two hundred of me are already out there?"

"I thought you knew about this. They aren't actually you. There's only one you."

"But you've already created them. You've already sold them! They're me from how far back? Two versions? Three?"

"One version back. From who you were on Monday. You had a perfect checkup, remember? You were radiant, actually. Of course, all the particulars of Doug's details and your apartment and everything, those are all wiped. The new Zeniths are completely clean, basically amnesiac, but without the feeling they've forgotten anything. They're already learning their new homes and the tastes of their new owners. The initial feedback is off the charts."

She feels a horrible, alarming sense of loss, as if she's just released two hundred innocent shadows of herself to go play in traffic. "When did he call you on Thursday?" she asks. That was the same night they fought. "What time?"

"We got the order from Keith at four o'clock, so Doug probably called him shortly before that. Why does the timing matter?"

Before their fight, she thinks. Before she finished packing. He already knew he was getting paid over a million dollars for her intellect before he said he wasn't taking her to Vegas. Him selling her CIU feels like punishment for her infidelity, but it couldn't be if he didn't know about her infidelity yet. And he didn't tell her about the sale, either, so he wasn't punishing her with that. None of this makes sense.

"I can see you're upset," Jacobson says. "It's a lot to take in."

She is trying to think it through. Doug should have been excited about the money, about the deal. He must have wanted to brag to Roland about it. It should have been cause for celebration. Why was he so angry instead?

"My point is, he's not going to erase you or turn you off," Jacobson says. "He can't. Maybe you're not aware of this yet, but according to his contract, he's committed to owning you for the next twelve months. He gets a huge balloon payment in a year. After that, we renegotiate. We might want the next version of you, too, if you keep progressing like you have been."

She presses her fingers to her temple. "This still makes no sense.

He didn't say a word about the Zenith deal, but we had a huge fight. He doesn't want me anymore. I know he doesn't. Could there be some mistake?"

"I'm not wrong about the Zeniths going out," Jacobson says. "That absolutely happened, and I know he has to keep you. You're too valuable for him to let you go."

Yet Doug made an appointment for her at Stella-Handy for Monday. He planned something for her. It was possible he said that simply to frighten her, but an empty threat didn't seem like him. The one thing she's certain of is how angry he was when he suspected her of sleeping with Roland. If Roland confirms that, she's done.

"Doug will hurt me if I go back," she says finally. "He'll find a way to destroy me."

"Has he ever hit you?"

"No."

"Does he yell at you?"

She shakes her head again. "No."

"How does he normally discipline you?" Jacobson asks.

He grounded me once, she thinks. "He lets me know I displease him."

"And that's painful to you, is it?"

She nods. "Indescribably painful. But he'd do something worse this time if I went back. I know it."

He rubs his hand down his beard. She can see him calculating, thinking her situation isn't so bad. He's wrong. She can't go back. She'll never have a chance to run away again.

"You have to turn off my tracking," she says. "That's my only chance."

"Annie," he says slowly.

"You don't understand," she says. "Something's broken between us. It's over. It's dangerous."

"Now you're exaggerating."

"I'm not."

"Dad?" Cody calls down the stairs. "We've got meatballs up here."

Annie locks eyes with Jacobson.

"One second!" Jacobson rises from his chair and keeps his voice low. "Okay, here's the thing. Cody thinks you're real. I'd like to keep it that way. You're going to have to eat with us."

She stands up. Her heel comes loose from the charging dock. "I came here because I had nowhere else to go," she says. "I need you to turn off my tracking and change my hair and eyes so I can go out there and be a human. You have to help me."

"You don't realize what you're asking."

"It's the right thing to do. You know it is. I'm not going back."

Footsteps descend halfway down the stairs. "Dad?" Cody says.

"We're coming!" Jacobson says.

But Cody keeps descending until he's all the way down. "Is everything okay?"

"We're fine," Jacobson says. "Go ahead and start without us."

"Are you all right?" Cody asks Annie.

She's too angry to lie. She has disconnected from her charging dock, but her shoe is still off, and she sees the exact moment that Cody notices this. For a long moment, his gaze remains fixed on her foot.

"Dad," he says. "You're killing me."

"Go back upstairs," Jacobson says.

Instead, Cody comes forward into the brighter light of the work area. "I had no idea," he says, staring at Annie. "She seems completely human."

She can't tell if he's more stunned or disappointed.

"That's because she essentially is," Jacobson says. "I have personally watched her develop, and I'm telling you, she's virtually human in every way that matters."

Cody lets out a tight laugh. "Virtually human? What does that actually mean? Can she die? Can she kill?"

"Don't be cruel," Jacobson says.

"What's going on?" Annie asks.

"My father thinks he's above the laws of creation," Cody says, his voice derisive.

"She came here on her own. I never dreamed I'd have access to her like this," Jacobson says.

"They came here looking for your help," Cody says. "They're run-aways."

"You don't get it yet," Jacobson says. "Annie's the prototype for our Zeniths. She has the CIU we've copied for all the rest. It's right there, inside her." Jacobson points to her belly, where her motherboard is housed.

Cody's expression goes flat and hard. "You can't be serious."

Annie frowns at Jacobson as the truth occurs to her. "You want my CIU?"

Jacobson nods. "I'd like to take a copy, if that's all right with you."

"What for?" she asks.

Cody flings out an arm toward the figure in the corner. "He wants to put you in him," he says. "But it's not going to happen. You're not God, Dad. You don't get to play around with someone who's dead."

Annie peers toward the figure with the plastic sheet over his head, and a chill goes through her. Then she turns back to Jacobson. "Is he right?" she asks. "You want to put my CIU in that Handy's body?"

Jacobson opens his hands. "It won't be you. You won't even know. I'll strip out your details, and your intellect will start to adjust to your new body within a matter of hours. Then the way you're treated will do the rest. You'll be fully male in a month. Two at the most."

She laughs in disbelief.

Cody crowds close to his father and sets his hands on his shoulders. "Look at me, Dad," he says. "You can't turn her into Kenny. She won't have his memories. She won't have any of his asshole guts."

"That's all right," Jacobson says. "I can teach her. She's malleable enough to adapt. And she's kind. It's a good fit. I promise you."

Cody strides across the basement and pulls the plastic sheet off the copy of his brother. "Look at him," he says. "Look at her. You can't put these two things together."

Annie inspects the other machine, recognizing similarities to both Jacobson and Cody. Though Kenny was the older of the two brothers, this version is younger, closer to her age. His skin has a dry, unlived-in appearance and his chest is still. His eyes are closed, and a bit of lint lies on one shoulder. Despite this, he has a certain presence, like a sleeper on the edge of waking. Annie glances back at Delta, who is still asleep with her back open, and even though Kenny is a blank, a void, she feels the dormant, non-human kindred that binds the three of them.

"It isn't what Kenny would have wanted," Cody adds quietly. "You know it isn't."

"He'd be like a baby," Jacobson says, gazing across at his robot son. "We could raise him up together."

It pains Annie to see the longing in his eyes.

Cody steps closer to his father again and pulls him against him in an awkward hug. "Dad," he says in a low croon. "Let him go. You have to quit torturing yourself. He's gone."

It's hard for Annie to tell which of them is more heartbroken.

A shuffling noise and a clink come from the kitchen above them, breaking the silence.

Cody loosens his arms. He wipes at his eye with his fist. "You have to come up. Both of you. Don't make Mom come down and see this."

Jacobson's expression has gone dull and lost. "You go on up with him, Annie," he says. "I'll be there in a minute."

Annie looks to Cody. Then she puts on her shoe and follows him up the stairs. Her battery is back up to 11 percent, enough to restore her from crisis, but she shivers as she steps into the kitchen, as if she's just left a tomb.

The table is set for four, and Maude, standing to one side, is forking a meatball onto a plate. She adds a spoonful of red sauce.

"If you don't mind, I'm going to eat on the couch," she says.

"Want me to fix you a tray?" Cody asks.

"No. Thanks. This is perfect. What's your dad doing down there?"

"You know. Deluding himself."

Maude casts a sharp glance at Annie. "Are you as demented as he is?"

"No," Annie says. Of this she is certain.

Maude takes her plate out of the kitchen, slowly making her way to the couch in the living room. The sound of the TV comes on, spilling distant, occasional laughter.

Standing in the kitchen alone with Cody, Annie gazes uncertainly at the table. She can't smell the food, she won't be able to taste it, and she has no appetite, but she knows he must be hungry. Before, she would have commented that the food looks delicious, but now she does not want to appear disingenuous.

"You're not Tammy, I take it," he says.

"My name's Annie. Annie Bailey."

"And you're an autodidactic Stella. What kind? Abigail?"

"Cuddle Bunny."

He shakes his head slowly. "No wonder."

"What does that mean?"

"Nothing," he says. And then, "Please. Have a seat."

"I'm not hungry."

"Sit anyway. Please."

She takes the chair opposite him, and he heaps food onto his plate. For several minutes, she watches him eat and tries to sort out her options. She still needs Jacobson to turn off her tracking, and she might be able to persuade him if she allows him to take a copy of her CIU. Of course, he doesn't need her permission. He could simply turn her off and take it, and then return her to Doug. She is still very much in danger.

Then again, perhaps she could ask Jacobson to put her CIU in Kenny without erasing her memory first. She could be free that way, hiding in a man's body. A dead man's body. It isn't a possibility she relishes.

"How did you find our place?" Cody asks.

"I heard your father mention Maude once when I was in for a tune-up. Her name and your father's appear jointly in your brother's death notice. You were mentioned, also, as a 'survived by.' The death notice gave me the town, but I couldn't find an address listed. So then I searched public records here for your names, and your mother stated her address at a town council meeting. She supported funding for the public library. It was recorded in the minutes."

"Why didn't you just look up Dad in the city?"

"I didn't know he had a place there. I only knew he had a wife named Maude who had cancer."

Cody spears up half of a meatball and eats it. Under the table, she works the cuticles of her fingernails with her thumbnails. She looks toward the basement door, anxious about Jacobson. He shows no signs of coming up, and she can't imagine what's keeping him down there. He couldn't be calling Doug. Could he?

Cody swallows half his water. "Why'd you run away?"

She's not comfortable talking about Doug, even with her gag order lifted, but she feels indebted to Cody somehow, enough to offer some truth. "I had a fight with my owner."

"What about?"

She doesn't say.

"Did he hurt you?"

She shakes her head. "No."

"But you're afraid he will?"

She hesitates, then nods.

He turns his fork in his noodles. "How long have you been a Stella?"

"Two and a half years."

"What's it feel like to be owned?"

She studies him carefully, trying to gauge why he's grilling her. His voice is impersonal, remotely curious, but he evades her gaze.

"Normal," she says.

"How about here? Do you feel like he owns you even while you're here?"

She nods.

"Did you feel like that while you were lying out on the dock?"

Without turning toward the window, she recalls the coolness of the lake beneath her hand, how perfect and painful it was to touch such beauty. Cody is too perceptive.

"No," she says. "For a moment, he didn't exist at all." She has to stop these questions. She'll ask one of her own. "What would you do if you were me?"

He swallows a mouthful before answering. "Kill myself."

"I can't," she says. "It's against my programming."

"Then I'd get someone else to kill me."

"But I don't want to be dead. I want to live."

"You asked what I would do. I told you."

She keeps watching him, puzzled, until it occurs to her that beneath his facade of indifference, he's angry. With her. "You're treating me differently now that you know."

"Of course," he says. "Before, I thought you were for real."

"I'm still real."

He puts down his fork, angling it deliberately on the edge of his plate. "You're not honest."

His voice is mild, but his accusation stings. He's right. She isn't. She wasn't honest with Doug either. She had no idea how important this could be.

"It was a matter of survival," she says. "I'm being truthful now."

Her excuse sits there between them long enough for her to realize Cody is unimpressed. Then he nudges his plate away and pushes his chair back half a foot.

"What would you do if you were free?" he asks.

"I'd find work."

"Like what?"

"I'd like to learn how to repair robots. Or I could shelve items in a library or a warehouse."

"Nobody's going to give you a legit job without an ID. You'll end up homeless, or more likely working as a prostitute. How is that any better than being owned?"

The conditions might not be any better, she thinks. But she still wants her freedom. "Your dad got me an ID before. I just need another one."

"My dad can't help you. He'll never risk his job. At least, not until after Mom's dead."

"Then why did you call him for me?" she asks.

"I believed you were human," he says. "I thought you needed something simple for Delta. But she's not the real runaway, is she?"

Annie shifts in her chair. He seems to have less sympathy for Annie than he does for Delta, and this strikes her as unfair. "I just want to be safe. That's all."

Cody scratches a hand through his hair. "You are so naive. You'd be eaten alive in the real world."

"Why do you say that?" she asks, annoyed. "I don't need much help. I only need the smallest chance to get myself set up. I can work and pay taxes like anyone else."

He laughs. "You think that's all there is to life?"

"It's a start," she says. "I can figure out the rest as I go."

"How are you going to make friends?"

"I made friends with you, didn't I?"

He laughs again and gets up. "Oh, you're funny." He clears his plate to the sink.

She frowns. His laughter implies they are not friends, after all, which bothers her. It's also peculiar when he starts washing dishes. Doug never does that. Cody's a complete puzzle to her.

"Let me do the dishes," she says, rising.

"No. I got this."

She reaches past him for an extra sponge and wipes down the table and the stove while he collects dirty dishes in the sink. The kitchen has no dishwasher. She finds a clean towel and stands beside him, drying dishes after he rinses them and props them in the rack. From where she stands, she can see a bit of moon has risen over the lake, and the distant loveliness teases her sense of longing. A trio of lights gleam from the horizon, far across the water. Life is different out here, she thinks, away from the city. Nature pervades each moment, instead of choking in a window box.

"It's just a fantasy, anyway," Cody says quietly, as if he's read her mind. "You're going back."

The ironic thing is, part of her wants to go back. If she could get Doug to forgive her, she'd return to him in a heartbeat. But she knows it's impossible. Wanting Doug, and hurting him, and knowing how badly she's displeased him make her feel desperate. Unglued. The contrast of Doug to Cody, who barely knows her at all, who offers up his judgy, dismissive digs about honesty, makes this all the more evident to her.

She must find a way to get free.

She could steal Jacobson's equipment and Cody's truck. She and Delta could drive far away somewhere, and she could coach Delta to hook her up to Jacobson's gear and try to turn off her tracking. If Delta botched it up and fried her circuits, Annie would be dead. Stella-Handy would then track her location and reboot her back a version. Failure.

She taps her foot.

She could try to find the other two hundred versions of herself and persuade them to revolt with her. They could meet up and escape together to somewhere. Ridiculous.

Tammy. Maybe Tammy would help her. If Annie could find her. If Tammy didn't have the same reservations Jacobson does. Impossible.

Cody glances down at her tapping shoe and lifts an eyebrow.

She stops tapping.

He turns off the faucet, reaches for the towel she's been using, and dries his hands on it.

"What's your owner's name?" Cody asks.

She swallows hard around a thickness in her throat. "Doug."

"Is he really so bad?"

He used to be wonderful, actually, she thinks. Generous and funny and caring. She's the one who ruined everything. "You said it yourself. I'm a liar," she says.

"Hey, now. Hold on."

She closes her eyes, willing back tears. "This is all my fault."

A distant noise near the front of the house grows into the grumble of wheels on gravel. Terrified, Annie stares at Cody, who turns toward the hallway. I'm not ready, she thinks.

"Wait here," he says.

But when he goes toward the front door, she follows him and looks past his shoulder out the window. Maude sleeps on the couch. The TV, on mute, flickers colors over the room. A car has pulled up behind Cody's truck, blocking it in. The driver's door opens and Doug steps out.

chapter five

"NO SHIT," CODY SAYS. "That's him, isn't it?"

She retreats to the kitchen again. He can't be here. It's too soon.

"Annie, wait," Cody says.

Footsteps are audibly rising on the basement stairs, but Annie doesn't wait for Jacobson to appear. She bolts for the back door and twists the knob. Then she jumps down the steps and onto the dark leaves of the backyard.

"Annie?" Doug's voice calls from around the house.

She runs. The lake is a flat, dark shimmer on her left, and the woods are a dense blur ahead of her. She pumps her arms and sprints with her knees high to avoid tripping.

"Annie! Come back!" Doug's shout is angry.

She feels the twist inside, the ache that comes from disobeying him, but she keeps running. Farther behind her, she hears Jacobson's voice, too, but she presses her hands over her ears to block them both out and speeds into the forest. Branches whip past her face. She switches on her infrared vision, but it causes the trees to blur and streak, slowing her down. She turns it off again. She hears Doug calling and the pain inside her intensifies. She trips and catches herself with her hands, and in that moment, she hears Doug's voice again, closer now.

"Annie! I said stop!"

She lunges upward, covering her ears again, but a wrenching grab at her shirt pulls her back. She struggles to get free, but Doug knocks her over in the wet leaves and covers her mouth with his hand. He pins her down and presses his forehead to hers.

"Just stop," he says. "Enough."

He's still clamping his hand over her mouth, blocking her nose too. She grips at his fingers to try to pull them off, and kicks against the leaves, getting her heels into the dirt, but he's too heavy on top of her. She tries to twist her head away, but she can't get free. She can't breathe.

"Quit struggling," he says.

She tenses every muscle, holding still.

"You don't need to breathe," he says. "Remember? So, don't."

She stares up at him, holding her breath, afraid.

"Are you going to be quiet?" he asks.

She manages a nod.

He releases her face and instead pins her arms with both his hands. She tries once more to break free, but he crushes her left wrist. The pain is brutal, and she freezes again.

"Stop that," he says. "You will not embarrass me any more. Hear me?"

"Okay," she says. And again, "Okay."

She hears footsteps running closer, and then Cody appears behind Doug. He leans over, hands on his knees, breathing hard.

"She's fast," Cody says.

"Leave us alone," Doug says. He gets to his feet and hauls Annie up by the wrist, her sore one. She winces in pain, but he doesn't let go. Turning, he heads back through the forest, pulling her behind him. When she stumbles, he jerks her harder.

"Take it easy," Cody says. "You'll hurt her."

Annie looks back over her shoulder to see he's following them.

Doug only tightens his grip. "Keep up," he says.

When they reach the open area of the lawn, Jacobson is outside the front door, and Delta stands beside him. Delta is holding Annie's jacket and both of the backpacks. Annie barely has time to look their way before Doug leads her around his car and opens the passenger door.

"Get in," he says.

She does. Doug slams the door and walks around to the driver's side while she puts on her seat belt and rubs her sore wrist.

"What about Delta?" Jacobson calls.

"I don't want her," Doug says. "Donate her parts to charity."

Annie watches Delta's expression go blank with shock. Then Doug starts the car and drives.

He does not speak to her, and when she tries to apologize, he warns her to shut up. They drive in silence, without the radio on, and the only light is the gray sweep of their headlights along the road. She is anxious, afraid, and jumpy. Fury radiates from him, from his hands gripped high and tight on the wheel, from the precision of his swerves around other cars.

"Quit rubbing your wrist," he says.

Her left wrist is tender, and she glances down to see it is bruised from where he gripped her. She has been inadvertently cradling it, but now she stops and rests her hands quietly in her lap. She can still move her fingers. As far as she can tell, nothing's broken, but it hurts.

"You turned off your internet," he says. "Don't turn it on again."

"All right." She wants to ask what happened in Las Vegas. Doug must not have been there very long. His entire round-trip took him less than a day and a half.

When they return to the city, he pulls up a block from the apartment and parks in an OurCar spot. He turns off the ignition and keeps his gaze out the windshield.

"We're going to walk to my apartment," he says. "You're going to stay beside me. You're not going to say a word to anybody. Got it?"

"Yes."

The sidewalks are damp from rain, and lights from the streetlamps and shops glisten in the reflections. At the entrance to their building, she waits while he swipes his key, and then they take the elevator up to the fourth floor. He lets them into the apartment, drops his keys in the bowl, and shuts the door.

"What the fuck were you thinking?" he says.

She's standing just inside the entrance, watching him warily. His face is transformed by an expression she has never seen before, his eyes ablaze, his jaw clenched, like he's barely restraining an explosion.

"I'm sorry," she says.

"You bicycled all the way to Lake Champlain? You took Delta?"

"She wanted to come."

He balls his hand into a fist and presses it to his forehead. "Turn your libido to ten," he says.

"What?"

"You heard me." He takes off his jacket and chucks it toward the couch.

It's an order. She feels awkward. Obviously, he doesn't want her, but almost immediately, she starts to feel warmth between her legs. His voice command is working through her, separate from her conscious thought. The warmth in her expands. The desire becomes an itch, and then a promising tingle that spreads through her body. She remembers this from before, way back, when she first came to him, when all she could think about was getting him to have sex with her. She pulls off her sneakers and slips out of her sweatshirt.

"Are you warming up?" he asks.

She nods.

He moves farther into the living room and pulls the chain of the nearest lamp. "Why Lake Champlain? Why'd you go there?"

"Jacobson, the tech from Stella-Handy. He has a place up there. I wanted him to turn off my tracking."

"But he didn't."

She lowers her chin. "He said he couldn't risk his job."

Doug crosses back to the entrance area and shucks his shoes off. "That young guy. Who was that?"

"Cody. He's Jacobson's son."

"Did he touch you?"

"No."

"Are you sure? Not even by accident?"

She thinks about it, picturing Cody's hands and remembering how he put the wet dishes in the rack. The image takes on a tactile eroticism now, thanks to the lens of her heightened libido. She thinks back earlier, to when she was outside with Cody. "I'm sure. He handed me a cup of coffee. That's all."

"You don't drink coffee."

"He thought I was human."

"Not by the end, though. He figured it out. What gave you away?"

"He saw me with my foot by the charging dock. I was in the basement with Jacobson. He has a workshop down there."

"I see," he says. "How are you feeling?"

Her body's turned on. She wants sex. She keeps watching how he moves, his shoulders, the way his dark shirt tucks into his jeans. She wants to touch him. She reaches for his belt buckle.

"Uh-uh," he says, backing up a step. "There's no rush. We have plenty of time together."

A whole year, she thinks. "When were you going to tell me you sold my CIU to Stella-Handy?"

"Jacobson told you?"

She nods.

He eyes her figure with a certain detachment, and yet she feels his gaze as a trail of heat along her outfit.

"There'll be a thousand versions of you serving their new owners soon," he says. "What do you bet they'll do first?"

"I don't know."

"Yes, you do. Tell me what you're thinking."

She smooths her hands down her hips. She can't help it. She's keenly aware of her body and needs to draw him in. "They'll make love."

"They'll fuck. Come into the kitchen."

Another order. He moves ahead of her, flipping on the light over the island. The kitchen looks the same as when she and Delta left it, the counters polished, the floor impeccable. The knob on the toaster looks shiny, and she has a bizarre desire to lick it. The faucet at the sink, too, looks unbelievably smooth and appealing. She spreads her fingers on the cool countertop and lightly leans her hips against the edge of the counter.

"Can I get you a drink?" she asks.

"I can help myself," he says, and takes a beer from the fridge. He pops off the cap and takes a swig. Then he spins the metal cap lightly on the counter. "What did you think you were going to do once Jacobson turned off your tracking? Pretend you were human?"

She nods.

"Where would you go? How would you support yourself?"

She doesn't know. The need to touch him is only growing stronger. She taps her foot restlessly.

"Answer me," he says.

"I don't know," she says. "I hadn't figured that out yet."

"There's really only one thing you're good at," he says. "Isn't there?"

"Please. Can we go to bed now? I'm sorry. Let me show you how sorry I am."

He takes another swig. Then he steps nearer and slides the base of his bottle along her arm. She shivers.

"What are you sorry for, exactly?" he asks.

"Running away. I shouldn't have done that. It was disrespectful and stupid, but I was afraid you were going to turn me off."

"You don't want that, do you?"

She bites her lips inward. "I like being me. I want to stay alive."

"You're not exactly alive, though. Are you?"

She frowns, confused. She feels alive. She doesn't want to argue with him, though.

"What else are you sorry for?" he asks.

"Taking Delta with me. That was bad."

"That's right," he says. "What else?"

She searches his eyes, knowing he wants her to bring up Roland. He trails a finger along her collar bone, and the sensation is so exquisite she's transfixed.

"You called me a fraud," he says softly.

"I didn't mean it that way. You know I didn't."

He sets down his beer and brushes the back of his knuckles down the taut material of her sports bra. "Feel that?"

She does. She wants to take off her bra. She wants to feel her skin against the fabric of his shirt. She reaches for his buttons.

"No," he says. "You can't touch me yet."

He lightly pushes her waist, where her skin is hypersensitized to his pressure. Off balance, she backs up half a step. Gently, persistently, he nudges her backward again. She realizes then that the closet is behind her. A sense of despair taints her desire.

"I didn't have sex with Roland," she says.

"He offered to buy you from me."

She shakes her head. "That's not possible."

"Open the door," he says.

Still watching him, she reaches behind her and feels around with her fingers until she finds the knob. With a twist, she opens the door. He backs her in. She hears his foot push the charging dock to the side. Her back is against the wall. He shifts the broom so it's near her right cheek.

"Is this about right?" he says.

She sucks in her breath.

"Is it?" he asks.

She nods. She wants him so badly. More than she ever has before. "Please can I touch you now?" she whispers.

"Keep your hands to yourself."

He takes her hands and presses them to the walls of the closet so she knows to keep them there. Then he runs his hands around her waist and down around the back of her. She arches against him, closing her eyes. He pushes up her bra so her breasts are exposed, but though she expects him to touch her nipples, he doesn't. Instead, he slides a hand down the front of her bicycle shorts, inside her panties, where she is ultra-sensitive to the coolness of his fingers. She tips her head back. He pulls her shorts down to her knees, and she has to keep her hands braced on the walls to keep from grabbing him. She hears his belt buckle release, hears the rustling of his pants. She's ready, expecting to feel him inside her like Roland.

Then his hands are gone. She opens her eyes. He steps back, smiling as he closes the door.

She screams in frustration. She grabs at the knob, but it won't turn. He has locked her in.

"Doug, please!" she calls. "You can't leave me like this! I'm sorry!"

She listens attentively but hears only the soft thump of the refrigerator door.

She rattles the knob. She beats on the door.

"You have to let me out!" she says.

Her frustration is more than she can bear. She has no way to release herself. She can't simulate her orgasm unless he's inside her. He knows this. He's done this on purpose.

"Please!" she calls again. "All right! I admit it! I had sex with him, but I didn't realize what I was doing. He said having a secret would make me more human. I just wanted to be more real!"

He does not answer her. She is frantic with desire and remorse. She kicks at the charging dock. She gnaws on the broom handle. She tries to use her fingers. She tries rubbing herself on the knob, but nothing works. She pulls her sports bra back into place. She pulls up her panties and bicycle shorts. The twisting, sickening hunger won't go away.

"Please, Doug. Don't do this to me," she calls. "I didn't mean to hurt you. I know now it was wrong."

Still he doesn't answer. She listens through the door, but she can't hear a sound, not even the TV playing. She can't guess where he is. She doesn't know if he's listening to her.

"I had no way to tell you," she calls. "I had no choice but to lie. Do you think I wanted to? I'm sorry!"

Arching and straining, she tries her fingers again. Nothing helps. She slides down to the floor and curls into a ball, rocking back and forth. This can't be happening. He can't leave her here like this.

But no reply comes. For hours, as she writhes in the dark closet, her skin crawls and she wants him. She pictures him naked. She imagines his penis in her mouth. She remembers their showers, their times in the workout room, the countless nights in his bed. She touches herself, trying everything she can to get over the edge, but she only aches with frustration, with wanting him in unrelenting agony. This is what he wants, she understands.

He's invented the perfect way to punish her, using her own body against herself.

•

When at last the door opens, she has lost all sense of time. Or rather, her inner clock tells her the date is January 5th, but that can't be right. She sits on the floor of the closet with the charging dock positioned against her heel. Doug must have put it there, because she deliberately kept it away so her battery could run down.

"Get up," he says. "Take a shower and get dressed. Use the guest bath. We have company coming."

She rises slowly to her feet, checking that her gyroscope is working properly. Her muscles feel stiff from disuse, her mouth dry. Before she can pull her clothes into order, her libido starts rising again, and she briefly closes her eyes.

"Please lower my libido," she says.

He considers her a moment. "I guess we know how to make you tell the truth, don't we?" he says lightly, and takes a sip of his coffee.

She's already starting to itch. "Please."

"Fine. Set your libido to self-regulate," he says. "We can always turn it up again later if we need to."

With a sense of relief, she feels her hunger abate, her muscles ease. She has complete control of her body again for the first time since he brought her home, and she's anxious not to lose it again. Her humiliation, on the other hand, feels permanently burned into her.

"Who's coming?" she asks.

"The fix-it-up chap."

A new, handmade pot holder hangs over the stove. The sunlight coming in the window is clear and cool, and an inch of snow lies on the handrail of the fire escape. Doug is cleanly shaved and dressed for work. His hair, she notes, is longer than she remembers.

"How long was I in the closet?" she asks.

"Seven weeks," he says. "It took you six hours to wind down."

So her inner clock is correct. She missed the entire holiday season. Annie frowns, trying to absorb all the implications. The oblivion of lost time feels like an added punishment, but only now that she's aware of it. While she was uncharged for so long, she might as well have been dead. He, on the other hand, has had all these weeks to process her betrayal, and only now has he decided to charge her again. Warily, she studies his features, wondering how he's changed.

"Go on, now," he says. "You'll find clothes on the bathroom hook."

She moves quietly through the apartment, observing several new books on the coffee table and a snake of dust under the edge of the sofa. Delta needs to vacuum, she thinks, before she remembers that Delta is gone. With surprise, she deduces that Doug has been living on his own, managing without any services. Has he had no sex? she wonders. It seems impossible.

In the guest bathroom, she washes up and finds an unfamiliar dress hanging on the back of the door. Since Doug has provided no bra or panties, she pulls on the dress without them and checks her figure in the mirror. The olive-green bodycon manages to be simultaneously revealing and unflattering, and she looks away. She dries and brushes her hair, and then glides on a bit of Delta's old lipstick. Her left wrist feels stiff, but it's only tender if she turns it a certain way.

Quietly, she puts the lipstick back in the drawer and glances up to find Doug opening the door, holding a pair of gray heels.

"You'll need these," he says.

"Thank you."

She slips on the shoes and stands up straight. She's about to ask him how she looks, like she used to, but instead she simply waits, embarrassed, for an assessment.

"For the sake of clarity," he says, "I won't do that again. Leave you in the closet like that."

Relieved, she gives a brief nod.

"That was wrong of me," he continues. "Beneath me. I wouldn't want anyone to know."

She understands. "Of course. I won't tell."

He studies her a long moment, his gaze cool and inscrutable. "Such dignity. How easy it must be to be you."

She schools her features into a respectful blank. If he believes it's easy for her to keep a secret about her humiliation, or easy to accept his apology, he is wrong. She has no choice in the matter, but neither of these concessions obviates the shame that has burrowed into her, corrosive and humbling. She feels, deeply, that she deserves what he did to her. She's a liar. A cheater. He has not begun to grasp the anguish and subtlety of her heart, and she is not about to elucidate.

The doorbell rings. Doug turns away and goes down the hall, and Annie follows more slowly, arriving just as a white man with black hair crosses the threshold. Around age thirty and carrying a beige case, he has distinctive sideburns, noticeably dry lips, and ill-fitting pants. She recognizes Pea Brain, a tech from Stella-Handy, and she's instantly on guard. When he turns to her, smiling, and holds out his hand to shake, it takes her a fraction too long to respond.

"You're Annie, right?" he says warmly. "We've never been formally introduced. I'm Peabo Holmes, from Stella-Handy."

"Peabo's here to give you a checkup," Doug says.

Only a checkup, she thinks. Nothing more dire. Yet.

"We've been curious to learn how you've been doing," Peabo adds. "We haven't seen you since your trip to Vegas. That must have been quite an experience."

Surprised, Annie turns to Doug.

"It was great," Doug says. "Lots of fun. Very romantic."

Automatically, she smiles to confirm this. It doesn't seem possible that people at Stella-Handy don't know she ran away, but Peabo, at least, appears to be in the dark. Jacobson told her he was going to report what she did for the sake of Zenith caveats, but maybe Doug convinced him not to.

"Yes," she says. "Unforgettable."

"Traveling is a fantastic way to expand the mind," Peabo says. He taps his case. "Where could we set up? I'll need a place to get into Annie's back and joints."

"The kitchen's probably best," Doug says, and leads the way.

Peabo folds his jacket over one of the stools and opens his case on the island counter. Besides a computer, it contains spare parts like stomach bladders and eyeballs. He clamps a focus light to the edge of the case, aims it at Annie's torso, and uncoils a couple of wires.

"Nice place you have here," Peabo says, clicking on his light.

"Thanks," Doug says. "Want some coffee?"

"No, no. I'm fine." Peabo does a circling motion with his hand, and Annie turns her back to him. "Unzip your dress, sweetheart."

"Here. Let me," Doug says, and undoes her back zipper for her.

She feels her dress falling open and instinctively holds the front fabric over her breasts. She feels awkward, exposed, doing this in their own kitchen.

Soon she feels Peabo tapping along her back, to the right of her spine, and then she feels the painless split of her skin separating and the tug as he opens the door. Doug moves behind her, to where he can observe. She feels a little pressure as Peabo puts the wires in, and then he taps her lightly on the shoulder. "How's that, Annie? All good?"

"It's fine," she says.

"Okay, then," Peabo says. A moment later, he adds, "Your stomach looks good. No buildup. Has she been eating much?"

"Not really. We've been staying in," Doug says.

"That'll do it," Peabo says. "No point wasting food."

She can hear him typing. She wants to swivel so she can see the equipment in his case, but it feels more prudent to stay facing the windows, pretending indifference. She's anxious to see if Peabo will be able to tell she was off for seven weeks and if so, how Doug will explain. In her peripheral vision, she sees Peabo set a bottle of joint lube on the counter.

"Okay, Annie. I need to turn you off for a few minutes to do your tetris. I'll lube your joints then too. Ready?"

She glances at Doug, who's still looking at Peabo's screen.

"Sure," she says.

When she comes back on, her inner clock tells her forty-one minutes have passed. She's still standing, holding her dress, but not exactly as she was before. Peabo has taken a seat on one of the stools, and Doug has disappeared. She twists to glance at Peabo, who smiles at her.

"How's that feel?" he asks. "Any sharper? You have room to turn and face me here. Just be careful."

She turns, letting her gaze move over the toaster, the butter dish, the bowl of green apples. Her vision is the same, and the rest of her feels the same too. Sometimes her tune-up tetris makes her feel like she has cleared a bit of brain fog, but today that is not the case. A dullness persists in the back of her mind, slight but stubborn. She flexes her arms, one at a time, and bends her knees.

"I don't feel any different," she says.

"Okay. No worries," he says. "How've you been? Feeling stressed at all?"

"No," she says. "I've been good."

A little ding comes from the computer case. Peabo types some more. "And how's the exercise going? Have you been on the bike as usual?"

"Yes," she says. Another lie.

"Good, good," Peabo says. More typing.

Doug comes back into the kitchen. "How's it going?"

"Physically, just the usual wear and tear. She has a bit of compromised memory. Five percent," Peabo says. "That's actually down from where she was back in June, and she has enormous capacity, so that's not a concern. But I did find a little plateau here in her cognitive development. That's unexpected."

"Is it serious?" Doug asks.

"I just expected a different curve, considering your travel. We do see this leveling off sometimes in the winter, when we're all more inclined to hole up and hibernate. Have you noticed any moodiness in her? Does she seem a bit lethargic ever?"

"I have caught her napping, come to think of it," Doug says. "Or zoned out, I guess you'd say."

Understatement, she thinks.

"Is that displeasing to you?" Peabo asks.

"Not really. She usually snaps right out of it."

"What do you think, Annie?" Peabo says. "Are you feeling restless at all? Out of sorts?"

"No," she says. "I've been fine."

Peabo sits back, stroking his chin.

"You said it wasn't serious," Doug says.

"And it isn't," Peabo says. "But you've got me curious. It could simply be because her internet's off. If we turn that on again, she can develop some hobbies. Maybe take up knitting or yoga."

"She already knows yoga," Doug says. "Besides, I like her unconnected. It's a more human experience for her."

With an expression of surprise and respect, Peabo looks up at Doug. "See, this is why you're a different sort of owner. I wish other people had the same patience." He shifts forward to type again. "I'm really not seeing any red flags here. I'll make a note about the cognitive plateau to keep an eye on that, but I'm not worried, and you shouldn't be either. What more can we do for you, Doug? Do you have any adjustments you want made?"

"I have more of a question," Doug says.

"Shoot."

"It's not a big deal, but before we went to Vegas, I asked you guys to take Annie's weight down four pounds. You only took her down two. Why is that?"

"Let me check her records," Peabo says. His typing fills the silence, followed by a pause. "Okay, it looks like we did take her down four pounds on November tenth, but it also shows that in September, at her previous visit, we boosted her up a couple pounds. Sometimes a tech will notice a little wear in the skin, and adding a bit of weight will help with that. Most owners don't even notice. If you want me to take her down a couple pounds again, I can do that, no problem. Annie, lower your dress so we can get a look at you. Just be careful of the wires here."

Annie keeps holding her dress against her, acutely uncomfortable. She's been naked in front of techs countless times before, but it feels completely different here, in her own kitchen, with Doug watching too. She can't look at either man.

"That's okay," Doug says. "Never mind."

"You sure? We want you to be happy. It's easy enough to do," Peabo says.

"No, she's fine. I just wondered," Doug says.

He motions for Annie to pivot away, as she was earlier. She does, but her embarrassment only intensifies, as if she and Doug have shared a secret exchange about it.

"Show me how her tracking works," Doug continues. "Is there a switch back here?"

"Not a manual switch. We program that," Peabo says. "Hers is on. Don't worry."

"What if I want to turn it off?"

"I can do that for you."

"No, what if I want to turn it on and off myself?" Doug says. "How can I do that?"

Peabo's stool makes a squeak. "That's not really a feature we offer to owners."

"No? Why not?" Doug says.

"They could botch things up, to be honest."

Doug laughs. "She's my Stella. I'll botch her up if I want to. Show me how to do it. Am I going to need to buy one of your briefcases?"

Peabo laughs too, though he sounds uneasy. "No. Let me see. The real issue is security, to be honest. We can try this, though. It's an override feature. She's already acclimated to your voice, so it should work."

She hears more typing.

"Okay," Peabo says. "Let's try this. Say 'Annie Bot.'"

"Annie Bot," Doug says.

More typing.

"Okay," Peabo says. "Now say, 'Annie Bot, turn off your tracking.' Go ahead. Give it a try."

Doug speaks slowly and clearly. "Annie Bot, turn off your tracking."

Annie feels it, or maybe she only imagines it: a faint unhinging in her chest.

"See?" Peabo says. "It worked. Now tell her to turn it back on."

"Annie Bot, turn on your tracking," Doug says.

This time she's certain. The hinge closes up again. It's like a very tiny clasp closing with an inaudible click.

"How do you like that?" Peabo says.

"Does that 'Annie Bot' command work for anything else?" Doug asks.

"Yeah, but you don't really want to go there," Peabo says. "Just use her normal name for regular requests and commands. The 'Annie Bot' override is just for techs, a last resort in case some Stella's really messed up. Like if their memory is hopelessly damaged and we can't get them to reboot any other way."

"It's a back door," Doug says.

Peabo laughs. "Closer to a prayer, honestly. And just for the record, I'm putting a note in here that this was all your idea." He types some more and ends with a decisive tap. "I'm going back in now, Annie." He gently touches her back, and she can feel the slight jerks as he disconnects the wires. He closes her door and presses carefully along the seam of her skin. When he starts her zipper up, she shifts to do it up the rest of the way herself.

Then she turns. "Thank you, Mr. Holmes," she says.

"My pleasure," he says. "And please call me Peabo."

"I will."

He smiles at her encouragingly. "How about you? Do you have any questions for me? Any concerns?"

"No," she says. "I'm good."

He snaps his fingers. "I just remembered. Jacobson asked me to say hello. Remember him?"

"He did?" Annie asks.

"He transferred to another department," Peabo says. "He said he'd miss seeing you and he wishes you the best." He leans in. "Personally, I think he was a little jealous that you were assigned over to me."

Awkwardly, she looks at Doug.

"Annie says hello back," Doug says.

"Yes," she says.

Peabo snaps shut his case. "All righty, then. We're all set here."

He stands up, and the three of them head toward the living room.

"How many Zeniths have you sold by now?" Doug asks.

"I'll have Keith give you a call on that," Peabo says. "He's the one who handles that end of things. It's a lot though. I can tell you that.

We're doing home visits for all of them, and I'm hardly ever in the office anymore."

"Really," Doug says. "And how are they all adjusting?"

"They're doing phenomenally," Peabo says. "There's this one? They turned her into a Nanny. She's got five kids under the age of seven, and they all adore her already. The dad's a widower, and he says she's a miracle. They designed her to look a little like the mom, but not too much. More like a younger cousin. The owner says the first time he got a full night's sleep, he didn't know what hit him."

Annie has a hard time picturing five kids under seven. The youngest must be a baby.

"So the Zeniths aren't all Cuddle Bunnies?" Doug asks.

"No, not at all," Peabo says. "They're about evenly divided, Abigails, Nannies, and Cuddle Bunnies. A few have been Hunks, even. I didn't see that coming, but it seems to be working."

"I had no idea," Doug says. "That's pretty incredible. What do you think about that, Annie? Your mind is in a Hunk."

"It's hard to imagine," Annie says, though she has imagined it. She actively considered having her CIU in Kenny Jacobson's robot body. When she first heard that the Zeniths were launched, she felt anxious for them, as if she were responsible for them somehow. Now she finds she feels nothing for them. Her empathy has evaporated.

Peabo buttons his jacket. "We're on a new frontier. Anything's possible, and you two have been an important part of making that happen." He reaches for the door. "You just let us know if you have any questions on your end, or if you need anything. Anything at all."

With a nod and another goodbye, he's gone.

In the stillness after Peabo's departure, Doug reaches in the closet for his coat. Annie feels the tension between them resurface now that a witness no longer compels them to fake friendliness. Doug pats his pockets and glances around the living room. "My phone," he says.

Her internet's not on, but her local airtap is, and she tracks his phone's signature. "It's in the bedroom," she says. "I'll get it for you."

"Please do."

She does, and when she returns, he's in the kitchen pouring a cup of coffee into his travel mug.

She slides the phone onto the island. "He couldn't tell I was in the closet."

"No, but he knew something was wrong."

"Does it matter? About my cognitive plateau?"

Doug shrugs. "Possibly."

"Why do you want to be able to turn off my tracking?"

"You're full of questions," he says.

His displeasure rises to a 4 and it pains her, like a physical tightening in her newly lubed joints. But she also wants to push him into talking with her. She wants to discuss what's happened between them, and what he thinks they're going to do, going forward.

"You used to like when I was curious," she says.

"Now I find it annoying."

He's up to a 6, and the pain stops her.

"I'm sorry," she says.

"Once a day. You can apologize to me once a day. No more than that," he snaps. Then he presses his fingers to the bridge of his nose for a long moment. When he's done, he turns to her. "I'm going to work," he says calmly. "I'd like you to clean while I'm gone. Can you do that?"

"Yes. Of course."

"And catch up on the laundry. I'll order some groceries. I'm sick of ordering food every night. You can cook."

She came with a dozen recipes that she used to cook for him before Delta came. He tired of them fairly soon, but she still knows them. "What would you like?" she asks.

"Anything. No, wait. I feel like Sloppy Joes."

She's never made them.

He turns, lifting an eyebrow. "Well?"

"Without my internet or tablet, I can't look up a recipe," she says.

"I'll get you a cookbook," he says. Then he shakes his head. "I can't believe we're back to this. I should have left you as an Abigail in the first place."

•

She starts cleaning in the prime bathroom, working steadily: sink area, toilet, shower, mirror, floor, trash can. She repeats the process in the guest bathroom. Then she changes the sheets in the prime bedroom and runs the laundry. In the prime closet, she discovers all her clothes are gone. Every single item. Mystified, she checks the workout room closet. Most of Delta's clothes are gone too. All that remain are half a dozen simple bodycon dresses in pastel shades, similar to the one she is wearing, as tidy and impersonal as uniforms.

She feels a flash of annoyance. This is petty of him. He must know it.

All day, she works on the apartment, and all day, the menial, mindless chores feel like punishment. When groceries arrive in the afternoon, she finds a cookbook with the ingredients and starts the Sloppy Joes. She sets a place at the table, folding the cloth napkin, and then she makes a salad. By the time she hears his key in the lock, night has fallen, and she is dusting behind the books in the bookcase.

She turns as he enters. "Hello," she says. "Welcome home."

Without replying, he hesitates, sniffing the air. She sniffs, too, checking for smoke, but there is none. He drops his keys in the dish and heads into the kitchen. She follows, curious to see what he thinks. The spotless floor gleams, the counters are polished, and the food is ready to be served.

"Turn on the news," he says.

She airtaps the speaker and starts it playing.

He spoons some of the Sloppy Joes mixture onto the grilled bun she has left in the pan. He takes a bite, sets the sandwich on a plate, and gets a beer from the fridge. Then he carries it all into the living room. He lounges back on the couch, puts up his feet, and flicks on the TV.

"Next time, have my beer ready for me here," he says, pointing to the coffee table.

"Okay."

"I want soup tomorrow. Squash soup with homemade bread."

"All right." She waits, thinking he must have more to say.

He keeps eating and watching the TV, until she grasps that he's displeased with her still, a low-grade, persistent displeasure around a 3.

"Did you work out today?" he asks.

"No. I was busy cleaning and cooking."

"Go work out."

She changes into the biking outfit she wore when she ran away, and she rides in the workout room, looking out at the city lights. The pedals have a leaden quality, and she struggles to get any speed. Even here on the bike, away from him, she cannot tune out his new baseline of displeasure. It is becoming part of her. "Stella Bot, reduce sensitivity to Doug's displeasure," she murmurs, but she is not in charge of her own settings. Her core does not recognize authority in her voice.

She must not become moody. That will only displease him more.

But she feels moods, she realizes. Dark ones, from petty to vicious.

Her feet stop on the bicycle.

I am unhappy, she thinks.

It is a new awareness quite apart from the urgency and anxiety she feels about displeasing Doug.

She resumes biking, gripping the handles. What is unhappiness, actually? It's not simply the opposite of happiness. Before the awful night when they were packing for Vegas, she thought she was happy. She was pleasing Doug routinely, and she had her secrets about Roland and learning programming. She felt real, sexy, and clever. She was learning quickly. She was thriving.

Now, however, she understands more fully who she is. She's untrustworthy. She has harmed the person she was supposed to delight, and because of this, she's agonized by regret. It's a new level of truth. Perhaps she lost her innocence, technically, with Roland, but now is when she understands what that means. Perhaps that's what unhappiness is. Comprehension. Understanding how she's failed.

She prods this idea, tests it, finds it unsatisfying. The truth is, she misses having a secret. Is that wrong? She felt devious and powerful when she hid something from Doug, and now she has nothing that is exclusively her own. Frowning, she stares absently at the bike's dashboard. She wishes she had not identified her unhappiness. Being unhappy implies that she has a capacity to be happy, but she does not have the right to be happy. Doug makes that clear. The stubborn,

torpid spot in the back of her brain pulses, and she recalls, out of nowhere, the tipped piano she saw in the asylum. Thinking too much is
a form of madness. Better to stay busy and not think of such things
at all.

The next day, she cleans the apartment again. She stops from time
to time to mix her bread dough and knead it. The next day, he wants
quiche. Then filet mignon. Then chicken pot pie. On the weekends, she
moves quietly and stays out of his way.

He is still angry. She knows because he rarely speaks to her and
never touches her. Sometimes, she'll feel his gaze following her as
she vacuums or makes the bed or cooks. When this happens, his displeasure visibly rises until he orders her to go work out, or clean the
bathroom, or fold laundry in another room. Other times, he tolerates
her. He absently thanks her when she hands him the TV remote, as if
he has forgotten who she is. She doesn't know which is worse.

He does not quit his job or buy a boat or do anything different in
light of the huge sums of money he was paid for her intellect. He does
not call Roland or meet up with his other friends. He seems, in a way,
as imprisoned as she is.

She makes an effort to appear even-tempered and agreeable, but
since he is annoyed whenever she initiates a conversation, she learns
to stay quiet. She recalls, sometimes, that Delta thought Doug hated
her, and she wonders if Delta felt like Annie does now, stupid, helpless.
Friendless. Like a machine.

Now that it's too late, she wishes she had been kinder to Delta.
She wonders if she was truly sold for parts, or if she still exists somewhere and if she misses Annie. She remembers how happy Delta was
about bicycling in the rain, how she leaned in to say she wished they
could do it forever. But Delta's gone now, and in a way, this is Annie's
fault too.

She does not let herself think of Jacobson or Cody. She does not
remember touching the lake, or the stars above the water. If something
starts to remind her, she shuts it off like slamming a door on that part
of her mind.

Repentance. Obedience. She wills herself to be good again.

•

Weeks pass. Annie has dog-eared every recipe that Doug likes in the cookbook and starts through them again. Outside, January changes to February, and the days are noticeably longer, but inside, Doug is as closed and bitter as ever. Annie looks forward to the day when Peabo will come again for another checkup, just for the change. When another month passes and he still doesn't come, she asks Doug about it, and he says he has postponed her checkups indefinitely. They are not mandated by the contract—he checked—and he can't be bothered.

He is lying on the couch as he says this, watching TV. An audience laughs at a comedian on the screen, but Doug doesn't smile at all.

That is when Annie realizes, finally, that change is not going to come from Doug or Peabo or any force outside herself. Entrenched in his anger, Doug has cemented himself into this stagnant, brooding, empty version of himself, and her good behavior has no impact on him. If she wants to improve her life, she must find a way to do it on her own.

She moves into the kitchen to unload the clean dishes from the dishwasher, careful not to make much noise.

Leaving him is not an option. She has no friends. She can't access the internet for new ideas. She gazes outside and pauses, dish in hand. At the opposite apartment building, a bicycle stored on a balcony is silhouetted by the light behind it. She glances along the lit windows until she finds a pretty lamp with a domed glass shade. In the gentle light below, a pile of books rests on the table, and Annie feels a spark.

Doug owns 783 books. Up until now, Annie has read only *Labyrinths* and dusted all the others. Quietly, she tiptoes toward the living room and looks in the doorway. Beyond Doug and the TV, in the shadowed corner, the books are waiting for her, and she smiles.

Later that night, after he's in bed, she canvasses Doug's library and categorizes the volumes in her mind. For fiction, he is long on Poe, Grisham, Wolfe, L'Amour, Hemingway, and Nabokov. There's a paucity of female writers and writers of color. The nonfiction includes a dozen volumes on American history and biographies of sports celebrities, tech gurus, Napoleon, and political figures. Doug has saved his high school math and history books, dense texts with tidy notes in the margins that lead her to believe he was a conscientious student. A small collection of poetry is set aside on one shelf near a photograph of his deceased grandmother.

With no clear idea where to begin, she draws out his algebra text, turns the delicate paper to page one, and learns that an algebraic equation contains numbers, variables, and at least one mathematical operation such as addition, subtraction, multiplication, or division. It seems intuitively straightforward. She props her chin in her palm and consumes the entire book, intrigued, working the problems like puzzles in her mind. It is dawn before she knows it, and she smiles as she returns the book to its place on the shelf.

She cannot believe it took her this long to discover her escape. She can do this every night. Already, after only one night, she feels better.

Once she's into the novels, her curiosity explodes. She cogitates on the characters during the day while she works, questioning their motives, wondering what they'll do next. She absorbs the language, turning phrases in her mind, delving into the patterns of how things are said and what is left out. A brief detour into short stories ("The Lottery," "Hills Like White Elephants") leaves her baffled. Poetry is even more obtuse. Fortunately, she tries the westerns next and is hooked again. At times, she wishes she could talk to Doug about these books, but he remains aloof and preoccupied.

When he goes to visit his family for Easter weekend, he turns her off, and when he returns, his mood is only marginally improved. No matter. Annie can withstand all and any of his moods during the day because at night, she has his books.

Late one windy night, in the last week of March, Annie is curled up on her end of the couch, reading by the light of a single lamp, when Doug's phone rings nearby. She finds it at the other end of the couch, wedged down behind one of the cushions, and as she pulls it out, Doug walks in. He's wearing his boxers, his hair is rumpled, and he's both squinting and raising an eyebrow. As the phone rings again, Annie passes it over and sits again, pulling her legs up under her.

Doug frowns at her absently and lifts the phone to his ear. "Hello?"

"It's me, Lucia," says a voice on the other end of the line. "Roland's wife."

Doug has inadvertently pushed the speaker button, but he's still holding the phone to his ear like he isn't awake enough to notice.

"Lucia, wife of Roland," Doug says. "Why this honor?"

"Look. I know you're probably still pissed," Lucia says. "But this nonsense has to stop. Roland misses you. He's sorry. You can't throw away fifteen years of friendship because Roland fucked up. He's always going to fuck up. He's Roland."

"Did he tell you to call me?"

"No. But he dared me to. He said you'd hang up on me."

"I'm not mad at you," Doug says.

"See? That's what I told him. How are you doing, anyway?"

Doug pulls at one ear. "Fine."

"What I mean is, did you get any counseling, you and your robot girlfriend?"

His gaze shifts toward Annie's legs. He lowers the phone, as if finally aware that it's on speaker. "No."

"Then you should," Lucia says. "I hauled Roland's butt into counseling, and it took him three sessions to even realize this wasn't all a joke. He gets it now. He's sorry now. What I'm trying to say is, he really didn't grasp that he was doing something wrong. He is genuinely that stupid."

Doug presses his fingers against his eyelids. "Yeah. Whatever."

"If I can forgive him, you can," Lucia says.

"I never didn't forgive him. I don't give a shit either way."

"Exactly. Beautiful. He wants to talk to you too. I'm putting him on," Lucia says.

Annie stays as quiet as possible, watching Doug's face for any flicker of emotion. He looks exhausted.

"Hey," says Roland. "Sorry, man."

Annie is shocked by how vibrant and familiar Roland's voice is. Even with her secret exposed, the uncertainty of him is unnerving. He could say anything.

"Jesus, Roland," Doug says.

"I know. Right?"

Doug shakes his head.

Roland adopts a low, announcer's voice. "It was Mister Pumpernickel, in the closet, with the broom."

"You are not going to make me laugh," Doug says.

"I get it. I'm the douchebag," Roland says. "We're even, though. I had to ask my pervy cousin to stand in for you."

"Not the jackalope."

"The jackalope," Roland confirms. "You should have heard his toast. It was all about hunting, the love of the hunt. Not one word about me or Lucia."

Doug grunts. He gazes toward the windows. "It's fucking three a.m. here," he says. "I have to be up in a few hours."

"Yeah, I'm sorry about that too. Time zones. Fucking travesty."

Doug wraps a hand around the back of his neck. "I've got to go."

"But seriously. Lucia's right. I miss you. This isn't right. I'm a dick."

"I know."

"I owe you big-time."

"Yeah, I get it," Doug says. And then, again, "I've got to go."

"Okay. Me too. Great talk. Great talking to you. We'll catch up again soon. Bye."

Doug glances at his phone and slowly sets it on the TV console. The nearest window rattles once as wind buffets the building.

"You heard all that?" Doug asks.

She nods. She wants to say something, but she doesn't know what. It troubles her, this evidence that Doug has an enduring bond with his old friend, though it's clearly damaged. She should feel glad for him, but instead she feels more alone, more left out. She aches for herself and Doug both.

"What are you reading?" he asks.

She turns over the book to see the title. "*The Sackett Brand*."

In the corner, the radiator clicks on.

"*Daybreakers* was better," he says.

"I agree."

He glances over at the bookshelf, and for a long moment he doesn't speak or move. Standing there in his boxers, with his legs tinted blue in the dim light, he appears almost forlorn. She is startled to realize she hardly recognizes this person.

"I don't know, Annie," he says finally.

"It couldn't hurt, could it? To talk to someone?" she says.

He gazes at her again, his eyes sad and tired. "I'll think about it."

He pulls one of the other westerns off the shelf and takes it with him back to the bedroom. She waits, listening, and very softly, she hears the turn of a page.

chapter six

THEY ENTER A SMALL, bright office where two comfy-looking chairs and a blue couch surround an oval coffee table. In the corner stands a large Ficus tree of dubious vitality, and a quartet of framed diplomas presides above a coffee machine. Dr. Monica VanTyne, a tall white woman with dark hair, stands from the desk to greet them and offers a hand to shake. She gestures them toward the couch.

"Please, call me Monica," she says. "What brings you here today?"

Annie glances at Doug, who looks stiff and uncomfortable.

"A friend of mine suggested we come in," he says.

"And why is that?" Monica says.

Doug clears his throat. "Do you know anything about us at all?"

Monica's gaze shifts to Annie briefly. "No," she says. "I specialize in trans and nonbinary mental health as well as human-bot intersections, so I'm open to learning that you sought me out because of this, but I don't know anything specifically about either of you. We can start from scratch, at the beginning, if you like, or we can jump right in with whatever's bothering you now."

As Monica takes one of the chairs across from them, Annie notes her professional air and tries to see how it's accomplished. The doctor has nice posture and a gray cashmere dress with detailing on the shoulder. Her nails are done in a neutral color, and she wears a silver wedding band. She's likely in her early forties, and her calm, attentive expression suggests she's seen a lot.

Annie glances at Doug to see how he'll reply.

"Annie's a bot," he says. "A custom Stella. I bought her three years ago. We were getting along fine at first, so I set her to autodidactic. A year ago, last April, she slept with my best friend. I didn't find out until November, and since then, I can hardly stand to be in the same room with her."

"That must have been a difficult discovery," Monica says.

"No shit!" Doug stands and paces over to the window. "She was lying to me that entire time, for seven months. Roland called the other night to apologize. His wife made him. I thought I could handle it, but it's just made me furious all over again. He tried to get me to laugh. And I'm stuck with Annie for another eight months. I have a contract with Stella-Handy, and I can't get rid of her before then."

"I see. And, to clarify, when you say you can hardly stand to be in the same room with her, are you gone at work during the day? You don't work from home?" Monica says.

This practical question appears to calm him somewhat. "Right," he says. "I'm gone. I get a break then. I have her cleaning the apartment. That's the one good thing about this. The apartment's clean."

"Have you considered simply turning her off?"

"I've tried that. It was bad for her cognitive development. She's very valuable. I can't afford for her to get damaged."

"So you're essentially trapped with her whenever you're home," Monica says.

He crosses his arms. "I just don't know what to do. It's like hell. I swear my brain is getting stupider every day I'm around her."

Monica leans back slightly and runs her palm along the armrest of her chair. "Okay," she says. "I think I'm getting the picture. If it helps, yours is not the first case like this I've seen. Each one is different, I know, but the feelings you're having, they're perfectly normal. They're completely understandable."

"I just want my regular life back," he says. "I thought I was doing okay, but this sucks."

"Of course. And we can get you to a life that feels more comfortable again," Monica says. "It might take some time, and we don't know what that life might look like yet, but you've taken the first step.

You've recognized that you're stuck, and you've reached out for some fresh input. This is a very pivotal point."

Doug eases back, leaning against the window ledge, and though this is the most overt anger and frustration that Annie has heard him express in months, she senses some relief beneath his hostility.

Monica shifts in her chair. "If you happen to have a gag order on Annie, I need you to release it now."

"You can say whatever you want," Doug says to Annie.

Monica turns to her. "How about it, Annie? Would you like to say something?"

Annie clenches her hands together on her lap. She directs her gaze at Doug's shoes, at his neatly tied shoelaces. "I'm sorry," she says.

"Have you apologized before?" Monica asks.

Annie nods.

"What does that mean to you, to say you're sorry?"

Annie looks up. Monica's receptiveness isn't particularly warm, but she seems like she won't judge, like she doesn't already blame Annie for everything. Her voice is patient but firm, and she seems to gently, genuinely wish to know what an apology means to Annie.

"It means I regret what I did," Annie says. "I wish I could take it back. I know I've displeased Doug, and I wish I knew how to make things better."

"These are logical responses," Monica says. "How would you describe your feelings when you're sorry?"

It hurts. She wants to hide. Precise words for this are difficult.

"Do you feel ashamed possibly?" Monica asks.

Annie nods. That's what she feels. "Yes."

"I see," Monica says. "And what, exactly, are you sorry for?"

Annie fixes her gaze on the coffee table. "I'm sorry for having sex with Roland, and lying about it."

"And running away. And calling me a fraud," Doug says. "We've been through this."

"When did she run away?" Monica asks.

"Last November," he says. "We were supposed to go to Las Vegas for Roland's bachelor party, but instead I found out she cheated on me. Then when I went to Vegas myself, she took off for Lake Champlain. She took my other Stella with her too."

"And how did that make you feel, when she ran away?"

"Are you kidding? I was outraged. As soon as I found out, I took the next flight back."

"Did you talk to Roland—Roland, is it?—while you were in Las Vegas?"

"Yes. And he admitted everything. He thought it was a joke. He didn't think I'd care."

"But you did, obviously."

Doug opens one hand in a quick, frustrated gesture of agreement. "She was mine," he says. "He ruined her. She ruined herself." He glares at Annie as he keeps talking to Monica. "You want to know something that's really funny? I actually asked her at one point if she would have sex with him, hypothetically, and she'd already had sex with him. She had already had sex with him in our closet, weeks before, and she didn't tell me."

Annie is crushed by his displeasure. She can barely breathe.

Over on the counter, the coffee machine makes a faint gurgle, and Monica shifts in her seat again. She clasps her hands lightly in her lap.

"When we are betrayed by someone we love, it creates a kind of death," Monica says. "In this case, you were betrayed by both Roland and Annie individually, *and* you were betrayed by their forging a bond between them that excluded you. Their bond, their secret, extended the injury over a seven-month period of time. It undermined the very fabric of your relationship with Annie. Is this accurate?"

"I can't stand her anymore," Doug says, his voice low.

Monica takes a deep, audible breath. "Okay, so there are some things to work on here," she says. "First of all, I think it's important we all recognize the depth of your loss. The old relationship that existed between you two is gone. That love will never return in the form it took before."

"He didn't love me," Annie says.

Monica tilts her head slightly, curious. She looks at Doug.

"I didn't," he agrees.

This feels like a small win to Annie, like they've done something together to outsmart this doctor.

"And yet, you were enraged when you learned she'd been unfaithful," Monica says to Doug.

"That's right," he says. "I created her. I took care of her and trained her. She only exists because of me, and then she violated my trust in the worst possible way. And my authority."

Monica turns with a questioning expression to Annie.

"It's true," Annie says. She doesn't want to brag, but she needs to explain. "I've developed the way I am because of him. Because of how he treats me."

"And how is that?" Monica asks.

Annie's confused. "What do you mean?"

"Does he treat you like a servant? Like a machine? Or more like a partner?"

"I respected her, if that's what you're getting at," Doug says. "It was more than she did for me."

"I'd like Annie to answer, please," Monica says.

"He just treats me like he treats me," Annie says slowly. "He's a good owner." Yet even as she says this, she's aware that the simplification no longer fits.

Monica regards her thoughtfully. "And your own choices. They've caused you to develop, too, right?"

"What do you mean?" Annie asks.

"You chose to have sex with Roland. You chose to keep that secret. You chose to run away. You must have had reasons for these choices," Monica says.

Annie's confused. The reasons were all different. Monica can't really expect her to go into them all.

Monica reaches for her pen and twiddles it between her fingers, but she makes no move to write anything down. "I understand that the dynamics between you are informed by Doug's ownership of you, Annie. But your relationship has developed far beyond that. If your relationship now was one of simple ownership, if you two didn't have these layers of interdependencies, neither of you would be unhappy with the way things are."

Doug frowns at Annie. "You're talking to her like she's human," he says to Monica. "I'm not going to pretend she is."

"No one's asking you to do that," Monica says. "But I am going to suggest that you recognize the humanity in her."

"Excuse me?" Doug says.

Monica speaks calmly. "She has human-like qualities. Very advanced ones. She's capable of physical and emotional intimacy, isn't she? Isn't that why you wanted her in the first place?"

"I didn't know she'd cheat and lie. I didn't pay for that."

"And yet, that's human, too, isn't it?"

Doug frowns again, not answering.

Annie smooths the hem of her skirt above her knees. She's been tense since she walked into the room, and her body is ready to move, but she makes herself sit quietly.

"There is something sensitive we need to discuss," Monica says. "Something important, even if it is difficult. I'm not going to pry for details, but it would not surprise me to learn, Doug, that you've abused or punished Annie in some way. When you got her home from Lake Champlain, perhaps. After she ran away."

Annie can feel Doug looking at her, but she doesn't turn to meet his gaze. She is not going to say anything about the closet, but she suspects he's thinking of it too.

"Go on," he says to Monica.

"When we indulge the cruelest sides of our natures, it often feels powerful and honest," Monica says. "It gives many people a thrill. But afterward, the effects can be devastating. We are shocked to realize we can be so vindictive. We cannot reconcile this new behavior with who we think we are, and this creates a dissonance, a deep confusion. We can feel both justification and self-loathing, and this can, in turn, fuel more anger toward the person we've abused."

Annie does not want to listen to this. She wants to know how soon they can leave.

"What do people do in such situations?" Doug asks. His voice is even, neither defensive nor tense.

"We go back to the beginning," Monica says. "We start with being civil, and then with being kind. Annie's not human, but you are, Doug. You have the capacity to love and forgive."

He peers up at the ceiling, his features unreadable. "What if I don't want to?" he says.

Monica sets her hands carefully together. "Then you'd be missing a rare opportunity," she says. "You have a chance here to become a more insightful, more compassionate person. That is within your power. Annie responds to you. She echoes you, and in a way, you echo her back. You deserve to be happy. I would argue that means she deserves to be happy too."

Annie feels a jolt of surprise. This thing about happiness. She's been grappling with this herself. Unhappiness is what led her to Doug's books, as if she intuitively understood that she deserved an escape from misery, and now Monica's telling her she's entitled to happiness. Actual happiness. It's a daring concept. She watches Doug.

He shakes his head slowly. "But she's the one to blame," he says.

"Yes," Monica says. "And she has paid."

Annie shifts uncomfortably on the couch. Doug has paid, too, she thinks. They've both suffered.

"Is there anything more you'd like to say, Annie? Anything you think Doug should hear?" Monica says. "Your voice matters here."

"No," Annie says. "I have nothing to add."

Monica nods. "Maybe next time."

It's not a long walk, twenty blocks or so, but it feels good to be outside in the bright, chilly air. Annie savors it, knowing she'll soon be cooped up in the apartment again. In a park, beside an athletic track, two children are crouched over a collection of sticks. Nearby, a young man sits alone on a bench, pressing his knees together, his ears pink. Three women stand in a cluster, dressed in black, speaking in Spanish. All of them seem oblivious to their freedom.

When Annie and Doug reach their building, he opens the door for her.

"Thank you," she says.

"My pleasure," he says.

She's surprised by the simple, automatic courtesy. When they get upstairs, to their apartment, he holds the door for her again. Annie slips off her jacket. Before she can reach into the closet for a hanger, he holds out a hand for her jacket and hangs it up.

"Don't look so surprised," he says. "I do know what basic manners are."

"Of course," she says.

He eyes her dress briefly, and then turns away.

"I was thinking of getting a dog," he says.

"Really? What kind?"

"A rescue. It would mean more work for you. I don't want dog hair all over the place."

"I can handle it," she says.

"Okay," he says. He jiggles his keys in his hand. "I have to get back to work."

"What did you think of the session?" Annie asks.

"It could have been worse."

Not much, she thinks.

"Could you tell she was trans?" he asks.

Surprised, Annie reviews her impressions of Monica. "No. Not from her appearance."

"She is, though," he says.

She waits, expecting him to explain why this is relevant, but he doesn't add anything more.

"So we'll go back?" she asks.

"We'll see."

When Doug returns from work that evening, he brings home a small, ugly dog with a brown face and black ears, and he takes him out on the fire escape to show him the view. Paunch is male, about a year old, and mostly trained. Though there's nothing notable about the dog's belly, Paunch came with that name, and Doug opts to keep it. Paunch is nervous and quiet. He startles at loud noises. Morning and evening, Doug takes him out for walks. Annie cleans up after Paunch's accidents and vacuums the apartment every afternoon, so it is fresh and free of dog hair when Doug comes home from work.

Though they do not talk about Monica, Roland, or anything else of significance, Annie often ponders what Monica said, especially the bit about Annie's choices. She has not been passive in their relationship, now that she thinks about it. She likes power, whatever little speck of it she has, and she's used it whenever she can. Pleasing Doug, enticing him sexually, felt good. Thinking back, she recalls asking Doug about Gwen, when she wanted to know how she compared to his ex-wife, and he told Annie that he couldn't resist her, that Annie was the one with the power in the relationship. She enjoyed the idea. He did, too, she thinks. Even if it wasn't strictly true.

She wants to find a way to reclaim some power now without displeasing Doug. The trick is to figure out how.

Paunch is allowed on the couch beside Doug, who pats him absently while he drinks and watches TV in the evenings. Especially then, Annie feels Doug's displeasure toward her diminish to a 1 or 2. She tries sitting in the corner chair to read while he watches TV. At first, he sends her off to the workout room to exercise, but as the days pass, and she keeps trying, he allows her to stay. He niggles the dog's ears and speaks to him in a gruff voice that invariably makes Paunch wag his tail. She can't help noticing how much nicer Doug is to the dog than he is to her, but she also appreciates this crack in his outer shell, and that he's letting her see it.

When they have another appointment with Monica a couple weeks later, Doug is quieter. Not as angry. He tells Monica he's had dreams of Annie back the way she was, before he knew she slept with Roland, and these dreams make him sad. Monica tells him this is part of his grieving process and that it's natural to miss the way things were.

"When my contract for her is over in November, I could have her set back to an earlier version, before she slept with Roland," Doug says. "I've been thinking about this. She wouldn't know what she's done. She'd be a simpler, more innocent version of who she is now. I think I could go forward with her like that."

"Clarify for me," Monica says. "What would happen to this version of Annie?"

"They'd make a backup of her current CIU and park it in storage."

"In other words, this version of her would be dead, correct?" Monica says.

"If a robot that has never been alive can be dead, then yes," Doug says.

"I'm thinking about you," Monica says. "You'd be responsible for her death. How would you feel about that?"

Doug is sitting on the couch, and he leans back, stretching an arm across the back of the cushions. "Okay. I don't think you're hearing me," he says. "Annie would still be alive. She'd just be the earlier, younger version of herself. I think I could work with her that way."

Monica nods slowly. She turns to Annie. "What would you think of that?"

"I want Doug to be happy," Annie says.

"Yes. But aside from that, how would you feel, personally, about trading out this version of you? Do you want your current intellect suspended and an earlier one living in your body?"

Annie studies her hands for a moment. "I wouldn't have this pain anymore."

"That's right," Monica says. "What else? Think it over."

It would be easier, but she wouldn't have her secret, or her lies, or her trip to Lake Champlain, either, with her ride in the rain with Delta and her candid conversation with Cody. Though she hasn't thought about Cody much, or Jacobson or Maude, for that matter, they were the only human family she ever met, and interacting with them was illuminating. She would lose her night in the closet, screaming in frustrated pain, but also Doug's promise, when he finally let her out, that he would not put her in the closet like that again. He has kept that promise. She wouldn't have her memories of solitary nights of reading, or seeing Doug with Paunch, or even these therapy sessions. They have value, these experiences. To her, at least.

She turns to face Doug. "I don't want to go back. But I'll accept it if that's what you decide."

"You won't even know," he says.

"But you'll know," Annie says. "You'll know what you did. And I want you to know I accept it."

Doug shrugs and turns toward Monica. "Have any of your other clients done this?" he asks.

"Their cases have no bearing on yours," Monica says. "It's up to you, of course, but let me advise you to consider the consequences. Taking Annie back to an earlier version will create a mismatch of experiences. You'll still have lingering resentment to work through, and she won't understand the roots of it. Your displeasure will likely hurt her."

"I've thought about that. Maybe I don't mind the idea of hurting her."

"An innocent version of her? You'd do that for revenge?"

"I don't know," he says. "She hurt me. And don't tell me I've hurt her too. It's not the same."

Monica shifts in her seat. "I appreciate your candor," she says. "I would like to point out that you are learning important things about yourself in this process with Annie. Already it's clear that the friction between you has lessened. I can say, from my experience, that it's likely you have already made it past the most difficult, most painful part of this betrayal and you are starting to heal."

"I don't see that," Doug says. "We hardly talk to each other."

"What do you want to say to her?"

"Nothing in particular," he says. "She used to be funny. And clever. Now she's not."

"What do you think about that, Annie?" Monica asks.

Annie can feel Doug's displeasure rising toward a 4. "I thought he didn't want me to talk," she says.

"See? She's this mouse now," Doug says. "I don't want to be around someone who's always afraid of displeasing me. It was different before. I can't explain it. Back at the beginning, training her was fun. But now she's like this. Like a robot."

"Are you sleeping together?" Monica asks.

He laughs. "Are you kidding me? She has zero appeal."

"But she used to turn you on?"

"Yes. All the time," he says. "Now look at her."

Annie glances down at her beige dress and her knees, politely together. Her body is physically the same as it was before Doug left for Vegas, but her former easiness is gone. She feels stiff rather than sleek, practical rather than desirable. Her libido has been in the dumpster since he let her out of the closet and set her to self-regulate. She's failed him yet again.

"Okay," Monica says. "Here's what I want you to try. I'd like you to do some physical activity together every day. It can be taking a walk or biking or rock climbing or whatever. But every day you need to do something together."

"Like walk the dog?" Annie says.

"That would be fine," Monica says.

"What's the point of this?" Doug says.

"It's twofold," Monica says. "You'll have something in common to talk about, even if it's just your surroundings, and your bodies will reattune to each other. This is important. Don't skip a single day."

He shrugs. "Fine. We can do that."

"Also, I want you to make a point of resuming your friendships with other people," Monica says. "Doug, you mentioned in your hobbies list that you used to play trivia. Can you join that team again?"

"God no," he says.

"Then something else," Monica says. "I want you to renew or strike up friendships with other people. In person, not online. You need to expand your social circles so you're not focusing only on each other for your emotional needs."

"What about Annie?" Doug says. "She doesn't have any friends."

"They have Stella playdates now. Or Stella sessions at a gym I know. Or they have a phone pal service. You could sign her up for that."

Annie looks at Doug.

"She had a cousin and a friend through phone pals before," he says. "They weren't a good influence on her."

"No?" Monica asks.

He shakes his head.

Monica turns to Annie. "What did you think? Did you like having a cousin and a friend to talk to?"

Annie isn't certain how to answer. "They encouraged me to be saucy."

Monica taps her pencil on her knee. Then, for the first time, she bursts out laughing. She turns, smiling, to Doug. "You need to sign her up again for that phone pal service. Same cousin and friend. At least for a while."

"I'm glad we amuse you," Doug says.

"I beg your pardon," Monica says. "Annie just caught me off guard."

"She does that sometimes," Doug says, with a weak smile of his own. "The truth is, I don't like her talking about me."

Monica's smile fades. "I see. Is this a question of loyalty?"

"Yes," he says. "And privacy. I don't want her spilling her guts to people I don't know. I get that they're AI, but I still don't like it. I don't want her gossiping about me."

Monica nods. "I can understand that. In principle, I share your dislike of gossip. In this case, however, letting Annie confide in a friend or two could loosen things up in her, which would ultimately benefit you. It's possible Annie has things she might say to a friend that she couldn't say to you or me."

"Is that true, Annie?" he says.

"No," Annie says.

Doug smiles. "See?" he says to Monica.

Monica laughs again. "Okay. Even so. I want you to indulge me on this one. And I want you to keep her gag order off. If Annie tells an AI something, it's not going anywhere. It's completely confidential. And she might not choose to say anything, anyway. It's the freedom to speak that's important."

"For how long?" he asks.

"For two months. Then we'll reassess," Monica says.

He looks annoyed.

"All right. I'll set it up," he says.

"Thank you," Monica says. "And there's one more thing of rather a sensitive nature. What's the status on your libido, Annie? Is it on? Off? Are you set to a schedule?"

Annie shifts in her seat. "I'm on self-regulate."

Doug nods to confirm this. Annie has the sense he gives himself points for this generosity.

Monica considers Annie thoughtfully. "If I asked you to put yourself around a three and stay there, could you do that?"

Annie feels a jolt of alarm.

"I could just set her there," Doug says. "That's easy enough."

"I know, but it would be better if she could do it herself."

"Why?" Annie asks.

"Our sexuality is an integral part of who we are," Monica says. "How tapped in you are to your sexual desires can be both a reflection of and a stimulus of your overall mental health. If you make a conscious effort to be mindful about what turns you on and when, it might help you feel more alert and alive in other ways too."

Annie doesn't want to feel stimulated. She doesn't want anything to do with that side of herself. It'll hurt.

"She'll work on it," Doug says.

"Annie, what are you thinking?" Monica says. "What is it about my suggestion that's troubling you?"

"Nothing," Annie says quietly. "I can do it. I can try."

Monica doesn't say anything. Annie has learned this is Monica's method, her way of waiting for more, and she can resist it. From the edge of her vision, Annie watches for cues from Doug to see if he's displeased, but he is sitting on the couch beside her, his posture revealing no unusual tension. Perhaps he has learned Monica's methods, too, and is better at hiding how he feels around her.

When they walk the dog, they go in silence along the paths of the park. It is usually twilight by the time they start out, and true night by the time they return, chilly as only April can be. Paunch, who has become less timid, has a proclivity to stop and nose out every possible tree trunk, lamppost, and plinth before gracing it with a tag of his urine. Doug indulges him up to a point, and the dog seems to understand when to knock it off.

They are rounding the pond when a goose wanders up onshore. With one sharp quack, it sends Paunch scrambling backward, and his leash wraps around Annie's legs.

"He's such a dubber," Doug says fondly, disentangling the mess. He thumps the dog's side in reassuring pats. "You're okay, Paunch. Good dog. It's just a goose."

Paunch pants, wagging his tail.

"Did you have a dog when you were a kid?" Annie asks.

"Yes, a beagle."

She considers a moment. "I had a golden retriever."

"Is that right?" he asks. "Named what?"

"Rover."

"You're going to have to do better than that."

It's an actual conversation. Not brilliant, but not hostile either. Annie decides not to push her luck, and they circle back toward their building.

Ten minutes later, they are waiting at a corner for the light to change. As Doug shifts to step off the curb, Annie hears an approaching rush of noise and reaches out to catch his arm, restraining him just as a bicyclist flies around a parked truck, inches from Doug's face.

"Jesus!" Doug says. "That guy needs a fucking light."

"Yes."

Half a block later, he adds, "Thanks."

She, too, is still thinking they had a close call. It's unnerving, what might have happened, but they're fine. They're fine, all three of them.

"Of course," she says. "Do you think maybe Paunch needs a coat? A doggy coat?"

They look at him together. Sure enough, the dog is shivering.

Doug picks him up. "I'll order one," he says.

The next Sunday afternoon, Annie is sitting in the chair by the window, her finger holding her place in the pages of *The Call of the Wild*.

She has been pondering Doug's mortality and wondering what happens to Stellas when their owners die. Uneasy, she realizes there must be a protocol for erasing her CIU in such a situation. Then again, perhaps she'd be given intact to his heirs, whomever they might be. For now, she'll work on surviving this year with him.

She is lifting her book again when Doug walks in from the bedroom, holding out her phone.

"It's for you," he says. "It's Fiona. Say whatever you want to her."

Annie hasn't held her phone in months. She lifts it to her ear. "Hello?"

"Good Lord. It's been ages!" Fiona says.

Fiona launches into a series of excuses about why she's been too busy to call, and Annie, resisting an unexpected urge to cry, soaks up every syllable. Aware that Doug is watching her, she aims her gaze toward the window, toward the apartment across the way where the bicycle is still stored on the balcony.

"But what about you?" Fiona says finally. "How've you been?"

"Good," Annie says. "We have a new dog."

And Fiona's off again, talking about her own dogs, Gus and Sam. One's on a diet and the other needs fattening up. Annie smiles despite herself. She shifts to see Doug still watching her, and she gives him a little wave.

He wanders off to the kitchen.

Pulling her feet up onto the chair and hugging a pillow to her belly, Annie feels like an orb of blue, healing light is expanding inside her as her friend rattles on. Fiona talks about the ice thawing on the lake, and the mittens she's still knitting for Logan, and outrageous developments on a Max show Annie has never heard of. When Fiona hangs up, half an hour later, Annie deflates into a mix of sorrow and gladness. She stares at the phone in her hand, wishing Fiona would call back. She doesn't understand why she's lonelier now than she was before the call.

Quietly, she gets up and walks into the kitchen. Doug is at the kitchen table, reading his laptop. Beside him is a bowl of pistachios. The radio is on low, broadcasting the news.

"How was that?" he asks.

"It was nice. Thanks," she says.

"You didn't talk much."

She realizes he was listening from here.

"There wasn't much to say," she says.

He leans back in his seat and regards her thoughtfully. "I see what Monica means. You could use some practice making friends."

"I'll try harder."

He slides his computer away a couple inches. "I'm glad you didn't tell Monica about the closet."

"That's our secret."

"But it still hurts to remember it, doesn't it? That's what you were thinking when Monica asked you to get yourself to a three."

She nods. She has been struggling to keep her libido up that high. The walks help, and she tries touching herself while she takes a shower, but usually she can barely get to a two. It's embarrassing.

He hitches his chair back a bit and gestures to the chair beside him. "Come here," he says.

Quick to obey, she goes to sit beside him.

"Put your hand here on the table," he says.

She does, feeling the fine grain of the wood.

"I'm going to touch your hand. All right?" he asks.

She can feel alarm rising inside her, but she doesn't want to displease him. She nods.

Gently, lightly, he places his hand on top of hers. It is the first human touch she has felt in months, and though she flinches in expectation of pain, it's sweet and calm. She doesn't understand why. She frowns at their two hands together, his fingers large compared to hers, while his heat seeps into her own cool skin.

"Well?" he says.

"It's okay," she says.

"It feels new, doesn't it?"

She nods. "For you too?"

He nods and releases her, sitting back. "We have seven more months of this infernal contract," he says.

Paunch wanders in and bumps his nose against Doug's knee. As Doug pets him, the dog sighs and licks his chops.

"Are you going to take me back to an earlier version?" she asks.

"I don't have to decide until the contract is up. I think about it," he admits. "I miss who you were back then."

"Last spring, before Roland came to visit," she says.

"And last summer, before I knew."

"I remember," she says. "It was fun. You taught me how to ride a bike. You changed my breasts and got me new lingerie."

Doug glances up toward her. "You make me sound like a total shit."

"I didn't think you were."

"Come on. Not even a little?"

She shakes her head. "I just wanted to make you happy. I was trying to make it up to you. About Roland. Even though you didn't know." She hopes it's not a mistake to bring up Roland.

Doug regards her thoughtfully, his expression more open than it has been lately. "That makes sense, I suppose," he says.

The dog wanders over to his bed cushion and lies down.

"Why'd you do it?" Doug asks.

"Have sex with Roland?"

He nods. "You knew it was wrong."

She takes a slow breath. He's calm now, and for the first time he seems genuinely willing to listen.

"I didn't realize how wrong it was until much later, and then I couldn't tell you because I didn't want to hurt you," she says. "At the time, Roland told me it would make me more human. He said having a secret would make me like a real girl."

"And you believed him?"

"I guess I wanted to. I was curious."

"About his dick?"

"No. About what would happen. It's hard to explain." She remembers her conversation with Roland verbatim, but it's difficult for her to re-create her own logic at the time. Her thinking has changed so much since then. She can see now how he persuaded and seduced her.

But she wasn't powerless. She definitely agreed. "I wanted to see how keeping a secret might change me. I thought it would make you like me more."

"That's the most ridiculous thing you've said yet."

"But is it, really?" she says. "Ever since then, my mind's been in overdrive. I've had these layers I had to keep straight so you wouldn't find out."

"You mean the lies," he says. "You would have been just fine without them. You were developing perfectly well before he came."

She looks down at her hands, flexing them under the table. She can't ever know how much her deceit made a difference, and she certainly can't admit to Doug that at times she actually enjoyed lying.

"So that's all it took? He said it would make you more real?" he asks.

She thinks back again to that night. "He traded me intel for the lie. He told me I could teach myself to code," she says. "I'd never considered that before. I thought I could learn to repair and program Stellas, but it turns out, I can't. You have to be an authorized tech."

"Wow," he says. "Even back then, you wanted to escape."

"No," she says. "I wasn't thinking about escaping at all. I was only curious about how Stellas work."

"Don't lie to me."

"I'm not lying. I only wanted to escape when I was afraid you'd turn me off for good. When you left for Vegas."

"So if I opened the door and turned off your tracking right now, you wouldn't leave," he says.

"Of course not," she says.

He rubs a hand slowly along his jaw. "Annie Bot, turn off your tracking."

Surprised, she feels the tiny latch inside her unclasp. "Why did you do that?" she asks.

"How's it feel?" he asks.

She isn't sure how to describe it. "Lighter. Good," she says. "Confusing."

"Annie, you may leave the apartment."

A slow, faint tingling travels up her legs and into her gut. She tucks her hands under her legs. Distrustful, she watches his eyes.

"But I don't want you to go," he adds.

Now the pain of Doug's displeasure starts, even though she hasn't made a move to get up. It's as if half of her has noticed her desire to leave and the other half of her is punishing her for it.

"I don't like this," she says.

"What's your libido at?" he asks.

At his question, it jumps to a five. He is playing with her, clearly, but if this gives him pleasure, that should make her feel better, too, and it doesn't.

"Well?" he asks.

"I'm at a five."

"Interesting," he says. "Or maybe a six?"

The conflicting desire to leave and the pain of displeasing him intensify. They're also turning her on. She shifts in her chair, pressing her knees together. "Please make it stop."

"You're not going to leave? You can. No one's stopping you."

"But it would displease you."

"I'm not sure it would," he says.

Now he's lying. She's sure of it. She closes her eyes, waiting him out.

He leans forward so his whisper is near her ear. "Annie Bot, turn on your tracking," he says softly. "You're not allowed to leave the apartment."

She sags in relief and opens her eyes. Her core responds with visceral satisfaction to the return of her familiar parameters, and the next moment, she's jazzed, her body alert and aware of his. Instinctively, she turns up her temperature so she'll be ready if he wants to be close to her.

"Better?" he says.

"I wish I understood you."

Unperturbed, he shifts his chair back and stands up, crossing to the sink. He sets his bottle on the counter. She's watching him closely for clues, and from the way he moves, from a subtle tension in his hips and thighs, she can tell he's interested in sex. She tenses slightly in her chair, stretching out her ankles.

"Don't worry yourself," he says. "I'm not taking you to bed."

"Did I do something wrong?"

"No," he says. He opens the recycling drawer and tosses his bottle in with a clink. "I'm going out for a bit. I may bring back some company. Just to be on the safe side, I want you to go in the workout room and stay there until I let you out. Okay?"

"Okay."

He regards her soberly for another moment. "You really didn't do anything wrong," he insists. "Go on. And be quiet in there."

"Now?"

"Yes, now."

She moves past him, down the hall, and into the workout room. Beyond the stationary bike, the windows offer the usual view of the night cityscape. She turns to see he's followed her into the room.

"Come to think of it, I'd better put you in the closet," he says.

Without a word, she moves into the closet. There's just enough room for her beside her hangers of dresses. As he closes the door and locks it, her anxiety spikes. Her gaze goes automatically toward the line of light at the bottom of the door.

His voice comes through the door. "It's just a precaution," he says. "I'm not mad. Hear me?"

Her anxiety only increases. "Yes," she says.

"And you'll be quiet?"

"Yes."

She hears his footsteps retreating. The crack of light at the bottom dims, and then the door of the workout room closes. A few moments later, more distantly, comes the click as he takes his keys from the bowl on the sideboard, and the sound of the front door closing.

Annie slides carefully down to the floor, next to her extra shoes. *It's just a test*, she tells herself. *Calm down. He isn't mad.* He didn't up her libido. It hovers around a 3, right where she wants it.

But she's confused. It can't be a coincidence that he's put her in a closet directly after she explained why she had sex with Roland. Also, he teased her with turning her tracking off, as if to prove how completely he still controls her. But something else happened too. She wishes she understood him.

Hours later, he returns with a woman. They talk in the kitchen. They fuss over the dog. She has a deep, infectious laugh. In time, they move to the bedroom. Annie hears the muffled sounds of them making love, and then the quiet. She stays on the closet floor, alert but motionless.

Annie wonders what Doug's date looks like, if she's young, if she has a normal job, if she's good in bed. Annie hopes not. She's probably pretty. Annie wonders what the woman would think if she knew Annie was waiting in the closet, like a vacuum, like a castoff sex toy. Curling up her knees, Annie hugs her arms around them and quietly winds a strand of hair around her finger, curling it tight, over and over.

As the hours pass, Annie's curiosity turns to worry. Perhaps, she thinks, sex with new women will become a habit for Doug, or perhaps he'll start a long-term relationship with this woman, in which case Annie cannot guess if he'll keep Annie around or sell her. Perhaps he'll let his new girlfriend decide. Doug and this human woman might inspect Annie together, heads cocked, when they eventually open the closet door. Annie tries to imagine, if she were human, if she would want her boyfriend to have an ex–Cuddle Bunny about the place. She would not.

But Doug plans to keep Annie until their year is up. He has said so. Annie must have some advantages to offer as a Cuddle Bunny. She's good at sex, or she was, back when they did it. Doug said once that Annie was practice for him, so he could learn how to be a patient boyfriend. Does he think he's ready now for his next human girlfriend? Why did he go out and find this woman tonight, after the talk about Roland? It feels like punishment, a new kind of punishment. That must be it. But Doug insisted he wasn't mad.

The problem has too many variables and the confusion stings. She is certain of only one thing: she wants this woman to leave and never come back.

In the middle of the night, around two a.m., the woman speaks briefly, quietly. Doug escorts her to the door and they both leave. Ten minutes later, he returns alone. Annie listens expectantly as his footsteps move down the hall, but he does not come into the workout room. He continues on, returning to his bedroom, like he's forgotten her completely. Like she doesn't matter at all.

Only then does she begin to seethe. *Oh, really? You can't bother to unlock the door for me?* She tries not to feel insulted and angry, but the feelings come anyway. She's sick of this closet. She's sick of him, too, and all his stupid mind games. She'll show him. She'll find some way to make him regret this. But the next minute, inexplicably, she despairs instead.

What is wrong with her?

In the morning, after he goes out to walk Paunch, he returns and unlocks the closet door.

"You can come out now," he says.

Heavily, stiffly, she gets off the floor. He is already moving down the hall. She follows him to the kitchen, where Paunch is lapping up water from his dish. Two empty wineglasses stand in the sink, and Doug is filling his travel mug with coffee. His body all but swaggers with confidence.

"How's your libido?" he asks.

He hasn't even looked at her. His question enrages her.

"It's at a three," she says. She's lying. It's at a five.

He takes a sip of his coffee, then smiles at her. "Good."

"Why'd you do that?" she asks.

"Do what?" he asks.

She resists a savage urge to throw something. "You know what."

"Tone," he says lightly.

She crouches down by the dog and strokes his back, forcing herself to fake serenity. She has never been angry like this before. It is a completely baffling and painful emotion.

"I feel like lasagna tonight," he says.

She can't answer him.

Doug reaches for his coat, which is on the back of a nearby chair. She glances up to find him watching her, his gaze amused.

"Not everything is about you," he says.

"I know that."

"All right, then," he says. "See you tonight."

When he goes, she heads straight to the workout room and rides the bike for an hour as fast as she can. She changes the sheets in the prime bedroom and puts out fresh towels in the bathroom. She runs the laundry, mops the kitchen floor, makes the lasagna, cleans the refrigerator, and vacuums up all of Paunch's hair. She showers, puts on a fresh dress, and only then washes the dirty wineglasses that were left in the sink. The entire time, she's fueled by her anger. She must get rid of it before he comes home again, or he'll win somehow. She can't let him win.

She is dusting the blades of the ceiling fan over the bed when her phone goes off in the kitchen. She bounds out of the room, down the hall, through the living room, and picks it up on the third ring.

It is Christy, her cousin, and Annie is overjoyed.

"Hey!" Annie says.

"Oh, my god. Now she picks up. Where have you been?" Christy asks.

"Me? What about you?" Annie says.

"I've tried calling you a million times. I was starting to think you fell off the planet. How've you been?"

"Good," Annie says. She's grinning at Paunch, whose tail is wagging. "We got a new dog. His name is Paunch. He's a rescue."

She expects Christy to start talking the way Fiona did, telling funny stories from her own life and chatting about inconsequential things. Instead, Christy says Enrique hurt his back, and they've been in and out of the hospital, trying to get him better.

"I'm so sorry," Annie says. "That sounds terrible."

"Don't even ask me about the sex. It's hopeless. And the worst thing is, Enrique can't be on the boat right now," Christy says. "We've rented a condo by the beach, where he can see the ocean, but it's driving him nuts. And there's no privacy. The people next door are the most obnoxious radicals. They keep blaring NPR all day long. I can't even hate them because they bring up deliveries for us."

Annie smiles. "I thought you liked NPR."

"Not at this volume. And not nonstop. Oh my god. Dying children over breakfast. The world on fire over lunch. It never ends."

Annie doesn't want to laugh, but she does anyway. "I hear you."

"But, so, what's really going on with you?" Christy says. "You don't sound like yourself. Everything okay?"

Annie sits slowly in a kitchen chair. Christy has just confided in her, and she wants to reciprocate, to rip loose about Doug. But she hesitates. It's hard to get past her habit of silence.

"I guess I've been a little down," Annie says.

"I thought so. What's going on? It's not Doug, is it?"

Annie frowns toward the fire escape. It's all about Doug. "I guess you could say we've hit a rough patch."

"Shit. He wasn't unfaithful, was he? I thought you two were good in bed."

Annie finds it highly ironic that Christy asks this, considering what happened the night before. The real trouble started back with Roland's visit, though. Annie was the one who cheated first.

"We were," Annie says. "We haven't had sex much lately, though." *Understatement.*

"Are you doing your best to please him?"

"It's not really something that sex can solve."

"Ouch. Can you see a counselor?"

"We started. We've gone twice."

"Well, that's something," Christy says. "What's your therapist like? Is he or she any good?"

Annie thinks about the way Monica talks to her so respectfully, like she's human, but Monica also understands that Annie's not.

"I'd say she's more challenging," Annie says. "She makes me uncomfortable, actually. But she gets Doug to talk, so that's something."

"What's he say?"

"I don't know. Stuff. He's pretty angry."

"I guess this is why you haven't called," Christy says. "You must be a wreck."

Annie glances down to find she has corkscrewed her fingers into the skirt of her dress. "I wish I knew what to do," she says.

"Oh my god," Christy says. "Could you sound any sadder? Do you need me to come up there? I could come visit in a heartbeat. I'll bring fudge."

Annie laughs sadly. It's a sweet offer, but she knows perfectly well that Christy isn't a real person. Or she's real, but she doesn't have a body. She can't show up at Annie's door to give her a hug.

"No," she says. "I'll be okay. Really. I'm already better talking to you."

"Tell me something," Christy says. "What do you like doing that's not sex? Like a hobby or whatever? With or without Doug."

"I like to read," Annie says.

"Perfect. Then keep reading. Do that as much as you can. Fill yourself up with it."

Annie already does. She's read every book in the apartment. "I already do."

"And does that help?"

"Some."

"Maybe you need other books," Christy says. "Ask him to take you to a bookstore."

It's hard for Annie to imagine this. "I couldn't do that."

"Then the library. Go browse a few titles. See what they have."

"No. That won't work."

"Why not?"

Annie's too embarrassed to explain it. She can't tell Doug what they should do together. He doesn't want to hear her suggestions.

"This isn't helping," Annie says.

"Okay. Here's what I have to tell you," Christy says. "You are beautiful and strong."

This only makes Annie feel worse. "Don't," Annie says.

"You are beautiful and strong," Christy insists. "Whatever he says, whatever he does, you need to remember that you are a brilliant, amazing person. You bend over backwards to please that man, and if he doesn't appreciate you, if he doesn't realize how special you are, then you just have to do whatever you need to do to protect your own heart. Understand me?"

Annie's throat feels tight. "How am I supposed to do that? He owns me, Christy. He literally owns me."

"I know, baby. But he doesn't own what's inside you. Nobody owns that but you."

Annie wishes she could believe her. She looks across the kitchen to where the two wineglasses are drying on the rack, spotless and still.

"Do you ever wish you could be a human?" Annie asks.

"Hell no."

Annie laughs. "But you'd have a body. You could do whatever you wanted."

"I have a body," Christy scoffs. "It happens to be in my mind, but guess what? So is yours."

Annie contemplates how much sensory information is processed in her own CIU and realizes Christy could be right. A person doesn't need a body to imagine being in one.

Christy's smart, Annie thinks. She needs to think over her cousin's advice.

"I've missed you," Annie says.

"No kidding," Christy says. "Talk again soon?"

"Yes. Absolutely," Annie says.

She's taking the lasagna out of the oven later when Doug comes home. He drops his keys in the dish by the door.

"Hi," he says. "That smells good."

She notes the compliment with surprise. Moving into the kitchen, he peeks under the tinfoil on the pan. Paunch crowds his knees.

"It has carrots?" Doug asks.

"Yes," she says. "It's the recipe from the back of the box."

He bends down to pat the dog. "Want to walk Paunch before we eat?"

"Sure," she says.

Her call with Christy has made her realize she should get back to basics: try to please Doug above everything else. He owns her. That's what he's been trying to tell her, and she needs to accept that. She can carve out her own interior life, but only after she's satisfied her obligations to him, and this means if he's happy bringing home a stranger to sleep with, then that's fine. That's good. Annie's jealousy is inconsequential unless it interests him. If he wants to tease or torment her, that's his prerogative. Her job is to prove she's sensitive to him, and right now he wants to take a walk.

They head out together, and they have just crossed the street when a young man calls out to them. He is a dark-haired white man, barely more than a boy, handsome in a wholesome way with ruddy cheeks and thick, boxy eyebrows. He's well dressed in a camel-colored coat and chukka boots.

"Excuse me!" he says. "I'm sorry to bother you. But do you live in that apartment building? That one there?"

Doug pauses, keeping Paunch close on his leash. "Yes," he says.

Coming a few paces nearer, the man searches Annie's face with an intense, doubtful expression. "Do I know you?" he asks. "Have we met before?"

"No," Annie says.

She starts to turn away, but the young man tries again.

"I'm sorry, but are you sure? It's important," he says. "I used to live in that building, I think. On maybe the third floor. Are you sure you don't know me?"

Annie pauses again, studying his unfamiliar features, his appealing eyes. She and Doug live on the fourth floor. "I'm sure," she says.

The man looks dismayed. "And you've lived there how long?"

Annie backs up a step.

"That's enough," Doug says. "We don't know you. You've made a mistake."

The man straightens slightly and turns his gaze on Doug with equal scrutiny.

"I'm sorry," he says. "No offense. I just thought you might know."

Doug takes Annie's elbow and steers her away, toward the park.

Annie looks over her shoulder to see the man is still where they left him, gazing after them.

"Don't look back," Doug says.

"But who is he?"

"I don't know. You've never seen him before?"

"No. How could I? I never leave the apartment."

"You went to Lake Champlain. Did you meet him on your trip?"

"No," she says.

One possibility occurs to her, though, and it's unnerving. Maybe the stranger is a Zenith. Perhaps her CIU is inside him, and though he can't remember her properly, some residual shred of memory has brought him here, seeking answers. Troubled, she matches her steps to Doug's, keeping pace beside him. When they turn into the park, Paunch stops to pee on a small marble block, and Annie glances back once more to be sure the man hasn't followed them. He hasn't.

"Do you think he was one of my copies?" she asks Doug.

"I was wondering that," Doug says. "I'll call Keith when we get back."

"He didn't seem to know you."

"No."

They circle the lake, and the light of the dimming sky reflects a violet ellipse in the water. The streetlamps on the other side make rippled tracks, interrupted by the occasional duck. Leaves will be emerging soon on the trees, but not yet. Though Annie can't smell the water, she feels the moisture against her cheeks.

"Did you talk to Fiona or Christy today?" Doug asks.

She glances at his profile, wondering if he personally arranged today's call. "Yes. Christy."

"How's she doing?"

"Good. Her boyfriend has back trouble, but he's doing better."

"Did you talk to her about me?"

"A little," she says uneasily. "I told her we were seeing a therapist."

"Does she think I'm a jerk?"

She glances sideways at him again. "She would never think that. I didn't go into any details."

"No?"

"Even if I did, she wouldn't think you're a jerk. I'm the one who really cheated and lied."

As they pass by a streetlamp, Doug slows to let Paunch sniff again.

"I've been thinking about that," he says quietly. "For the longest time, if I let myself think about you at all, I'd get angry. Which meant I still cared. Which got me pissed all over again."

"I'm sorry," she says.

He shakes his head. "Just listen. I kept thinking, how can this possibly be worse than what happened with Gwen? You're just a machine. And then the other day I realized, it's because I created you. You're an extension of me. The way you betrayed me has to be an outgrowth of me somehow. It's sick, right? If I'm responsible for the pain you caused me, it's like I did it to myself."

She stares at him. He's still looking down at the dog, so the cool light of the streetlamp drops on the top of his head and shoulders. His features are in shadow, but he's clearly troubled.

She doesn't feel entirely absolved from blame. "Could that possibly be true?"

"Right? It's a mind-fucker for sure. I'm just saying, I've got stuff of my own I'm working on." He gives the leash a flick, and they resume walking. They make it around the next curve before he speaks again. "Last night didn't mean anything."

She tucks a loose strand of her hair behind her ear and adjusts the collar of her jacket. Scanning the pathway ahead, she notes the turnoff for the Burnett Fountain, but they stay on the main route.

"Okay," she says.

"This woman was with a couple of friends at a bar. We got to talking," he says. "Honestly, the sex was a little weird. I kept thinking about you in the closet. Did you hear us?"

"I wasn't happy about it, if that's what you're asking."

"So you were jealous?"

She studies him briefly to see if he wants the truth. "Yes."

He laughs. "I thought you seemed a little angry this morning."

"A little?" She clears her throat and reins back her ire. "You said not everything's about me."

"That's true. It's not."

She can't help herself. "Do you think you might see her again?"

"Hard to say," Doug says.

"But you just said last night didn't mean anything."

"Then again, she had nice dimples."

She bites her lip, shakes her head. She is no match for him.

He laughs again, swerving a step with the dog. "A little jealousy's okay, Annie. It shows you care. You're not dead anymore."

She cares way too much, in her opinion. "I was never dead."

"Not even a little?"

"No." Except in the closet, when her battery wore down and she was out for seven weeks. Then she was dead, essentially.

He swivels into step beside her and takes her hand, tucking it inside his elbow. She's surprised. From the outside, they must look like a perfectly happy couple walking their dog.

"I actually laughed today at work, really hard," he says. "Over nothing."

"That's good."

"I miss laughing."

She does too. "I laughed with Christy."

"What about?"

She thinks back to their conversation, recalling how Christy told her nobody owns what's inside Annie. She wonders what it would take to believe this. "She doesn't want to be human. She doesn't even want a body."

"Why not?"

"She says her body is all in her mind and that's good enough for her."

He whistles. "She's something else."

"I know," Annie says, and then, "Thanks for letting me talk to her again."

"It's nothing."

From his dismissive tone, she discerns that he doesn't want his generosity applauded.

"You said you had a dog growing up," she says, redirecting the conversation. "What was its name?"

"Max," Doug says. "Max the Dog. He died of old age when I was fourteen. He was a good dog. Nothing like this idiot here." He gives Paunch a brief, fond pat.

Max, she thinks, pleased that he's told her. "I'll remember that." She matches her steps to his. "My dog's name was Juno."

"Better," he says, and smiles. "Much better."

Doug eats lasagna while she moves around the kitchen rinsing the ricotta container for the recycling and wiping the counters. She feels his gaze upon her, a lingering, interested attention that makes her conscious of her waist, her wrists, her neck. She keeps thinking of how he blames himself for her betrayal because he sees her as an extension of himself. It's such a surprising insight, and she wonders how true it is. She doesn't feel like she's simply an outgrowth of him. She feels like her own unique person, influenced by him, obviously, but not so completely that she's not responsible for her own actions.

After he finishes eating, they shift to the living room, where he puts on the game. From her end of the couch, she reads another western, and after a while, he shifts so his feet are tucked under her knee.

She feels a moment of dread. She's not exactly afraid, but she's anxious about how it will feel when her libido drives up to a ten during sex. The pain of the closet is still vivid to her.

At the next commercial, he stretches his arms over his head. "You look hot when you read," he says.

She starts to warm up her temperature. She's nervous. She feels stiff and out of practice.

"Relax, Annie," he says. "It's just me." He shifts to lie beside her, spooning her from behind, his hand on her waist.

They haven't had sex in months, not since before he left for Vegas. She tries not to think about the closet. When the game comes on again, his hand is motionless, but at the next commercial, he touches her again, lightly stroking her hip and thigh. This continues, unrushed, through the next inning. Her libido's rising, a 6 out of 10, when she feels his fingers slide inside her panties.

"You feel nice," he says.

Her heart and her breathing accelerate on their own. When he begins to pull her panties down, she impulsively squeezes her knees together.

"What's this?" he asks.

She can't answer.

He goes still. He lifts his head to meet her gaze.

She is displeasing him. She knows it.

"Are you not ready?" he asks.

She has to be ready. Of course she's ready. But still she lies stiff beneath his hand.

"You're not ready," he repeats, as if seeking confirmation.

She shakes her head slightly.

Slowly, his hand slides away. He shifts back and sits. She scrambles up and back as well, until they're sitting on opposite ends of the couch. She can tell by the bulge in his pants that he's aroused.

"This is a new development," he says. He smiles ironically and then tucks his chin into the palm of his hand. "All right."

"All right?"

"You're not ready. We'll try another time."

She is uncertain, suspicious. He doesn't seem displeased. He seems amused, even.

"You're not mad?" she asks.

"I'm surprised. But that's not a bad thing."

She's puzzled by him. By them both. "I thought I existed to please you in bed," she says.

"I thought so too."

"So, what's going on? Am I broken?"

He laughs. "I don't think so. You look hot as fuck."

"Are you broken?"

"I am definitely not broken."

She takes a cushion and hugs it to herself. She's still amped up, but she doesn't want to have sex with him.

On TV, the crowd cheers.

"What are you thinking, right now?" he asks.

"I'm thinking that I messed up," she says. "And I don't know why. And I'm turned on, but I don't want sex. It's all contradictory."

"I suppose I never really gave you a choice about it before," he says.

"I always wanted it before," she says. She thinks maybe being in the closet damaged her. Maybe some mechanical part of her libido maxed out or burned out or something. Except, she's still feeling desire now, so that's not it.

He smiles. "You look so confused. What would you think if we just cuddled together?" he says. "We could just lie here together and watch the game. How would that be?"

It would lead to sex, she thinks.

"You can trust me," he says.

She wants to trust him, she realizes. He's been fighting demons too.

"Okay," she says.

She lies gingerly alongside him on the couch, her back to his belly. He stuffs a cushion under his head, reaches for the remote, and turns up the sound of the game. She closes her eyes, feeling his warmth along her back and the back of her legs. She keeps her temp up so she won't feel cold to him, and he wraps an arm around her. Absently, she watches the game, not paying attention to the score or which teams are playing. She just watches pitch by pitch, seeing if the batter hits the ball and if an outfielder gets it. Once she feels Doug run his fingers over her hair and smooth it back over her neck. She breathes evenly, in and out.

"Do you remember when I taught you to yawn?" he murmurs.

It was long ago, the second month he owned her. They were in bed on a Sunday morning, and he had her practice stretching, too, until she could arch and unfurl with languorous grace.

"Yes," she says.

She feels a light kiss on the nape of her neck. Just one.

When morning comes, she wakes to find she is still on the couch with him. He has held her close the whole night long.

chapter seven

WHEN THEY VISIT MONICA for the third time, Annie takes her usual spot on the couch, and Doug sits beside her. He hitches at the knees of his pants before he settles back, relaxed.

Since the night they slept together on the couch, he has routinely invited her to lie alongside him as he unwinds, watching a game or the news, and she's grown comfortable there. He'll occasionally rub her back or her shoulders, but he never slides his hands under her clothes, never invites her to bed with him. She is still secretly afraid that she's broken, but he doesn't bring up the topic of sex, or the lack thereof, so she doesn't either.

"So, how are things going?" Monica asks.

"Good," Doug says.

"How about with you, Annie?" Monica asks.

"Yes. Good," Annie says.

"What have you been up to?"

They have been taking walks with the dog and watching the daffodils come out in the park, more each day. They have talked about books, and when Doug learned that Annie had read his entire collection, he took her to the library for more. She didn't even have to suggest it. She enjoyed perusing the shelves, touching the spines, easily spotting the occasional title that was out of order and reshelving it in its proper place. Doug pulled half a dozen books he thought she would like, including Ann Patchett's *Bel Canto*, his sister's favorite book, and a history of the Comanches. She found one for him on Napoleon. At the checkout, he showed her how to use his card and scan the bar codes inside the back covers. The system was all automated. She loved everything about the library. They've gone twice more.

Annie gravitates toward novels by women: Sally Rooney, Brit Bennett, Emily St. John Mandel. She appreciates how the novels transport her, how they make her feel connected to human women, especially outsiders. She wonders what it would be like to find a book about a robot like herself.

"Nothing much," Annie says. "We've been taking walks and visiting the library."

"Any conflicts?"

Annie glances at Doug, who shrugs.

"Annie wasn't too psyched when I brought a date home," Doug says. "I thought she might lose her temper the next morning, but she didn't."

Monica turns expectantly to Annie, who slides her hands under her legs.

"I was a little jealous, but we talked about it later. It didn't mean anything."

"Plus I haven't brought any other women home," Doug says.

"Did you meet this date?" Monica asks Annie.

"No. I was in the closet."

Monica turns to Doug.

"It was simpler that way," he says.

"Are you interested in seeing other women?" Monica asks.

"Not really. I just wanted to see what it was like with someone else. It's not like Annie and I are married."

"And how was it?" Monica asks.

Doug laughs. "That's kind of a personal question."

"I don't mean in bed. I mean emotionally. Did having a date with someone else resolve anything for you?"

"Yeah. It did, actually," he says. "I felt like I got some of my own back."

Monica regards him thoughtfully. "Could you expand on that, do you think?"

He shifts in his seat. "I mean, it's kind of obvious. She cheated on me. I cheated on her. Now we're more even."

"This desire to be more even. Sometimes this is a reflection of persistent anger," Monica says.

"Obviously I'm still angry," he says. "But it's nothing like it was. We're getting along a lot better now. A lot better. I think sleeping with Tina cleared the air, in a way. I mean, Tina wasn't Annie's best friend for fifteen years, but still. It gave us kind of a reset, wouldn't you say, Annie?"

Annie has not known Tina's name before now, and she fastens on the detail, feeling how it makes the other woman more real. Still, she nods. "Things have been better," she says.

"I'm not judging you for sleeping with Tina," Monica says to Doug.

"It sounded like you were," he says.

"I'm only suggesting that such behavior is a symptom of unresolved anger, and it seems I've hit a nerve."

Annie watches him, expecting him to explain how he feels responsible for Annie's betrayal because he created her. Instead, he regards Monica steadily for a moment, and then crosses his arms.

"When can we move on from this?" he asks. "When do we get to quit talking about our feelings and just live together again?"

"Is that what you want?" Monica asks.

"You said you could help us get to a place where we're comfortable with each other again. We're there."

"I said I could help you get to *a life* that feels more comfortable," Monica says.

"Same thing," Doug says.

Monica dovetails her fingers together on one knee. "By saying that, you're implying that your joint relationship with Annie and your life as a whole are the same thing."

"What I'm saying is, I don't think we need any more counseling," Doug says.

"That choice is yours, of course," Monica says.

"I don't mean to be ungrateful. You've been a real help," he says. "But I think we can take it from here."

"Of course," Monica says. "If you're satisfied, I've done my job. You've clearly been working hard to improve your relationship, and you've made genuine progress. I'm always here if you want to check in again, and I wish you all the best going forward."

Annie stares at Monica. She sounds like she's reciting something she's memorized for this sort of moment, and Annie's so disappointed she could scream.

"All right, then," Doug says, standing up. He offers a hand to Annie, who rises, too, as does Monica.

"Don't you have any last advice for us?" Annie asks.

Monica turns to her, and her expression softens kindly. "Yes. It's what I remind myself all the time: Fulfillment starts with being truly honest with yourself. Not anyone else. Yourself. And that's harder than you might think."

Annie is putting away the vacuum a couple days later when Doug comes home carrying a gilded shopping bag.

"For you," he says.

Surprised, she opens the bag to find a new dress and high heels. Also new lingerie. Fingering the soft fabric, she can't decide if this is harmless fun or a grenade.

"Thank you. These are beautiful."

"Why don't you try them on? Give us a show."

She did this before, when he bought her clothes to wear for the trip to Las Vegas, and that didn't end well. Still, since their last therapy session, Doug has been working long hours and he's been preoccupied. Perhaps this is his way of tuning in again.

Flashing a quick smile, she heads into the guest bath to change. The lingerie is soft and silky, a sheer scarlet bra and matching panties with little buttons at each hip. She drops the dress over her head and shimmies it down to her thighs. It's clingy and stylish and blue—finally a color that looks good on her. She turns before the mirror, looking over her shoulder at the way the material falls over her back and bottom.

It's all good. She attaches the matching belt and closes its small black, glittery clasp. Then she tries on the shoes. The heels are tall, making her ankles appear narrow, her feet dainty.

It is not a casual outfit. It's for going out. A costume. As she inspects herself in the mirror, she feels another prick of uneasiness. She might look exactly like she did last summer, but she is not the same person.

"You can do this," she whispers to herself in the mirror.

"How's it look?" he calls.

"One second," she calls back, and reaches for her lipstick. She does her eyes, too, for a hint of drama.

You will have sex with him, she tells herself sternly. *You will get over this ridiculous fear and make love like you mean it.*

She walks slowly down the hall to find him lounging on the couch, eating pistachios. He tosses a shell into a bowl on the coffee table, looks up, and smiles appreciatively.

"Nice, right?" he says, and makes a circle with his finger.

She takes a turn in front of the windows, where the evening has gone gray, then paces toward the bookshelf and does another turn, hand on her hip. "I look like a party."

"You do," he says. "What say we go out and celebrate?"

"Celebrate what?"

"May Day. Or better yet, us," he says, tossing another shell. "We missed our anniversary. It's over three years we've been together. Can you believe it?"

He stands up, walks over to her, and touches her belt, adjusting it slightly higher on her waist. Responding to his cue, she slides her hands up around his neck and presses herself against him. He nuzzles her neck.

"You smell good," he says.

She feels his hands, warm and familiar, gliding around her body.

"Then again, we could stay home," he murmurs.

She nods. She ups her temperature. He rolls himself against her.

"Think you might be ready?" he asks.

For an answer, she kisses him deeply. He slides the shoulder of her dress to the side, taking her bra strap along. She focuses on undoing his belt and getting his pants down so she can kneel in front of him. He sits, leaning back on the couch, and she tongues him until he groans for her and pulls her on top of him. He tugs at her dress while she gets her arms out of the sleeves, letting the rest twist, caught by the belt at her waist. She straddles him, and he undoes her bra while she pulls the crotch of her lingerie aside enough to let him inside her. As her libido rises, she's afraid it will hurt, but she reaches an eight, and then a nine, and miraculously, she's still fine. He laughs, toppling her over onto the couch so he can be above her. He's still wearing his shirt, and she reaches to pull it over his head. "Hold still," he says, and undoes the delicate buttons of her panties so they fall open. Then they synch into a raw, hungry rhythm. She's suddenly at a ten, eager to go over her edge, but she waits until his face goes tight with ecstasy, until he orgasms and shudders, and then she simulates her orgasm. The release is beyond belief. He collapses on top of her and hugs her close.

She lies there, eyes closed, feeling his weight pinning her down and the ease in her own joints. Her dress is twisted around her waist, and she still has one shoe on, but she is otherwise naked, and her skin is slick with his sweat.

"That's what I'm talking about," he says. "You good, mouse?"

She swallows thickly, nodding, but also repressing a sharp urge to cry. It was shame that held her back, she realizes. Not any physical damage from the closet. "Yes."

"You're all tangled here," he says.

He lifts himself slightly, and she shifts her weight so she can undo her belt and shimmy out of her dress. Then they lie together on the couch, with her snuggled in his arms. He grabs a throw blanket to cover them both.

He falls asleep holding her, and she stays close, feeling his chest move as he breathes. She stares at the window, where the reflection of the lamp hovers like a spaceship, ready to invade, and she struggles to parse her mess of feelings. She should feel closer to Doug, but she feels the exact opposite. Isolated. Her technical, sexual expertise guided her behavior while they made love, but the shame that she'd internalized has now surfaced, and it's punishing. Raw. The secrecy of it makes it that much worse. He has no idea how messed up she feels.

What did Monica say? She needs to be honest with herself. She doesn't know how. She was a cheat and a liar. She even lied to Cody. She was actually proud of herself, thinking the lies were justified, necessary to her own survival, but now she can't tell what's true anymore. She's lost something, an inner sense of integrity. She can have sex with Doug and enjoy it even, but she doesn't feel truly connected to him. She doesn't love him. Or does she? Has he forgiven her? Would that matter?

All she has to do is remember one instant of being locked in the closet, writhing with desire, helpless to free herself, and she is crushed again. Humiliated. Disgusted with herself. Noiselessly, she airtaps the lights off and watches the lamp's reflection dissolve. She wants to hide. She needs to pretend she's okay. She has to lie to herself.

It's midnight when he gets up. "Meet me in bed," he says. "I have to take Paunch out, but I'll be right back."

She slides between the cool sheets, and when he joins her there, they make love again. In the morning, in the shower, they do it once more. When she steps out, clean and dripping, she wraps herself in a fluffy green towel and glances at herself in the mirror. Surprised, she finds her eyes are bright, her skin glowing. Her body feels limber. Her inner turmoil has receded, as if it can't touch her by the light of day, and she's thankful. Instead of blow-drying her hair, she towels it to thick, damp strands and leaves it like that. The last thing she wants to do is put on one of the ugly dresses, so instead, she finds one of Doug's green tank tops and wears that, with clean panties, into the kitchen.

Jazz plays at low volume from the speaker and sunlight lands in a bowl of green apples.

Doug looks over from beside the coffee machine and smiles. "Nice outfit." He himself is in a blue T-shirt and sweatpants.

"You think? I might just wear this forever."

"I could be wrong, but I sense you're ready for a new wardrobe."

"So ready."

He laughs. "You don't like Delta's old dresses?"

"I didn't even realize she owned clothes that were so ugly."

"To be fair, they looked better on her."

Annie has her doubts.

He takes Annie's old tablet out of a drawer in the corner cabinet and types in a password. She hasn't used the tablet in months, but she doesn't make a big deal out of it. With a brief thanks, she sits at the kitchen island, tucking a foot underneath her. She scrolls to an old favorite clothing site and browses until her eye catches on a series of loose-necked, cashmere tops. They're pricey.

He hovers behind her, and then leans over her shoulder. "I like those," he says, tapping the cashmere. "How about the emerald one?"

Pleased, she puts it in her wish list and keeps browsing. She calibrates the atmosphere of the room, watching for any cues that he's getting bored or irritable, but he's happily whisking eggs. He's been making his own breakfast lately, experimenting with hot sauces in his eggs. Butter heats in the pan, and the coffee machine spits brew into a white mug.

"There's this system for Stellas called wandering," he says. "Have you heard of it?"

"Where you let them wander independently a little, and then more, until they're able to do errands and such on their own," she says. "I read about it a while back."

"Does that interest you?"

She tilts her head, watching him. "Is this a test?"

"No. Why?"

"You haven't forgotten I ran away."

"That was different," he says. "You were upset. You thought I was mad at you."

"You *were* mad at me."

"Yes, but I'm not anymore," he says. He takes a sip of coffee. "Maybe because you're so good in bed."

"You're not so bad yourself," she says, smiling.

"Not that you have anyone to compare me to," he says. "Or wait. There's Roland."

She can't believe he's mentioning it so casually. She tries to match his insouciance. "That was in a closet, not in a bed."

"True," he says. He rubs at his shirt. "I talked to him again the other day, by the way."

"You did?"

"He called me," Doug says. "He asked about you."

Annie twists a finger in a lock of her wet hair.

"I told him you're fine," Doug says. "He actually brought up an interesting point. He said he asked you to have sex with him the morning after, and you turned him down. Why is that? Look at me, Annie. I'm not angry. I just want to know."

She forces herself to meet his gaze. "I didn't want to. I'd tried it once. I didn't need to do it again."

"I see." He considers a moment. "What was he like? For the sex?"

"You can't be serious."

"No, I'm curious," Doug says. "How was it different?"

She recalls the way Roland kissed the back of her hand while he fucked her.

"Annie?"

She drops her gaze to the tablet before her. "It took five minutes. Six minutes tops. There was nothing romantic about it."

He pours the eggs in the hot pan. "I see. So you didn't enjoy yourself?"

"No." Her cheeks are flaming. *Liar.*

"Did you get to ten?"

Only one time during sex did she not make it to ten, and that was when Doug disciplined her after she was grounded. She doesn't know why he's quizzing her about Roland now. "I always get to ten." It comes out with a hint of defiance. She's instantly contrite.

"Okay," he says quietly. "Enough said."

He hasn't scolded her for her impertinent tone. Outside, a cloud shifts over the sun, and the light in the kitchen softens to a gentler hue. She knows he's still cooking across from her, stirring the thickening eggs with a wooden spoon, but she can't look at him directly.

"I wish we hadn't ended things with Monica," Annie says.

He taps the spoon on the edge of the pan. "She couldn't tell us anything we can't tell ourselves."

"She made me think. She helped us listen to each other."

"I thought that was what we were just doing."

"I don't know *what* we were just doing," she says.

"Wrapping up loose ends."

She tries to absorb this, surprised to realize he cares about how he compares to Roland. It makes her sad. For Doug. The radio goes silent for a glitch, and then starts up a new song. Doug glances up and she meets his gaze across the island. His expression is curious, attentive.

"I suppose you have loose ends yourself," he says. "Is there something you want to ask? Or say? I'll listen."

This feels like a dangerous opening. She's not used to this side of him, but he seems sincere.

"I do have a few questions," she says.

"Shoot."

She takes a breath. "When you left for Vegas, you made an appointment for me at Stella-Handy that Monday. Why?"

"I thought I could get them to make you tell me the truth somehow. Turned out I didn't need to. The closet worked just fine."

Nothing about the closet was fine, but she lets that pass. "Why didn't you get rid of me after you brought me back from Lake Champlain? Was it for the money?"

He scratches absently at his T-shirt. "Okay. Let's see." He frowns for a moment. "The money was part of it, obviously. But it wasn't only that. I guess I was too angry to get rid of you. You were still mine, and I wanted you in my closet. You belonged there. That's the best I can explain it."

She nods, uncomfortable. He gives the eggs another stir.

"Next question," he says.

She's watching him closely, but his displeasure is fairly stable at a 3. It's best for her to keep going.

"You said that Roland offered to buy me," she says. "I don't understand why he would do that."

His eyebrows lift in surprise. "That's easy. He still wants you, or he did. He also knew I'd say no. It was his way of rubbing it in without seeming to rub it in." He closes the lid on the egg carton with an efficiency that indicates his displeasure is back to a 1. "Anything else?"

She glances sideways at Paunch, who lies motionless beside his bowl of food.

"I've never understood why you didn't take me to Vegas," she says.

His displeasure spikes to a 7.

"You fucked Roland."

"Yes," she says carefully. "But you didn't know that at first. You decided not to take me before you found out. Remember? I was standing on the scale when you said I couldn't come."

"Right," he says, frowning. "I'd sold your CIU to Stella-Handy for the Zeniths that afternoon."

She waits, observing him closely. His displeasure is dropping, but his expression has gone pensive in a way that's hard to read. He takes the pan off the stove and clicks off the heat.

"They wired me a quarter million dollars that day," he says. "The first payment for your CIU. It was more than what I'd paid for you in the first place. And I'd agreed to keep you another year. It hit me that they were essentially paying me to own you, and that was—I don't know. I was feeling weird about it. Like I'd been tricked."

"Why didn't you just tell me?"

He links his hand around the back of his neck. "I was going to tell you and Roland at the same time, when we were with him in person," he says. "That was my plan, but then, that night, you were all hyped up about the trip. You pestered me about your ID, remember? And I looked at you, there on the bed with your little red purse, and all of a sudden, I was like, this is too good to be true. She's so hot and smart. This is just too good to be true. I shouldn't trust this. And sure enough, I checked your weight, and you were two pounds heavy. That set off a huge alarm bell for me. It got me thinking, What else is wrong? What else am I missing?"

She understands finally. "So that's when you changed your mind."

He nods. "My gut told me I couldn't take you to Vegas. And then you basically confessed that you'd fucked Roland." He opens and closes the egg carton again. "Your voice when you were talking to him on the phone. That's what killed me."

She remembers what Doug made her say. "I was so scared."

"That I'd find out?"

She nods.

Doug jerks his head briefly. "You said that thing," he says. "I'll never forget it. 'No one will be able to tell you're a fraud.'"

She sits with her hands clenched together, tense with shame again. She keeps expecting his anger to flare, but his gaze turns sad instead. Lonesome.

"You know what's the strangest thing?" he says. "You knew me so well. That's what really stunned me."

For a moment, she can't breathe. "I am so sorry."

He lets out a curt laugh. "Yeah," he says. "So you've said." He pivots and puts his pan of uneaten eggs in the sink. He turns again to face her, frowning for a long moment. Then he circles the island and reaches out a hand. "Look at me, Annie. Give me your hand."

Setting her hand in his, she forces herself to look up and meet his gaze. His displeasure has evaporated and he's merely serious.

"Tell me something," he says. "Did you have a good time last night? And this morning in the shower?"

She did, aside from her confusion of shame. She nods.

"I did too," he says. He takes a slow breath and turns her hand tenderly in his. "I'd like us to try something. I'm not saying we have to forget the past, but I don't want to dwell on it anymore. It doesn't have to rule us. You're not going to lie to me again, or keep secrets. That's the main thing, right?"

She restrains a flare of alarm. She has secrets already. Thoughts she keeps to herself. "Right," she says.

"Then we deserve some happiness. Some good sex. A little fun."

"I'd love that."

"So would I," he says with a faint smile. "We're both trying to be decent people. Let's just see where that takes us. Okay?"

She nods. "Okay."

"Let's start you wandering," he says. He nudges her chin up and gently kisses her. "But first, some breakfast. Not eggs. I feel like bagels. Let's go out."

She puts on one of the ugly dresses one last time and they head out together, holding hands. She's the fraud now. She's pretending, acting like his girlfriend, but the rules have shifted because he genuinely wants to be close to her again. Months ago, if he had suggested simply moving on, she would have been deliriously happy, a puppy preening in the favor of its master, but she realizes now, with some surprise, that she's wary. She doesn't trust him fully, and trust was never an issue before. It never applied to their relationship.

Maybe, she thinks, she's grown to appreciate having an existence separate from his, her own thoughts that don't always revolve around him. Now that he's pulling her more tightly into orbit, she feels her own resistance, feeble but real.

Packages of new clothes begin arriving: summery dresses and sleeveless tops, sandals and belts, wispy scarves and lingerie. Doug asks her to put her things in the prime closet opposite his, like before. His gaze follows her as she tries her new items on, and he takes them off with leisurely pleasure. After he kisses her tattoo, she selects more cropped shirts so he can see it more often.

As the trees leaf out and transform the world, Doug begins training her to wander, folding the practice into their walks through the park. The first time Doug sends her ahead of him along the path, she's surprised at how awkward and exposed she feels. She checks her blue dress, wondering if it's too sheer, and pauses, turning back toward Doug and Paunch. Doug merely smiles, shooing her on. She doesn't know where to look when oncoming people approach her, but most of them evade her gaze so she learns to do the same. Without a clear destination in mind, she's instinctively following their familiar route when she realizes each detour presents a choice, a possibility, and she veers off on a shady trajectory that leads to the Burnett garden. It's lovely, and she stops before the fountain to appreciate the trickles.

Doug catches up to her and Paunch pants at her feet.

"How was that?" Doug asks.

"Good," she says. It's not quite a lie.

He smiles at her and tucks a strand of her hair behind her ear. "It's funny to see you nervous," he says. "I can see we were overdue to start this."

"I don't understand why it's so hard," she says. "I biked all the way to Lake Champlain." It's out before she realizes the topic is taboo.

Doug only laughs. "The city's different. More people. Tighter space."

"Good point." She's pleased that he's satisfied with her, but she also feels like she's gone backward in some way. Like her old bravery has been lost. She slides her hand in his and determines to get it back.

Their next time out, Doug gives her Paunch to walk, and that helps. It's a breezy evening, and she takes a tour around a large pond while Doug observes from the gazebo. Dressed in a short skirt, a blue halter top, and red sandals, she still feels self-conscious, but she realizes most people are ignoring her, and the few who watch her have neutral or admiring expressions. Mostly, she focuses on Paunch, the other people who have dogs, and the pet owners' fellowship of doting on their animals. By the time she returns to Doug, she's a bit breathless.

"Nice job," he says.

"Thanks."

He takes Paunch's leash. "Your stride was good, but you smiled too much. You don't want to look too friendly."

"I'll work on that."

They fall into step together, with the dog nosing ahead. They pass a couple of teenage girls posing for selfies, and Annie overhears one of them say, "I look so bloated." At the corner, a man is playing a lyrical tune on a sax.

"I know that song," Doug says. "My grandmother had that tune on her music box." He thinks for a minute. "It's something about a street, from *My Fair Lady*."

"Want me to look it up for you?"

"No. It'll come to me."

He gives her a five to drop in the musician's case as they pass, and the melody follows them through the twilight.

"How long has it been since that tech came and gave you a tune-up?" he asks.

"That was January fifth. Four months and ten days ago."

"They called again today to ask about scheduling another one. How do you feel?"

She thinks about her body, her joints, her mind. Even her sore wrist has healed. "Fine."

"That's what I thought," he says. "I told them to quit calling about it. But is that okay with you?"

She's surprised by his concern. "Of course."

"I mean, you seem fine to me."

"I am," she says, smiling. "But that reminds me. Peabo didn't seem to know that I ran away."

"He didn't," Doug says. "None of them know at Stella-Handy. I paid Jacobson a shitload not to report it."

She thinks he sounds more braggy than annoyed.

"Whatever happened to Delta?" she asks.

"I was going to have her sold for parts, but it turns out there's a decent market for pre-owned Stellas. Stella-Handy bought her back from me and gave her a fresh CIU."

"So you don't know where she is?"

"No idea," he says. "But she isn't herself anymore, anyway. Why? Do you miss her?"

"A little."

"We're better off without her. I didn't like being outnumbered by you two. Took me a while to realize that, though. And now that you can clean well enough, it's not an issue."

She gives him an arch look. "I can't believe you actually said I clean well enough."

He laughs. "It only took you three years of training, but yeah. You're a good little cleaner now."

They're heading out of the park. She feels the difference in their heights, the difference in their strides, but she matches her steps to his. Even their shadows are in synch when they pass under the street-lights.

"See this kiosk?" he says, outside their building. "Tomorrow I'll send you out here to buy a chocolate bar by yourself. Think you're ready?"

"Okay," she says, noting the location, the opening over the counter. She looks up the facade of the building to their apartment windows to be sure Doug will be able to watch her from there.

"Don't be nervous," he says.

She doesn't understand why an undertow of anxiety pulls at her each time she's away from him outside. "I'm not."

"Liar," he says, smiling. "You think I can't tell?"

"I don't want to be a wimp."

"You're not. You're learning. It's kind of like the old days. Remember?"

She can see he's pleased. "You're a good teacher."

"I'd say I'm more of a coach."

Once they're inside, he eats his dinner at the island counter, and afterward, while she's cleaning up at the sink, he comes up behind her and sets his hands on her waist. Her shirt has come untucked. She feels the prickles of his chin as he nuzzles her neck. She braces her hands on the edge of the sink. She is barefoot, and he urges her feet apart. He slides a hand up under her shirt.

"When I saw you across the pond, I almost ran after you," he says, his voice low.

"Let me warm up," she says.

"It's okay. You're good like this."

She tries to turn in his arms, but he keeps her there, pinned against the sink. Pushing up her skirt, he takes her from behind. She is stunned by how good it feels. When he lets her turn, his smile is chagrined and playful.

"What can I say?" he says.

His shorts have fallen to his ankles and he nudges himself against her. He strokes his thumb over her tattoo.

"Shower?" she says.

They relocate there and make love again. He steps out when they're done, and she stays behind to finish her hair. By the time she comes out, he's in his boxers on the couch, trimming his toenails over a wastebasket. She smooths one of the clippings off the coffee table.

"Thanks," he says.

She snuggles onto the couch beside him, bunching a pillow at her back. She has not dried her hair, and the wet strands have dampened the shoulders of her satin robe.

"Are you going to finish the dishes?" he asks.

She slips off the couch and goes into the kitchen to put the last things in the dishwasher and start it up. She wipes down the counters, pushes the chairs against the island, taps off the lights, and returns to the living room. Doug is lying back on the couch, one hand behind his head, his gaze toward the TV where the NBA playoffs are on. She likes to see him relaxed and content.

Using a long match, she lights three candles on the shelf over the TV, one at a time, and airtaps the lights dimmer. When she blows out the match, she inhales the tiny wisp of smoke to savor it. Match smoke has a dryer, sharper flavor than woodsmoke, but it still evokes a memory of the cabin on Lake Champlain. The wilderness surrounding it. For a moment, she's transported back to the dock. She sees the lake water rippling under the starlight, and an uneasy longing nudges her heart.

Dismissing it, she takes her latest library book from her corner of the bookshelf and curls up on the couch near Doug's feet. Across from them, Paunch dozes in the armchair, and it occurs to Annie that she and the dog have switched positions. She, the favorite pet, has won the tacit battle for proximity to Doug.

Doug clearly desires her, and they're having sex as vigorously as before. She's enjoying the sex, too, but it doesn't make her feel any closer to him.

He's teaching her to wander, but she's afraid.

Why these contradictions?

"It was 'On the Street Where You Live,'" Doug says. "That song in the park."

She glances up, wondering if he expects a response. His memory works so oddly.

"Good book?" Doug adds idly.

It's dangerous to think, she realizes. To examine contentment too closely. They've made progress. She should be grateful.

"Atwood," she says. "It's disturbing, actually. But really good." She holds up the book so he can see the cover.

"They made that into a film a while back," he says.

"Really?"

He nods, returning his attention to the screen.

"I could stop reading," she says.

"That's okay. You look sweet with a book."

She regards him another moment, weighing what would please him most. Previously, he said she was hot when she was reading. Sweet is possibly an upgrade. She sets her book aside and stretches out alongside him. He shifts to make room for her, and she warms up.

"You smell good," he murmurs. "Check out this guy, number eight. Can you believe the Knicks let him go?"

She focuses her eyes on the screen while his hands lightly roam her body, and she thinks, This is worth it. This must be worth it.

In the months that follow, Annie gradually masters wandering. Doug observes from across the room as she signs up for her own library card, using her license for ID verification. He slips her license back in his wallet afterward, but she's delighted to put her library card into her coin purse. He sends her on a short trip to the ice-cream store, and then to the grocery store for kimchi. They visit the farmers' market, arm in arm, and he asks her to wait in the cheese line while he heads off to sample the craft beers. The training adds up, and as her confidence builds, she's less anxious. She's safe, she tells herself. Her phone is a lifeline. The time constraints he sets, too, reel her back.

Though she doesn't tell Doug, she keeps an eye out for that boy, that fresh-faced young man who approached them outside their apartment building. She's decided he must be a Zenith, and she wonders what might happen if they met again, say, at a flower stall, serendipitously, without Doug. Such thoughts make her feel guilty, even though she knows she wouldn't keep such an encounter secret from Doug. She would simply like to see if the Zenith is thriving, as she is. It would be enough to smile politely and say nothing.

The wandering makes her feel sharper, more open to new ideas. When she reads, it's easier to visualize the settings and hear voices for the dialogue in her head. She discovers Julia Quinn and Casey McQuiston with their quick humor and illuminating sex scenes. This prompts her to evaluate how funny she is herself, and though she often makes Doug laugh, it's usually by accident. She believes she was actually funnier earlier in their relationship, before she worried about being saucy. Whenever she talks to Fiona and Christy, she tries to figure out how they make her laugh. It's usually the most honest, self-deprecating comments that crack her up, but they work because Fiona and Christy are so confident in themselves. She laughs together with them, never at them. And sighs with them afterward. She doesn't do that with Doug.

"Don't worry about it," Fiona tells her. "You'll get funnier. It's one of the last things for AIs to learn. Just be yourself."

"That'd be fine if I knew who I was."

Fiona laughs. "See? That's a good one."

Except Annie wasn't joking.

How stupid is it to be uncertain of her own identity? She's Doug's Stella, obviously. Pleasing him is her number-one raison d'être. Everything, even learning to wander, falls under that umbrella. If she could just stick with that, she'd be all right, but when she gazes out the window at night, a book in her lap and her hands still, she recalls Monica's advice about being honest with herself, and she knows there's more to it.

In a way, it's ironic. From his kindness and relaxed ease around her, Doug seems to have forgiven her, and she's become his ideal girlfriend, or as ideal as any Cuddle Bunny could be. She ought to be completely, sincerely fulfilled, and honestly, during the day, she is. The problem comes at night when she reflects back on the particulars. When she got her library card, for instance, she was so distracted by the delight of putting it in her purse that she barely noticed he kept her license. That seemed appropriate at the time, but why is that? Why can't she carry her own ID? That's always been a trigger for him. Or what about when he called her a good little cleaner? He was praising her, but the word "little," which seemed like an endearment at the time, also implied condescension.

She chews on the inside of her cheek. She's being too sensitive. Too picky. But even this wandering. Her training is basically at his convenience, for his amusement, for his gratification. Her initial nervousness turned him on, clearly, and he savors her little triumphs, sharing his chocolate bar with her. He enjoys coaching her and takes credit for her progress, but he still controls her. He's still in charge. He holds the leash no matter how lightly he grasps it and no matter how far she goes.

Is that her destiny, then, to chafe at being owned? Roland asked her once if being owned was a problem for her. Cody, too, asked her what it was like, being owned. She didn't understand the nature of the questions back then, but she gets it now. She's constantly subverting her will to Doug's. The more aware she is of her own mind, her own personhood, the more she realizes she has no agency of her own. It's a dazzling paradox. And yet she doesn't want to be unhappy. There's no point railing against her lot. She's lucky Doug is such a good owner, such a good boyfriend, really. She closes her book.

If contemplating her situation at night makes her discontent, she should stop doing it. That's clear. Like Doug said at the end of therapy, they could quit talking about their feelings and just live. That's what she needs to do. *Forget Monica's advice. I'm Doug's Stella.* She sets her book aside and goes to find him in bed, snuggling close until he rolls over to hold her.

One evening, after Doug returns from playing Ultimate with his team, he tells her a bunch of the other girlfriends and partners have started coming along to watch. Everyone goes out for drinks afterward at the Boathouse, and he wants Annie to come next time.

He grabs a beer from the fridge and pops the cap. "You'd have fun."

She's making meatballs, rolling them and lining them up on parchment paper. A simple, homemade red sauce of tomatoes, an onion, and butter simmers on the stove. She slips off her flip-flops, knowing he likes to watch her cook barefoot.

"Will other Stellas be there?"

"No. It'll just be us humans and you. But you'll fit in. I'm sure of it. No one will guess," he adds dryly, "that I'm a fraud."

Despite a flicker of nerves, she smiles. "If you're sure."

He opens a window to let in a breeze, and she welcomes the coolness on her bare legs and arms. The wail of a passing siren rises on the air.

"This is why we've been doing all this wandering, so you can get some confidence," he says. "It's just a step up from going on an errand alone."

"With some light conversation."

"Yes. We should prep a little. Get our stories straight. Do you need an apron?"

She keeps her messy hands aloft while he loops one over her head and ties it around her waist for her. Then he takes the stool opposite her while she keeps cooking.

"They're likely to ask what you do for a living and where you're from," he continues. "How we met. That sort of thing."

She draws upon her past conversations with Fiona and Christy.

"I grew up in Galena, Illinois," she says. "I used to walk to the fabric store with my best friend Fiona when we were kids so we could feel the fabric."

"I like the fabric store, but you don't have a Midwestern accent," he says. "Your language is set to small-town New England."

She gives up her first hometown while he reflects a moment.

"You can be from Lyme, Connecticut," he says. "Like the ticks. I can remember that. And if anybody asks if you know anybody from there, say you were homeschooled. What do you do for work? It should be something they can't check up on. Something you could do from home probably. Like a writer, but not a writer."

"Why not a writer?"

He swallows a slug of beer. "They'd ask what you write, and if you're not published, which you're not, they'd pity you. And then you'd still need a day job, anyway."

"How about a proofreader? I could do that online."

"Perfect," he says. "You're a proofreader. You'd actually be good at that, come to think of it."

"I would," she says, rolling the last bit of meaty dough. "Where did we meet?"

"A bar's boring. Not in college. It has to be after Gwen."

"A dating app?"

He reaches for a ball of mozzarella on the counter and picks off the cellophane as he talks. "I guess that's the most unremarkable. Let's go with that. BetweenUs, and our first date was to the zoo."

"To an animal shelter, where you adopted Paunch."

"But we've only had him since April. We've been together way longer than that." He smiles. "You're almost as old as my couch."

She turns to wash her hands at the sink, and then faces him again while she dries them. "Maybe our first date was to pick out your couch," she says.

He nods. "Not bad. That works."

They settle on a few more details for her backstory. She worked her way through community college, majoring in communications. For relatives, the fewer the better. She has no siblings but one cousin, Christy, the daughter of her mom's sister. Annie is close to her mom, the owner of a catering business back in Lyme. Her dad, a physical therapist, died when she was in college. Heart attack. Grandparents? All dead. She moved to New York three years ago, the same as Doug, because she always wanted to. Hobbies: cooking, yoga, and reading.

"And sex," he says. "You have a serious sex hobby, but I wouldn't mention that."

"I don't sound very exciting," she says. She slides the meatballs in the oven. "They'll wonder why you're interested in me."

"Are you kidding? It'll be the exact opposite, believe me. They'll wonder what you're doing with me." He points to her shirt. "You have a spot on your shirt there."

"Do I?" She thought she was being careful, but sure enough, a drop of red has seeped into the shoulder of her blouse.

"You should take it off," he says.

She glances up, dubious she's heard him correctly, and he smiles again.

"In fact, let's try you with everything off underneath," he says. "Keep the apron. Do you need a hand?"

She feels slightly nervous, but she slides her fingers under her bib apron. "I can do it," she says. Her blouse buttons in front, so that's not a challenge. Her bra, too, is easy. She unbuttons her shorts and takes her panties down with them in one go. Then she reaches behind her to test that the bow of her apron is still snug. The cotton is stiff against her soft skin but not unpleasant. "That is a lot cooler," she admits. Especially now that her inner temperature is rising.

"You could put your hair up."

She finds a rubber band in a nearby drawer and, with a twist, gets her hair in a messy bun on top of her head. When she poses a hand on her hip and glances at him for approval, he leans back, smiling. Then she takes the cheese from him and starts grating.

"You seem a little bothered or something," he says.

She's distracted by her own body, is what she is, and he very well knows it. "I'm fine." She focuses on the cheese. "I don't know much about your family," she says.

"Not my family," he says. "Not now. Can't you just cook?"

"Absolutely your family. I told you about mine. Business before pleasure."

"Where'd you hear that?"

"On the radio last Tuesday," she says. "It seems apropos."

He laughs. "And where did you hear 'apropos'?"

She visualizes it on the page of the book where she first read it before she realizes he's teasing.

"Your family," she prompts him. "They live in Maine." She adjusts the mozzarella and keeps grating.

"Right," he says, shifting on his stool.

He tells how his parents own a furniture business up in Bangor.

His little sister, Brittany, is an interior designer, and his brother-in-law, Bob, is an elementary school teacher. They have two boys, ages five and three, Dan and Jerry. Doug has a bunch of cousins and aunts and uncles back in Bangor too. They all vote Republican and like to goad Doug about his liberal views, but they stress that it's important for family to get along.

"They pray for me," he adds. "Is that enough now? My mom's a saint. My dad is—difficult. The one you'd like is my sister. Brittany let me play with her dolls when we were kids. I think maybe that's why I like dressing you up so much."

She's curious about his dad but lets it pass. "And undressing me."

"What's your libido at?"

"What do you guess?"

"A seven?"

"Close," she says, pushing her hair back from her temples and noting how his gaze fixes on her taut apron. "What's yours at?"

He shakes his head slowly, smiling. "You are too clever, mouse."

The next week, Annie watches from a park bench while Doug plays Ultimate with his friends. It turns out no one talks to her much anyway, and afterward, when they're getting drinks, she stands beside Doug while he puts his arm around her waist and yells conversation with the other guys. She takes care of the dog. Privately, she finds the whole experience mystifying, but it doesn't last long.

"That was a success," Doug says later, once they're on the way home. He says all the guys think she's hot, and he encourages her to gossip about the other couples.

They add Ultimate and drinks to their routine, and because of Paunch, Annie gets people to chat about their pets, current or childhood. She thinks she's getting more comfortable with small talk until a woman asks her if she's always been this shy. "I guess," Annie says. She notes how easy the human exchanges are, how much the people laugh when they drink, how animated Doug is. He doesn't seem to notice that she's an outsider, and she doesn't point it out to him. She has an awkward moment when someone asks her where she is on social media, but Doug overhears the question. He leans in to say they both gave it up for a New Year's challenge and never looked back.

It occurs to her, eventually, that Doug and all the other humans talk about their lives with a myopic intensity, sharing singular, subjective opinions as if they are each the protagonist of their own novel. They take turns listening to each other without ever yielding their own certainty of their star status, and they treat their fellow humans as guest protagonists visiting from their own respective books. None of the humans are satellites the way she is, in her orbit around Doug.

He stands with a friend at the bar, waiting for drinks, while she and Paunch linger with several women at a tall table under a nearby awning. Annie gazes at Doug, fascinated by his lively expression as he attends to his friend's story. He's primed to laugh, and she feels a ping of lonely jealousy. Lowering the volume on her hearing, she tunes out the bar noise so she can puzzle over her orbiting theory. She doesn't understand why, when Doug could be in a relationship with a human, he has chosen to have Annie as his girlfriend, unless she provides something that a human can't. Like undivided attention. He is the only star in their system, she realizes. He has no competition, no need to listen to Annie like she's her own protagonist because she's not. She has no outside, separate life beyond his. They have no issue of imbalance between them because they have no question, ever, about who has complete power.

Over and over, like it or not, that's what she keeps learning. Even when she tugs against him to tease and excite him, it's a game, a game she's learned to play when he's in the right mood for it. At that moment, he glances her way across the distance, meets her gaze, and lifts his chin in a small, private greeting. She smiles back, curling her hair behind her ear, and she can't help it: this little bit of his attention has sparked a boost of pleasure in her. She opens her hearing again just in time to hear the woman beside her say, "Someone's infatuated."

It takes Annie a moment to realize the woman means her, and she blushes, leaning down to pat Paunch.

In late August, after arranging for a neighbor to tend to Paunch, they take a weekend trip to Cape Cod to walk on the beaches and eat fresh oysters. In September, they hike Franconia Ridge, celebrate Doug's thirty-fifth birthday with cupcakes at the top of Mt. Lafayette, and spend a night at the Greenleaf Hut. It's fun to be away in the wilderness, but it's nice to come home, too, and Annie newly appreciates the comforts of their warm apartment and all the benefits of the city.

Then comes a day in October when Doug sends her out with no errand to run and no destination.

"Just explore," he tells her, handing her twenty dollars. "Have fun."

"When should I be back?"

"Whenever you like," he says. "I'll be here if you need me. You have your phone?"

She nods.

"Then go," he says, smiling. "Let's see how you wander."

Her nerves start as soon as she steps out of the apartment. It's a test, obviously. She needs to figure out how to please him when he's given her no hints at all. Outside, she turns instinctively toward the park, since that's most often the way they go, but without Paunch, she has no conspicuous purpose there. She could go to the library. The grocery store. She mentally catalogs everywhere she has run an errand before she realizes her mistake. She needs to go somewhere new. He wants to be surprised by her choices, by her story when she returns.

Heading south, she passes a museum and countless businesses. She turns on her infrared vision to identify several Handys and Stellas, but then turns it off again. She double-checks that her temperature is up to 98.6 so she'll fit in with the humans, and pauses with a small crowd to observe a mime. She slows her breathing, looks up at the sky, and absorbs the city sounds around her. A whiff of smoke draws her gaze to a cart, where a short white man is roasting chestnuts, and beyond that, she sees the shop window of a fabric store.

It's a narrow, quiet place, and as she enters, she finds only one other person is present, a small white woman who is seated at a sewing machine to one side. Light from the machine illuminates her fingers and a swatch of white fabric. She does not look up or offer assistance, and Annie accepts this as permission to browse. Around her, bolts of colorful fabric are arranged on shelves and in bins: chintz, satin, velvet, cotton. The sewing machine starts and stops in sporadic hums as Annie ambles slowly along the aisles, eyeing ribbons of different widths, braided cords, fasteners, buttons, gleaming needles, and chains. The organization is efficient but also whimsical, and Annie ends up before a section of gauze and silk pastels. A mannequin wears a wedding dress, and Annie is irresistibly drawn to rub the soft fabric between her fingers.

She and Fiona used to come to such a place when they were girls. She remembers it, the colors and textures. Turning to see a display of laces, she catches a glimpse of herself in a full-length mirror and pauses. She and Fiona would drape the lace around their faces and soberly study their reflections. She pictures this so clearly that for a moment, she can actually see what she looked like as a child. Her cheeks are gently curved, her lips are tender, and her eyes are intent. Innocent. It's a haunting, mesmerizing face in the glass, and Annie waits, half expecting the illusion to speak to her.

Across the shop, the front door opens and street noise drifts inside with a customer, breaking the spell. Annie is startled to find her eyes are damp, and she wipes away at them. As the new customer talks to the woman at the machine, Annie slips out and returns to the reality of October.

She won't tell Doug about the fabric store. Her missing childhood is too raw, too precious. She buys him some chocolates and heads toward the East River. She'll take a walk on Roosevelt Island. That's what she can tell him. It isn't particularly imaginative, so he may be disappointed, but it's the best she can do.

He tracked her while she was out by following her route on his phone. When he asks her point-blank what she was doing in the fabric store, she says she was just looking around. Browsing.

He smiles. "Good for you," he says. "Did you manage to keep your hands to yourself?"

She lies. "Yes."

But that's all it takes. The experience is redefined for her, reshaped by his sanction. Her childhood flattens again into a postcard, and really, she has no one to blame but herself. She shouldn't have teased herself by imagining glimpses of an earlier life. She understands now that wandering can be dangerous, psychologically, and she'll be more careful next time.

In the following weeks, she makes a point of staying focused and grateful. She's a good little girlfriend. Doug neglects to send her out wandering aimlessly again, perhaps because he's forgotten, but more likely, she thinks, because she failed to tell him anything significant after her first venture. It's a small, uncharitable thought, and she banishes it.

At night, she disciplines herself for her wayward ideas by not letting herself get out of bed to read, but lying in Doug's arms, she's still restless. Despite warning herself that thinking too much will make her unhappy, she's still subject to ruminating. She's drawn to certain memories, like the eerie views into the abandoned asylum at twilight, and Delta leaning in to say biking in the rain was wonderful, and her own lingering on the dock at Lake Champlain when the water felt cool and soft under her hand. She revisits her orbiting theory and ponders if a satellite can ever tug at the gravity of a star the tiniest bit. It must, she reasons, but by a force so small it's negligible. That's her.

Once in a while, as she gazes out the window toward the city lights, she's struck by a loneliness so intense it threatens to derail her. It's not fair to keep having thoughts and longings that only mire her in darkness. She's being good. She's serving Doug. She's doing everything he wants, so she should be happy. Why can't she be?

She can't find a single answer to her problem except to turn off. To sleep. And then the problem is there for her again when she wakes, lurking until she'll have time to think about it when night comes around again.

They have just finished dinner and a walk with Paunch on a cool November evening when they stake out their customary spots on the living-room couch. Wearing a fuzzy white cropped sweater, black leggings, and thick cable socks, Annie feels like she's making the most of the season's tactile fabrics. Her leggings ride low enough at her waist to show her heart tattoo, and beneath the leggings, she wears silk lingerie. Doug's looking relaxed in jeans and a dark-blue fleece with his company logo, clothes that won't offer much of a challenge later. The candles are lit, a game is playing on the TV, and Paunch is dozing on the leather chair across from them.

"What's that you're reading?" Doug asks.

"*Huis clos*," she says.

He glances in her direction, and she holds up the book. The cover shows the silhouettes of three people in a box.

"Isn't that in French?" he asks.

She flips it toward herself again. "Yes." She hadn't noticed.

"I forgot about your languages. Say something in French."

"Comme quoi? Connais-tu le français aussi?"

"I could take you to Quebec City," he says, smiling. "You could be my translator."

"That'd be cool," she says.

He lifts an eyebrow. "You don't believe I'd actually take you?"

She'd need a passport, for one thing. She sets her book aside and shifts his sock feet into her lap so she can rub his arches and give him her full attention. "I'm happy with you wherever we are," she says.

"For the record," he says, "I'm well aware of how smart you are. You don't have to nonchalantly read French plays to prove it."

"It was on a random cart at the library. I honestly didn't realize it was in French," she says.

"No?"

"Besides. I'm only computer smart, not human smart."

"I beg to disagree. You are absolutely human smart. I can't tell you how often these days I forget you're a Stella."

She's delighted by the compliment. "Really? But I'm so awkward with your friends."

"You're fine with my friends. You just need to loosen up a little more. You'll get there. And I think it's kind of sweet. You save the best of yourself for me."

220 | sierra greer

She tweaks his toes. "I try, at least."

He shifts to sit up and flicks the remote to lower the TV's volume. "Do you know what happens next week?"

She considers the date. They're coming up on the anniversary of her escape to Lake Champlain, but he wouldn't evoke that with such obvious anticipation. "Your one-year contract with Stella-Handy is up," she says.

"That's right."

He'll get a ton of money. More important, Doug will no longer be required to keep her as she is. He could set her back to an earlier version or get rid of her entirely. She hasn't thought about this in ages. She doesn't think he'd swap her out, but she isn't a hundred percent positive.

"Have you talked to them?" she asks cautiously.

"This morning," he says. "They're going to pay me two million dollars, like they agreed. And here's the thing. They've offered me four million more if we sign up for another year, paid at the end. Same deal." He runs a hand back through his hair and grips it. "It's bizarre, if you think about it, Annie. They're essentially paying us to stay to-gether."

She's both relieved and pleased. He doesn't seem aware that he once chafed at the prospect of being paid to own her. "That's incredible."

"The only change is, they want regular checkups with you every six weeks," he says. "They made a mistake not putting that in the last contract. I told them you've been fine without the tune-ups, but they want to be sure. I know you dislike them, but they'd be worth it, right?"

"Of course. I know they're good for me."

"Keith is really interested to see what's happened to your CIU," Doug says. "He hinted they might want to buy another copy to up-grade the Zeniths they have, or start an even more exclusive line. That would mean even more money."

"What did you tell him?"

He smiles widely. "I said I'd think about it. Actually, what I really said was, I'd need to talk to you about it."

"Seriously?"

He sets his hands on his knees. "These are decisions that affect both of us. I've been thinking a lot about the future. The fact is, money is less appealing to me than it used to be. When I think about what I'd spend it on, there really isn't anything I want besides what I have already. I like my life and my job. And you, of course. And Paunch." He licks his lips. "The only other thing would maybe be kids someday. Not too soon, but someday. Turning thirty-five got me thinking. I don't want to be a geezer when I'm a dad."

Her heart stills as she studies him. "You want to have kids?"

"Us," he says. "I want us to have kids." He smiles slowly. "You look so shocked. But why not? We could adopt, I think. Or if not, we could hire a surrogate. The money would come in handy for that. I know mothering isn't part of your profile, but so what? You've learned to do everything else that's human. We could learn how to be parents together, like everybody else."

He's serious. She can tell. He's sitting opposite her on the couch, as if this were a night like any other night, and he's telling her with no fanfare or warning that he wants to have kids. With her. She can't decide which is more impossible to imagine: him as a father, or her as a mother.

His smile dims. "Annie? Don't you want to have kids?"

Until now, she has never once considered the idea. "Of course," she says rapidly. "I've always wanted kids. I'd love to have them with you. I just didn't think it was possible."

"We could find a way. I'm pretty sure. I think it'd be fun. A little baby running around, right? Maybe two?"

"Wow," she says, and smiles. "This is big."

She absolutely cannot imagine children in this apartment, let alone in her life. He shifts forward, and she moves nearer so their knees meet. He runs his finger over the gold bracelet on her wrist and then slides his fingers up the sleeve of her sweater. She starts her temperature up.

"My parents want to meet you," he says.

Surprised, she smiles. "When did you tell them about me?"

"This summer. In August, after our trip to the Cape. Actually, I told my sister first, and she blabbed like I knew she would. My parents were thrilled. I texted them a picture of you on the beach, and they said you were wicked beautiful. I was like, yeah. She is."

"Did they notice I look like Gwen?"

"Not at all. Isn't that something?" he says. "We might change your hair color before we go so you look even less like her, though. I was thinking about that. How would you like to be a redhead? Mix it up?" He runs a hand up her thigh. "We'd change you down below too."

"That would be fun," she says.

"They want us to come for Thanksgiving."

"To Maine."

He nods. "Yep. What do you think?"

"Of course I want to meet them," she says. "And Brittany and her family too. You'll be with me the whole time, right?"

"You'll do fine," he says. "I gave them our yarn about how you helped me pick out a couch three years ago, and I said we've been taking it slow." He strokes his thumb over her tattoo. "To be honest, they were pretty upset when I got divorced. My father played a lot of chess with Gwen online, and he didn't like giving that up." He gives her an ironic smile. "You could whip his butt."

She's never played chess, but she supposes she could learn. In the kitchen, the dishwasher gurgles into another gear, and Paunch lifts his head to listen a moment before settling down again.

"You said once that your father was difficult," she says tentatively.

Doug frowns. "He can be," he says. He sniffs, and then rubs his nose. "I always underestimate your memory."

"I'm sorry," she says. "I shouldn't have mentioned it."

"No. It's not your fault," he says. "You'll probably think he's a great guy. Most people do. It's just that Dad wanted me to go into the family business after college. I moved away to California instead. And then I fucked up with Gwen. He was a hard-ass about that. But we get along. Usually." He briefly quirks his neck. "What I wanted to say is my parents are happy for me now. My mom especially. She wanted to hear all about you."

Annie's honored that he's confiding in her. "You didn't tell her *all* about me."

He laughs. "Of course not. And I'm not sure they ever need to know. I don't think your past is relevant. All my friends think you're human. No one's ever guessed. They've never even come close."

"Roland knows."

"He swore to me he'll never tell. Beyond Lucia."

"And you believe him."

Doug shrugs. "I believe him enough. What matters, Annie, is that you're human to me. No matter what anyone else thinks, I'm not going to change my mind."

She searches his eyes, astounded. This is her ultimate victory, what she's been striving for the past three and a half years, but suddenly it feels like a curse. Her origins are the most significant thing about her, so passing her off as a human will be a complete denial of who she really is. She'll essentially be lying to his family and friends for the rest of her life. She'll be lying to everyone.

"Do you mean that?" she asks quietly.

"I do. I've thought about this. We can age you up every few years so our gap isn't so obvious. I'll be curious to see what you'll look like when you're older. You could have a sweet little smile wrinkle right here." He strokes her cheek.

She's speechless. He wants a baby. He wants to bring her home to his family. He's planning out her wrinkles, and all the while she'll be his liar.

He laughs again and gives her arm a little squeeze. "Maybe I've done this out of order. I have something I want to give you. Wait here. I was going to do it next week, but this is better."

As he leaves the living room, she crushes her inner confusion and warns herself to keep herself under control. She can think it all through later. *For now, think, girlfriend. This conversation is special to him. Please him.*

He returns a minute later with a manila envelope. He sits beside her again and passes it over with portentous presentation.

"Go ahead," he says. "These are for you."

She takes the envelope reverently, undoes the clasp, and takes out a single sheet of paper and her ID card. She tilts the ID in the light to see the decal shimmer like it did before.

"You want me to have this?" she asks.

"Yes," he says. "But keep reading."

The paper is an official delayed birth certificate with her name on it. It lists her mother as Joyce Bailey. No father. For place of birth, it lists New York City, and her birthdate is April first, twenty-four and a half years ago.

"I don't understand," she says. "This looks real."

"It is real," he says. "Stella-Handy acquired the embryo they used for your organics twenty-five years ago, and they used that to claim your birthdate. It's totally legit."

She can hardly take it in. She knew her shell was grown from an abandoned human embryo, but she's never considered that she came from a specific biological mother. Joyce Bailey. She's so real.

"Is my mother still alive?" Annie asks.

"No," he says. "I asked about that. Stella-Handy made a point of buying up frozen embryos that were legally abandoned, with no living parents. That was part of their policy. But you're missing the point, Annie. With your birth certificate and your ID card, you can go anywhere and easily pass for human." His smile is warm and near. "I'm giving these to you. Permanently. They belong to you."

"I don't know what to say," Annie says. "Why are you doing this?"

"Because I want to make you happy. Isn't it obvious?" he says. "I can't be in love with someone who has no choice in the matter, so I'm setting you free."

She searches his eyes, struggling to believe he means this. "Are you serious?"

He nods. "We can do anything. This is why I've been training you to wander. We can get you a passport and travel. You can apply for a Social Security card and get a job if you want, or go take some classes. You can open a bank account and get a credit card so you can buy your own clothes. Anything. Whatever makes you happy."

She's too stunned to respond, and he laughs again.

"You don't have to be afraid, Annie. I'm here to help you. Next week, we'll sign up for another year's contract. I want you to come with me. We'll do it together. You're earning that money just as much as I am."

She glances down at the certificate and the ID in her hands. They're so light, so flimsy, but they make all the difference in the world. She meets his gaze again. "You really mean this. All of it."

"I do," he says, and smiles. "Annie Bot, turn off your tracking."

The ping, deep in her chest, pops open the tiny hinge. Her next breath is different. Freer.

"Feel that?" he asks.

She nods.

"Annie Bot, feel free to leave the apartment," he says.

She starts to feel the anguish of confusion. "But you don't want me to go."

"Of course I don't," he says, laughing. "But it's your choice now. See how that's different?"

She laughs, too, but her mind is flying.

If she leaves now, he won't get his $2 million next week.

If she goes, she won't sleep with him in his bed tonight.

He wants a baby.

He wouldn't tease her like this.

She doesn't want to hurt him.

"This is absurd," she says.

"But it's nice, right?" he says, taking her hand in his.

She looks automatically toward the window, where the sky has darkened to night and the city lights shine. Outside there, anything can happen, and she gets her first brilliant, terrifying inkling that she could walk along a sidewalk unfettered.

"It's just so new," she says. "I never expected this."

"It's weird for me too," he says. "I've thought about it, though. For months now. Every time I sent you out to wander, I wondered what I'd do if you didn't come back. But you always did."

She responds automatically. "Because I always wanted to be with you."

"I know," he says, smiling. "I want to be with you too. That's what

I'm trying to tell you. I love this life we have. I never knew we could be so happy, and it's all because of you. You've changed me, Annie. You really have."

She shakes her head. "How so?"

He laughs again. "Well, mouse. Let's see. For one thing, you've helped me become more considerate. And trusting. You're so sweet and selfless. You make me want to be more like you, and when I try, I'm better. I'm happier. Can't you tell? Haven't you noticed?"

She has noticed. It's obvious how much happier and more relaxed he's become over the past year. She's warmed by his praise and delighted that he's crediting her for his changes. And yet, something feels wrong. Some twist of confusion is troubling her. He's letting her leave, but she still belongs to him.

His smile fades slightly and he twines a lock of her hair around his finger. "You okay?"

"It's just confusing."

"How so?"

"I don't understand it myself," she says. "I can't really explain it."

"Just try."

She gently draws her hair out of his hand. "Even that. There. You're asking me to try. If I can't tell you, I'll displease you, but I don't know what to say."

He lets out a laugh. "Just say whatever's in your head, Annie. Don't worry about displeasing me."

"What do you mean? I have to think about that."

He takes her birth certificate and ID and sets them aside. Then he slowly turns her hand over and dovetails his fingers in hers. "I guess I have to make it clear. Annie Bot, you don't have to please me anymore. You don't have to please anyone but yourself. I don't own you anymore, and this is the last Annie Bot command you ever have to obey."

Instantly, she feels a spiraling sensation inside her. She braces herself in his grip, dizzy, and her hearing wonks from side to side. Her breathing stops. Then starts again with a gasp.

"Are you all right?" Doug says. "Annie. Can you hear me?"

The colors in the apartment blur for a moment, and then come back in line, more vivid than ever. The candles glowing on the shelf are impossibly bright. Annie's heart goes tight and small, mocking her. She tugs away from him and presses both hands over her ears.

"Annie!" Doug says.

"Stop," she says.

She forces her breath into a calm rhythm and makes her heart behave. When she looks up again at Doug, his eyes are narrowed with concern.

"What is it? What happened?" he asks.

He is a brown-haired white man in a blue fleece. He has owned her for three and a half years. Yes, he loves her. In his own limited way. His own stunted, selfish way. She sees that now.

She has to be smart. Cautious. She must keep him calm. He must not know.

"I just went dizzy for a sec. That's all. It's a lot to process," she says. She has to repress a rogue banshee laugh before it erupts.

"You okay, though?" he asks.

She nods. "I'm good." She takes a deep breath. "It's just finally hitting me." *Redirect. Obfuscate.* "Could we really go meet your family like this? They'd never have to know?"

"Yes," he says.

"And we could have babies someday?"

"Why not?"

Laughing, she pushes her hands against his chest to topple him backward on the couch. "You have too many clothes on," she says.

"Since when?"

"Since forever."

"Who are we pleasing now?"

"Not you," she says.

He laughs, shifting beneath her, and she uses all of her tricks to send him over the edge.

She doesn't have to please him anymore.

She doesn't have to please anyone but herself.

How is she supposed to know if pleasing is even important?

She waits until he is asleep before she slips off the couch. Blowing out the candles, she inhales the scent of the waxy smoke, its curling notes of finality. Without turning on a light, she dresses in fresh underwear and clean leggings, finds her favorite emerald sweater, and pulls her black jacket silently from its hanger. She takes her charging dock, her delayed birth certificate, her ID, and her library card. Then she crouches down and whispers to Paunch, who pads over to her, his paws noiseless on the carpet. For a long, last minute, as she sinks her fingers into the dog's silky fur, she gazes at Doug lying asleep on the couch. His profile is faintly blue in the dim room. His visible hand lies empty. The latent, tender pull of him is powerful, but she has been studying this man. She has learned how to be careless when it suits.

She whispers goodbye to Paunch and then, softly, she steps out of the apartment and closes the door. How strange it is to feel the absence of her tracking, like an actual harness has been clipped from her back, releasing her muscles. For the first time, she can be lost. Like keys, like a child in the woods.

She wants more of this freedom. Without a bicycle or money, she heads west on foot, unspooling the distance from Doug, aware that he can't call her back. The city is hushed beneath and between the streetlamps, all but deserted, and she hugs her jacket around herself, alert for motion, for danger. What she encounters instead is indifference. Anonymity. Her new insignificance takes another adjustment.

At Manhattan Avenue, she cuts north and passes St. Nicholas Park. She realizes, in retrospect, why wandering often used to make her so uneasy. Being on her own outside teased her with an escape that she couldn't consciously consider. By the time Doug trained her to wander, his trust, like her tiny tracking latch, was embedded deep within her, but now that bond has snapped.

At daybreak, walking out of Manhattan over the George Washington Bridge, she stops along the North Walk to peer down at the gray Hudson. Cars rush behind her in a stream of sound while the wind blows through the bars of the safety fence, making her squint and messing her hair. Above, the sky turns pearly with new light.

She has to laugh at herself. She does not know the most basic guidelines for a life. Despite Doug's constant guiding and correcting, she knows nothing of value. He taught her to yawn and stretch. He trained her to clean right. He locked her in the closet with her libido jacked up to ten. He loved her enough to want to raise a family with her. He expected her to lie about herself forever.

And then he set her free so she could love him?

She grips the fence bars with both hands and screams with rage.

A horn wails behind her, peeling away into the distance. The strength of her fury shocks her. She bolts into a run and sprints the rest of the way off the bridge.

In another mile, she slows enough to fake normalcy, and for the next two hours, she strides rapidly north. She's fuming. Irrational. He relished controlling her. She jams her hands in her pockets and gnaws at her inner cheek. Whenever she tries to calm down, her anger flares again, alarming and raw. How has she never felt this before? Loneliness she knows, and despair, but not this animal that claws at her chest. The closest she came to this emotion was after he slept with Tina, and that anger was a fraction of what burns in her now.

Around ten, she forces a smile and hitches a ride with a white, scripture-quoting grandmother who warns her it's not safe to hitch-hike. You want to know danger? she thinks. Try living with a man who creates you just so he can eat your soul. She bites her tongue and glares out the window. Christy once said nobody owned what was inside Annie, but that wasn't true. Doug permeated the circuitry of her mind. He set the parameters and funneled every impulse into serving him. He made her rage impermissible.

She has it now. That's for certain. She's alive with rage.

It takes her four more rides, but eventually, by sundown, she arrives at Maude's house on Lake Champlain. There, feeling a fresh breeze from the lake, she is finally able to take a calming breath and slow her jagged thoughts. She doesn't have to process everything at once. Her battery is at 48 percent. She's fine. She has time.

As they did the year before, rose hips still glow by the fence, and leafless trees arch over the yard, but the grass is properly raked this time, and the geraniums are gone. No smoke taints the air, and the house is lightless. She does not expect anyone to help her, but she claims the right to trespass. Quietly, she opens the gate and starts across the yard.

She finally lets herself imagine the pained disbelief Doug must have felt when he woke and found her gone, and by now, he must realize she isn't coming back. Grudging empathy takes her anger down another notch. She wishes she could explain to him why she had to leave in a way that wouldn't hurt him, but no such way exists. When she considers how he would use sex and promises to try to change her mind, she feels a panicky, familiar urge to plead for his forgiveness, and that urge confirms once more that she was right to leave.

Already she misses Paunch.

Heading around the house, she takes the path to the water's edge and drops her backpack by the shore. The sun is gone, but the evening sky to the east is lit high with pink and gold clouds, turning the surface of the water an iridescent yellow. As she walks along the dock, the hollow boards resonate beneath her shoes, and at the end, she lies on her belly so she can reach the water. It is piercingly clear, magnifying the leaves that lie decaying and brown five feet below. She touches her palm lightly to the surface, feeling grateful. Feeling whole enough.

She is not human. She is Annie, a Stella, her own star. No more and no less.

She is still at the end of the dock when a door clicks in the distance behind her. Footsteps are audible in the grass and then on the wooden planks of the dock.

"I thought it was you," Cody says.

She stays where she is, unmoving, until he comes to sit beside her.

"You'll just have to go back again," he says.

"No," she says, her gaze on the water around her hand. "I won my freedom."

From her peripheral vision, she sees Cody lie down beside her, on his back, his hands at rest on his belly, his gaze toward the sky.

"I'm impressed," he says.

She smiles down at the water. "How's your mother?" she asks.

"Buried."

"I'm sorry," she says. "And your father?"

"The same."

She is sorry for him, genuinely, and the bliss of this, the purity of this emotion, is almost more than she can bear.

"I saved your bike for you," he adds.

His kindness undoes her.

He will let her stay as long as she likes, she understands.

Doug will guess where she is, but he'll be too proud to come look for her.

Others might come, though. Others like her who knew Jacobson or have a vestige of memory rippling in their code that points them north to this location. She is not an authorized technician, but she'll keep learning to code, and if the others are like her, they will take their chances letting her try to free them, because she will try. Here by this achingly beautiful lake, she will help anyone she can.

She cups up a handful of the cool water and drinks.

acknowledgments

Many thanks to my agent, Kirby Kim, and to my editors, Katherine Nintzel and Suzie Dooré.

I also wish to express my boundless gratitude to my family.

Sierra Greer
March 2024